A Distant Land Beyond

Dee Verhagen

MELBOURNE, VICTORIA

Dee Verhagen C/- Intertype
Unit 45, 125 Highbury Road
BURWOOD VIC 3125
www.intertype.com.au

Book Layout ©2020 Intertype Publish and Print

Ordering Information:
Quantity sales. Special discounts are available on quantity purchases by corporations, associations, and others. For details, contact the "Special Sales Department" at the address above.

A Distant Land Beyond by Dee Verhagen —1st ed.
ISBN: 978-0-6488714-5-3

Dedication

For my daughter who realised I was secretly writing a book, even if she doesn't like the last page.

For my husband who encouraged me to have it published, so I would spend more time on the book rather than annoying him.

But not for my son. Get off the Xbox and read my book!

If you want to change the world, start off by making your bed.
-Admiral William H McRaven

"I can't find her," he yelled, "the link doesn't lead me anywhere. It just pulls up towards the sky. I've climbed to the peak and still it pulled higher," he said pacing the floor, "I can go no higher. How can she be higher than the highest mountain? It makes no sense." He stopped and faced the Master "for the past five anoks I have tugged on the link and it doesn't answer. Five anoks!" his hands covered his face as he shook his head "I'm 20 and can't find my link," he said as he slumped into the chair, "It makes no SENSE!" he turned and faced the Master "Why? Why? Why?" he begged.

"You say it pulls up and only up, no one answering?" asked the Master, rubbing his chin as he sat in his chair.

"Yes, up and only up," he said watching the Master, "what does it mean?"

"There is only one reason it pulls up, she is not in this land," the Master stood, "she is living in a distant land beyond our skies." The Master began pacing "There is only one I know who was stolen in the past 20 anoks. She was presumed dead," he stopped "if I am correct…" the Master trailed off and raced out of the room at great speed leaving Rorien stunned and even more confused.

"Stolen? Distant land? Beyond the skies? What is going on? Who is she?" he said frustrated as even more questions plagued his mind. "I just want to find my link!" he yelled, shaking his head as he rose and walked out to find the Master. It was getting late and Rorien hadn't located the Master. He returned to his casa and flung himself on the couch looking up at the ceiling. "Another land?" he said out loud to no one. His hands covered his face as he replayed the conversation over. *How am I to find her if she is in another land? How do you get to another world? Who is she?* His thoughts played havoc on him, his confusion increasing and no answers came.

He lay there for a long time trying to figure it out before he rose, crossed the room and paused before the door realising it was very late. *I will find the Master on the morrow, he* thought as he headed to bed, slumping fully clothed on it. Again, his thoughts wandered to solving the riddle, a riddle riddled with more riddles. *How do I find the answer if I can't understand?* He questioned himself. All night he tossed and turned, paced the floor and moved from bed to couch and back. He could not sleep, he could not rest, he could not find an answer, only frustration filled his body.

As the sun began to rise, Rorien got up and bathed before changing his clothes and seeking the Master. He knocked on the Master's door.

"Enter Rorien. I am about to eat, join with me" said the Master from his chair. Rorien slumped into a chair, still confused and frustrated and just wanted answers.

"Please give me answers. I don't understand. I have been tortured enough. Where is she?" he asked.

The Master began to eat, offering food to Rorien. "Sixteen anoks ago a daughter was born to Elena. She was called Elentari. Her parents were thrilled to be having a child in their 400s. It was their first and their only child. She was a mesik old when she was taken from her crib. A search was conducted for over an anok with many spending much of their time to find her. Although she was never found her mother knew she was alive as she could still feel her attachment. Babes keep the attachment alive until they walk, it keeps them feeling safe, but although Elena could still feel the attachment, she could not find her. The attachment leads the mother to her babe, like the link, but Elena said it only seemed to pull her up. We scoured the texts and discovered pulling towards the sky, pulling up meant they live beyond the sky in another world. Unfortunately, our discovery was too late to find her, the attachment was cut and we were unable to know where she was taken."

"Another world!? My link is in another world!? How do I find her?" Rorien pleaded. He needed her, needed to find her, needed her to feel complete.

"It is going to take time. You have four anoks until she begins her awakening. She will need you then if she is in a world which does not have our kind it will confuse and terrify her. When you are not performing duties or training, you will search for her. After supper tonight, meet me in the library" the Master responded. Rorien looked at the Master, wondering what was to come but the Master waved his hand to dismiss him. Rorien rose and left, still feeling confused and frustrated.

The morning wore on, high sun came and the dia dragged out. He was performing on auto. He couldn't stop the questions plaguing his mind. He had to find her. All dia his mind was racing, questioning, screaming and searching but no answers. Supper came and he ate without tasting, more concerned with finding answers and finding her. He raced to the library hoping to find answers quickly yet the Master was not there, no one was there, he had to wait. He paced as he waited, his mind still in overdrive, wondering if he would ever feel settled and quiet. Time past and Rorien was still pacing, getting more and more agitated. *Where is the Master? Why is he not here? What is taking so long?* he thought as the door finally swung open and the Master entered.

"The King required me," was all he said as he moved through the library to the rear. The Master turned left and stopped in front of two bookcases against the rear wall. He placed his hand between them and the right bookcase swung open revealing a hidden stairwell.

Rorien stepped back amazed, curious and bewildered. "This is an ancient passage to the ancient texts. They are kept underground to preserve them and as there are many, a lot of space is required. Many have long forgotten they exist" spoke the Master as he descended the stairs, Rorien following close behind.

The Master lit the lamp at the bottom of the stairwell lighting part of the room. As Rorien looked around, the Master moved quickly to light the candles near a passage and one on a desk near the passage entrance.

They were in a large room, the out room used to study books, with at least 50 tables scattered throughout, each with two chairs and a candle. The walls were fully lined with books, ceiling to floor and twelve feet high. Along the far wall, were four passages, parallel to each other, all stretching straight out into the darkness.

"You will need the maps of all the lands and worlds to find your link. The maps are scattered amongst the books along each passage," said the Master with his hand stretched towards the passage. Rorien glanced down the passage, he could see no end, only darkness beyond the candlelight.

"What is this library?"

"It is all the books ever scribed, all the information ever to have existed, information on each power, on each village, cuedel, everything concerning our lands. The library above is information taken from here," replied the Master.

"So, the library above is large and only a part of what is contained here?" he said groaning at the realisation of his task. The Master moved down one of the passages. Rorien noticed the ancient symbols etched above the door and as he got closer, he could make out the symbol for air, his power. The Master was scanning the shelves using his hands to guide him, searching top to bottom as he moved slowly along the left side. His hand reached above and removed some papers from between the books. He partially removed a book to mark the spot and walked back to the desk. Rorien followed unsure of what was happening. The Master opened the papers fully and laid them flat on the table.

"You will use your link as you concentrate on the map, use your hands to travel over the map as you pull on the link. It will pull you to the map if she lives there otherwise…"

"Up," he said. "How many maps are there?"

"Many and they are scattered throughout the books. Return them to their correct location when you finish. The books near them are texts regarding those lands, information and data of those lands. It is time to see if this is where she is."

Rorien looked from the Master to the maps. He moved to stand above the map and hovered his hands over them, moving them over the map as he pulled on his link. Up it called back. He slumped into the chair and let out a breath. He knew the first map wouldn't be the one but still, he hoped. The Master took it and folded it up. Rorien tried the next map and the next and the next, but none pulled him towards them, none were where she lived. He felt empty and slumped back into the chair. If only it was that easy, that one of them was her map and he could be with her, feeling whole and complete. The Master returned the maps and turned to him.

"You have the answer on what to do. Come here when your duties and training are complete. Replace everything you move and when you leave, blow out the candles. There are more candles beneath the stairs. Good luck Rorien, find her," and with that, the Master left.

Rorien sat, not sure where to start. He walked back to where they found the last map and stared. He could make out a lamp hanging from the ceiling further along the passage and lit it. Another lamp came into view but no end to the passage. He let out a long breath and began his search, not feeling confident and ready to scream. His eyes looked towards the passage end. "The things I am doing to be whole, complete and loved. She had better be worth this," he said out loud.

Every evening Rorien spent his time in the ancient library searching for Elentari. After four dias, Rorien had hardly moved along the shelves. He groaned and left heading back to his casa not sure how long it would take and was getting impatient. He had to find her, he needed help. He had only four anoks to find her and at this pace, he would need forty. He changed direction and headed to Jasper's casa. He knocked, entered and slumped onto the couch. "I need help," he said.

"We know," said Jasper.

"Ha funny. I'm serious."

"Ok, what's up?" asked Jasper. Jasper and Rorien worked together in the King's army and spent time together when off duty. Rorien explained all which had been happening for the past four dias. Sarina sat down on the arm of the couch beside Jasper partway through Rorien's story.

Jasper was five anoks older than Rorien and Sarina was Jasper's linked. It was when Jasper and Sarina took their linking vows that Rorien started his search for his link. He was fifteen. It was the specialness of Jasper and Sarina's relationship which inspired Rorien, how they complemented each other and knew each other, their love and tenderness. He longed for a relationship similar to theirs.

"We will help you," said Sarina.

"Yes, and we'll get Lorcan and Fendton to help too, about time they were useful," said Jasper grinning as he elbowed Rorien, hoping the dig would cheer him up a bit.

"Great idea. Talk to them on the morrow and let's meet at the library after supper," said Sarina. "We will find her Rorien." She reached behind Jasper and placed a hand on his shoulder. Rorien smiled. He felt better, more hopeful and his spirits lifted slightly.

After supper the next dia, the five met in the library and Rorien led them to the ancient texts and lit the candles.

"Oh wow," said Sarina as she stepped into the out room scanning all around. "This is amazing! Who would have believed there were so many books?" The rest followed behind her and headed off in their own direction to explore the room.

"If only there weren't. There are more down the passages, heaps more. I would find her quicker if there was only the library above to search," said Rorien.

"With the five of us, we will find her."

Rorien explained what they were looking for and to make sure everything was returned exactly where it came from. Lorcan and Fendton continued where Rorien last looked and Jasper and Sarina starting at the beginning of the right side.

"How long are the passages?" asked Lorcan.

"No idea," replied Rorien.

"Umm let's see." Lorcan used his firepower to light along the floor. Slowly he spread his fire down the passage but no end was found. "Nope can't find the end."

"It has to have an end. We are on the mountain top and the passage is flat, it will end eventually. Can't go further than the other side," said Rorien turning and walking away back to the out room.

"The top is about 600 across, surely it can't be that far?" Lorcan was concerned, looking to the others. Their faces mirrored his concern but no one said anything to Rorien.

"We won't find her unless we start looking. Working out how far the passages extend isn't going to find her. Start searching," said Sarina. "I have some maps Rorien." She looked puzzled wondering why Rorien was bringing a table into the passage.

"Saves time walking back especially when we get further along," he shrugged.

"Yes, it will. Here are some maps."

Most nights all five of them searched together and some nights it was just Rorien. An anok had passed when they had completed the air passage and started on the water passage. At times the maps seemed to be the same and he wondered if there were copies scattered throughout. There were two more full passages to search and he was getting frustrated. At the rate they were going, they would need at least four anoks to search every passage and map, they had completed two and now only had another two passages and only two anoks to find her.

The Master came to check on progress and help as he could. As a Master, he had more duties to perform and less free time. Every spare moment he had, he dedicated to helping find Elentari. The Master knew the grave importance of finding her and his presence was to ensure she would be found.

By the end of the second anok, they had completed the air and water passages and had started on the earth passage. All five were losing hope of finding her. The others stayed to help Rorien, their friend and brother of the Kings army, all sensing his need and his desire for his link, his frustration at not finding her and having her near him. They could feel his loneliness at her absence and continued searching to bring happiness into his life.

By the end of the third anok, hope was almost lost. "I only have one more anok to find her."

"We will," encouraged Sarina, "we only have this fire passage to search. Her map will be here. We will find her land and you will find her there. We are nearly finished Rorien, nearly done."

Four vikas past when Sarina placed a pile of maps in front of Rorien on the table. Rorien began hovering his hands over each map, when he reached the fourth map, he felt the sensation of being pulled in towards the map. Rorien's face changed to shock. "I found her," he whispered, "she is here," he said. His eyes grew wide as the realisation hit him. "She is here. This is her map!" he yelled, grabbing Sarina and hugging her tight. Jasper, Lorcan and Fendton came running. "I found her lands!" he yelled letting Sarina go and throwing his hands high in the air falling to his knees. "I found her. Finally, I have found her. We have found her, her map, her. We found her."

"Yes!" the males yelled, fist-pumping the air and doing their own victory dance. They raised Rorien off his knees, laughing and congratulating each other, excited their search was finally over and were closer to Elentari. This part of the journey was over, the map was found and now they had to bring her home. Rorien raced out of the library heading for the Master's casa.

Sarina returned the other maps to their spot, leaving a book partially out to mark where Elentari's map was found. They cleared the library, leaving the table and map in the passage, and left.

Banging loudly on the door Rorien yelled, "I found her! Master! Master! I found her!" A sleepy Master opened the door, Rorien grabbed him. "I found the map where Elentari is. I found her!" The Master looked at him, his face slowly changing at the realisation of what Rorien was saying.

"Show me," the Master stated as he raced towards the library, meeting the others along the way. The Master entered the out room

"Where?" he asked as the others entered behind him with Lorcan lighting the candles.

"We found the map in the fire passage," said Rorien heading quickly down the passage as the Lorcan lit the way. "Sarina found it, this map is hers," he said with his hand on the map.

"Show me where you found this," said the Master.

"Here," Sarina said. Her hand pointing to the partially removed book. The Master began scanning the books nearby. "What are you looking for?" she asked.

"There will be a book with codes to this world. It will be filled with many codes and we will need to find the correct one."

"Please tell me there are not as many codes as maps" Rorien sighed slumping against the wall of books and sliding to the floor. Jasper placed a hand on his shoulder.

"Not as many. Codes will be similar and you will need to find the one closest to her otherwise you won't have time to find her."

"What do you mean won't have time? How much time do I have?"

"Once you open the doorway you will have seven dias to find her and return with her. On the seventh dia, the doorway will reappear and open. If you do not enter, the doorway will be closed and you will not have a way to return." The Master was removing books and checking them before returning them. "Elentari was taken to this land against her will and the doorway you open will allow her to return with you. Understand, YOU MUST enter the return doorway." The Master continued to scan the books. "This one, her doorway is in this one." He walked the passage back to the out room taking the map with him. Jasper grabbed the table to return its place in the out room.

"The codes in this book are all similar. You are looking for codes with this symbol." The Master's finger pointed to a mark in the top right corner of the map. "See how this one has this symbol in the code." Rorien looked at where the Master's finger was in the book. His finger was on a paragraph containing the symbol. "As you find each code, you will need to tug on your link to see if she is close. There will be more than one code which will pull you towards it. It is essential every code in the book is scanned. Each code which pulls you, scribe it onto parchment, one code, one parchment." The Master opened a drawer under the table and removed a quill, ink and parchment. "Once you have all the codes, we shall narrow it down. Make sure you scribe it EXACTLY as it is written, the slightest variation in the code will cause the doorway to open in a very different place."

Rorien looked at the size of the book and to each of his friends. He had not listened or paid attention in class when they learnt the ancient text symbols, now he was regretting not learning. The book was full of the ancient text and these symbols made no sense to him. Finding the code, the mark, amongst all the lines, squiggles and characters was going to be hard.

"Yes, we will help you," Jasper said, knowing the question was about to be asked.

"Thanks."

"Good luck Rorien." The Master patted Rorien's shoulder and took his leave.

"What does he mean by the code for the doorway?" Fendton asked.

"I guess to get to these lands we have to open a secret door between lands" answered Rorien "a hidden, invisible door maybe."

"Alright, you pull on the link and when you have a code, we will scribe it. On the morrow, we will start taking turns to help you search. Sarina, you take the next search after me, Lorcan then Fendton and back to me. We will find all the codes, Rorien, and narrow it down. She is close," said Jasper.

They stood around the map and book, looking at them trying to work out what it meant, lost in their thoughts. "Until the morrow," said Sarina, taking Jasper's hand and leading him out. Fendton moved to blow out the candles and Lorcan placed a hand on Rorien's shoulder.

"On the morrow Rorien, the morrow. Let's get some sleep," he said guiding Rorien out.

"Yes, on the morrow Elentari, on the morrow I shall take the next step to find you," said Rorien to the room as Lorcan pushed him up the stairs, both hands on his back to keep him moving.

The following dia, Rorien was in the out room when Jasper arrived and they began scouring the book for codes. Each night, his friends took turns to help him. It was near four vikas when they closed the book after searching all the codes. They had found eight codes in total.

"On the morrow, I will take these to the Master and find which is hers," he said leaning back on the chair letting out a long breath.

"This has been a massively long journey and finally it is nearing the end. Finally! This has been a pleasure to help you Rorien. Even if you have taken four anoks away from me," said Jasper jabbing him. "Now bring her home, bring her home."

"Her 20th birthday is only a few dias away and her awakening is nearing. I must find her before it begins. What if the world she is in, is not like ours?" he said with a quizzical look on his face.

"You will know soon enough."

"She may need some being to help her. What if she doesn't want to return or believe me?" he asked, concerned and a little frightened.

"You will be there to help her when her awakening begins and she will believe you," Jasper said, placing a hand on his shoulder.

He turned to Jasper, "I cannot thank you enough for all the help you have given me. All the time you have devoted, all of you have devoted to finding her. I am forever grateful," Rorien raised his hand to his chest and bent his head to show his gratitude. Jasper slapped Rorien on the back.

"Just find her, Bro. It will be worth every moment to see you happy and whole and not this miserable male and to finally meet this female who has taken four anoks to find," he said grinning.

"Thanks," Rorien said, grabbing the book to return it. Jasper gathered the parchments together and cleaned the out room. He was leaning on the stair rail when Rorien returned.

"It will be great to finally meet her, my link," said Rorien.

"Yes. Meet the female who has consumed my miserable friends' life." Jasper handed him the codes and they left.

On the morrow after breakfast, Rorien headed to the Master. "Master these are the codes my link led me to. There are eight all up. So, what do we do now? How do we find the right one?" asked Rorien.

"Spread them out on the table so you can see them all," Rorien spread them out. "Use your link to guide you to the strongest pull. This will be her code and the doorway closest to her."

Rorien began moving his hands over the parchments and used his link to find her. He removed two codes which felt weak and tried his link again. Another two codes he removed. He shuffled the parchments and used his link. He removed one, three remained. It was getting hard to know which is stronger. Shuffling the parchments again he moved his hands over the codes and shook his head. None were strong. He stepped back stretched and lined them up side by side. Changing the placement, he placed his left hand over the left code and his right hand over the right code. Pulling the link, his left hand felt stronger. He moved his right hand over the middle code and again the link pulled left. He checked over all the codes against the left one to ensure it was the correct one.

He sat down "This is the one. This is her code to her doorway," whispered Rorien tears welling in his eyes. She was close, his heart was racing, he would see his link soon. He would bring her home, his Elentari, his link, his life.

"Excellent. On the morrow, I will come to your casa and prepare for opening the portal," the Master said.

"Master, where is Elena?"

"She is no longer with us. The sorrow with the loss of Elentari became too much for her. Her will to live faded and she died when Elentari would have turned four. You would have been eight at the time."

"So, it's only me she will have?"

"Her mother is gone. You are her link and will need you to help her understand."

Rorien rose and made his exit, taking the parchment with her door code with him. In his casa, he placed the parchment on the table and a rock on top to keep it safe and headed out for training. The dia dragged on, time seemingly standing still as if the dia would last forever. Frustration and discontent filled him. He wanted the morrow to come for on the morrow he would find her, on the morrow he would find Elentari.

At high sun, the Master entered Rorien's casa. Jasper, Sarina, Lorcan and Fendton had arrived just after breakfast and were trying to keep Rorien calm. He had been pacing all morning, agitated, restless and tense. Nothing his friends did or said could calm him. He wanted only her, wanted only to find her and get to her.

"You are required to drink this to enable you to see the entrance and speaking the code will create the doorway." The Master carefully placed the bowl filled with liquid on the table. "Once you step through you will be in her land and use your link to find her. Your power may not work in her lands, but the link will. Observe those around you to fit in and not stand out. No weapons." Rorien removed his weapons. "Keep to the shadows and out of sight as much as you can. You must find her within seven dias before the doorway reopens." The Master added a word to the code. "You need to convince her to return. If she does not enter the door, there will be consequences for these lands. Drink this and speak the code" said the Master as he handed Rorien the bowl "Good luck and find her, she is one special female."

Rorien looked from the bowl to the code, the Master and to his friends. His friends were all smiling encouragingly, nodding for him to continue. He grinned and said, "To finding Elentari." He raised the bowl to his lips, downing the liquid before speaking the ancient text.

> *tossen twee entco fis dili potor*
> *vun kier kuto hapa tut calmina*
> *maxhori wala portel hus af kun casa*
> *miwass e autas kib forei*

A light appeared in front of Rorien, it grew until it was a silver circle, 7 foot in diameter. Coloured fluid-like substance began to seep from the frame, flowing towards the centre to fill the void, meeting and swirling about in the centre and filling towards the edge. The doorway shone full of moving colours similar to the way light reflects off a bubble, blending and swirling. A doorway into the unknown, into a land beyond the skies. He looked at his friends, his grin wide, eyes dancing with joy and stepped through.

"Go find her!" yelled Jasper. He could see no door but knew it was there by the distortion of objects in the space before Rorien.

He stepped into the doorway and into the void between the worlds. The void was nothing, no noise, no smell, no warmth, no coldness, nothing. Pure whiteness engulfed him stretching in every direction. He was unsure where to go as there was nothing to see or hear, nothing to guide him. He could see nothing and felt nothing. He moved his feet forward hoping he was moving in the right direction and entered the new land, her land. His heart was beating fast with excitement, anticipation and fear. He turned and faced the doorway as it shrunk to a bubble and popped. There was no turning back, he was here for seven dias and had a duty to fulfil, finding his link.

He surveyed his surroundings turning fully around and opened his senses. He was amongst trees on the side of a hill. There were no fruit trees that he could see, just evergreen trees. The trees were different from those in his world, there were no birch, oak or pine trees he could see, the leaves were thick and leathery, and bluish-green. They smelt minty, pine scent with a touch of honey. He spotted buildings in the distance and could hear the noise from the nearby cuedel which started at the beach and headed beyond going between the hills. The ocean wasn't as blue as it was in his world and the buildings were much, much larger. It seemed buildings were on top of buildings. It was very strange and the cuedel was bigger than his, much bigger. If it wasn't for the link, he felt he would never find her.

Rorien pulled on his link, he felt a very faint touchback. The link drew him towards the cuedel. He began to walk slowly towards the community, taking in everything around him. There was much to see and to hear compared to his world. It was different yet also similar. He found a path leading to the beach and followed it. Staying hidden amongst the trees, he observed those on the beach, wanting to make sure he fitted in. There was not much difference other than their clothing and the way they interacted with each other. They wore less clothing with more exposed skin. Males wore similar clothing but their pants were short. Females seemed to wear clothes like males although he could see a few females wearing dresses. They kept distant from each other, keeping to themselves and going about on their own. At home, all humanoids joined in festivities and activities together but here they were completing activities by themselves.

He noticed a strange large metal object moving along a wide straight black path. No paths in his world were that wide, not even half as wide. He had never seen a creature like this before. He watched it move along and stop on the path's side. The creature opened its wings and a male and female stepped out. Rorien took in a sharp breath as he stepped back horrified as to what it was. He kept watch, taking in all that was happening. More metal creatures moved around only on the black path and inside each creature were more humanoids and all walked on the white path beside the black path. He watched for a long time until he felt a touch on the link.

He moved past the beach and between the buildings, keeping his head down, avoiding all and staying on the white path. He had closed off his hearing for there was too much noise in this world. As he walked, he scanned the buildings. These must be where they live, they looked like very large casas with small flimsy walls surrounding each of them. It seemed strange to have individual walls around each casa which would keep no one out and why not surround the whole cuedel. He kept following the link, all the paths he followed were straight, wide and even. The link was getting stronger. He must be getting closer.

He arrived outside two separate casas on a hillside with a wall separating them, his link strong. It seemed he had walked in circles to get here. The link pulled him towards the rear casa which seemed to be two casas placed on top of each other and he wondered which was hers. The link pulled him on, urging him. He could see no way to reach the top and there was only one door at the bottom. He quickly walked to the door, his heart bursting with excitement and anticipation. His excitement waned wondering if she would know him. She was within his reach, his link so close to him, and he worried she might not know him. The Master hadn't said anything about her not knowing him and he didn't know what he would do. He hadn't thought about her not knowing who he was. In his world, you knew your link when you saw them. He paused at the door, his heart leaping in his chest, he knocked.

CHAPTER 2

Annie groaned as she woke, placing her hand on her forehead where the pain was, feeling like she had a hangover even though she hadn't been drinking. She opened her eyes to find the world was fuzzy. She sat up in bed, her nose stuffy, feeling like she was coming down with a cold. Her ears were muffled like they were underwater and her mouth was dry, so very dry. She had work today, but not uni, and would not be much good with her head the way it was. She reached for her phone and managed to text through fuzzy eyes that she was not coming in.

She swung her feet out of bed and touched the floor. The floor seemed different to usual, the carpet harsher. Her toes wriggled over the carpet as she made her way into the kitchen feeling the smooth, cold tiles beneath her feet. She poured herself a mixed juice and took a sip, it tasted different to normal, fuller of flavour. She could taste all the different juices individually and each very distinct. Her eyes read the label and saw it was still in date. It seemed whatever she had was playing havoc with her taste buds.

Her phone buzzed in the bedroom. Grabbing some bread, she put it in the toaster and turned on the kettle. She walked back to the bedroom to read her message and left it on the bedside table before heading back to the kitchen.

Moving to the cupboard she took out the teapot, a cup and a plate. From the fridge came butter and blueberry and raspberry jams. Placing the loose-leaf tea into the teapot she heard the toast pop. It seemed louder than usual with her ears no longer muffled, everything was loud and her ears were over sensitive. They had gone from being muffled to everything on loud like someone turned the world upon full. As she buttered the toast, she heard it loudly crunching under the knife blade and the kettle began to boil. It was almost like she could hear every bubble as it popped. She poured the hot water into the teapot and instantly smelt the tea, all the different scents filling her nose. She could smell the difference between the four varieties which made up the black tea blend. Her nose was super sensitive to the different fragrances. She began to worry about what was happening to her.

She placed the teapot, cup and toast on the table before sitting down. hesitating before taking a bite of toast. Her mouth was alive with flavour, another one of her senses enhanced. She poured her tea and took a sip. Her mouth was dancing with all the flavours as her taste buds were extremely receptive and picked up each flavour separately. It seemed strange to be able to taste each flavour so distinctly. There were four different black teas to create this one style and she wasn't tasting as one tea but individually as if she was drinking four teas at once. She could pick their different varieties as she smelt and tasted her tea. Her taste, touch and smell senses were heightened. She was puzzled as to why her senses were so strong and began to freak out. Her breathing increased and she began to panic not understanding what was happening.

Her head was no longer pounding and her hearing had increased. She heard her neighbours discussing where they would meet after work to go out for dinner as they got in their car. She could just make out what they were saying. Annie had never heard them before and her anxiety level increased as she paced the floor, shaking her hands.

"I don't understand. I can smell everything, taste everything, hear everything. What is happening?" she said aloud hoping for an answer. She crumbled onto the couch crying, scared and unsure, feeling the fabric weave beneath her fingers. Her cold wasn't a cold, it was more like she was getting superpowers. She sat up.

"No superpowers are in movies and are not real. Superman, Blade, Wolverine, Hulk, Thor, Daredevil, Wonder Woman, Aquaman all the imagination of creators. They are not real. So why are my senses stronger?" she said. It was making no sense superpowers were just imaginary and don't just happen. She had no answer to why she could hear, smell, touch and taste better.

She calmed down and decided since she was home for the day, she would take her senses for a test drive to get used to them before returning to the outside world. Find out how strong they were and what she could do to stop them. Using her nose to guide her she began her search in the kitchen which may not have been the best option to start with. She could smell the dank manky dishcloth and went to throw it in the bin. As she opened the bin cupboard, an overload of musty and putrid smells hit her. Having large bins and only one to fill them meant she emptied them once a fortnight on bin night and they were due to be emptied.

The food scrap bucket needed emptying and cleaning. She could smell mould growing on the decaying food scraps, not wanting to begin to work out the smells. The recycle box wasn't bad with mainly paper except the juice containers were beginning to smell bad. She grabbed all three bins and headed out the back door to empty them. As she opened the door, the noise hit her like a ten-ton truck, birds, cars, buses, dogs, cats, people, music, air conditioners, multitudes of sounds rang through her ears. It was deafening. She yelped as she dropped the rubbish to throw her hands over her ears. She raced inside quickly closing the door and slumped to the floor in tears, her anxiety increasing. To step outside which meant getting to work, to uni or even go to the shops would be difficult. What had begun as an exciting experience had now become limiting and frustrating. She had shopped last night on her way home and would not need to go shop again for a few days.

Calming down, she stood up and headed to the bedroom. Standing there in her room she could smell her eight different perfumes, her bedding, her dirty clothes. She grabbed the washing basket and headed downstairs to throw a load in the washing machine. Her unsureness began to turn into excitement as she imagined the possibilities this could bring her.

Heading to the pantry, she took out the chocolate blocks to try out her taste sense. Any excuse to have chocolate is a good excuse. There were eight blocks of chocolate to taste. The 80% was much more bitter than the 73%, quite strong and not tasty. The 73% was edible, just. The sea salt flavour really came out. The salt seemed to fill her mouth like waves of the ocean washing over the beach. She liked the way the chocolate and salt flavours flowed through her mouth together. Hazelnut, almond and macadamia blocks were similar in feeling with the rough hard nut mixed with soft smooth chocolate. The two textures caused her mouth to feel rough then smooth as they moved through her mouth. She craved the sea salt chocolate except she had eaten it all and began to look for more salty foods.

She continued to play with each of her senses, learning them, discovering them. Annie was enjoying these new abilities all except the hearing. The supersonic hearing was too much and one she could very much skip. She became aware of a high-pitched sound which was causing her angst. She could not make out where it came from and began to slowly walk through the apartment tracing the noise to the TV. The sound was from the TV being in standby. Heading through the house she turned off all power points to stop any and all squeals.

It was just before lunchtime and Annie was confused as to what she was experiencing and why. Her emotions were on a roller coaster, excitement to unease, enthusiasm to frustration and so on. She sat cross-legged on her bed with her laptop open to Google search. Her mind wandered back to waking up and played out her discovery trying to work out what it meant. Her senses were going wild and it did not add up. Even Google was no help with its vague suggestions of hormonal imbalance or pregnancy. She knew pregnancy was out as it required a man for that to happen and she had not been with a man. Hyperesthesia is the increase in sensitivity to any or all senses but it didn't answer why she had it all of a sudden or how to stop it.

She got up and hopped into the shower, hoping it would make her feel better. As the water hit her body, she could feel every drop on her skin and could feel the little rivers of water running down her body. It felt weird and exhilarating. Opening the body wash the smells hit her, ginger, lime, grapefruit. The soothing foam on her body felt softer and silkier than normal, taking on a creamier texture which felt amazing.

Everything she did was enhanced. It was frightening and exciting at the same time. She stood for a long time in the shower enjoying the sensation of the water flowing from her head down her body. It was soothing and relaxing, just what she needed to take her mind off everything.

Touching things was an experience. The surfaces were different to what she was familiar with. Some surfaces rougher, being able to feel each ripple and bump, and others smoother to the touch. Fabrics felt different on her skin. She had changed her clothes a few times while getting dressed to find the best fabrics against her skin with cotton feeling the best. She decided to overhaul her wardrobe, it was crowded and could do with a cleanout. After all, she took up both sides of the 'His and Her' walk through robe and the feel of the fabric against her skin was going to make it easy, anything itchy or rough will be discarded and with that, the clearing began. Each item removed and tossed aside or returned to the hanger. Annie stepped back after tossing the last item and surveyed her clothes still hanging. "Let's hope they all match" she murmured as less than half remained and is now fitted in the 'Her' side of the robe.

She dressed and made her lunch, stepping out onto the balcony to eat, forgetting the noise factor until it hit and hit hard. She rapidly stepped back inside and slid the door closed with a bang, almost dropping her lunch. She needed a plan to cope with noise before she went insane, a way to stop the noise, to turn it off, turn it down, to shut it out. With no clue on where to start, she was becoming alarmed. All her other senses didn't scare her but this did. She could hear those out on the street, her neighbours, the animals, vehicles, everything. It was frightening especially with no way of stopping it. She sat at the table eating attempting to shut off the noise. Today was Thursday and she had four days to figure it out before uni. If only she had noise-cancelling headphones.

Some parts of her new found sensors she enjoyed. The oil reeds placed in her home, the flavours on her tongue especially chocolate, the sensation of touch through her feet and fingers. So many new experiences. Some parts were not so good with burps and farts quite fragrant and certainly not nice to smell. A new dilemma arose, heading back to work and uni, she would be able to smell the uni students and her work colleagues and even know when they farted, be able to hear it and smell it. That became an unsettling thought. She was already avoiding a few classmates as their scent was overpowering and some days, she could smell them from the other side of the room. She was going to have to find a way to stop smelling. Things with barely a scent, she could pick up. Walking past the bookcase, on the way back to her room, the smell of books was similar to walking into an old book store. It was strange to be able to smell different items through the unit, even items she did not expect to have a smell, like the DVDs.

Standing in front of the pile of clothes on the floor, she sighed. It was no use putting it off, it all needed to go out and so she bundled the discarded clothes into bags and placed them into the boot of her car, the crinkling of the plastic garbage bags sounding strong. She paused at the car door dreading what was to come. Slowly opening the door, she eased herself into the driver's seat, closed the door and put on her seat belt. "You've got this," she said as she sat holding the wheel and pushed the button to open the garage door, bracing herself for the sharp noise to follow. The noise of the door opening sent shivers down her spine as the chain inched its way up, the grinding sound grating on her.

Her fingers reached for the start button and pushed. Her face cringed as the engine awoke and the radio blared to life with a Silverchair song. Her fingers pressed the down volume button on the steering wheel stopping as the music became bearable. Her feet touched the pedals and the car moved out of the garage. She kept encouraging herself, willing herself to keep going, not wanting this to stop her from living. Many obstacles she had overcome and this was another one she would climb and conquer.

She and Donna had managed to conquer many things together. They began scheming and getting what they wanted at age 8. Nothing stopped them, they always found a way. At 16 they convinced their parents to allow them to trek Kokoda trail. They found ways to make money to pay for their trip, researched it and presented them with their decision. All questions and concerns were fulfilled until their parents had no options but to say yes. Nothing stopped them working together to achieve what they wanted. Trekking with gorillas, backpacking through Europe and extreme adventure holidays through New Zealand were all conquered without parents' help. This was how she ended up with her job at the travel agency. They saw potential in her, in how she planned and brought their trips together.

Her ears heard every gear change, heard the engine changing revs, the fan and a lot of other noises she'd never noticed or knew. A car park was directly in front of the op shop bins. Annie parked her car, opened the boot and hurriedly grabbed out the bags putting them on this sidewalk. Her mind was going crazy with all the information being presented, a rock concert would be quieter. The smells and sounds were overstimulating as she quickly transferred the bags to the donation bins and raced back into her car hurrying home to safety. It wasn't until she was safe back in her garage that her heart began to slow and she calmed down. Raising her head from the steering wheel, she let out a long breath knowing she had tackled the world and won. She left her car and she headed back upstairs to survey her wardrobe.

The strange sensation in her chest near her heart was getting stronger. Before lunch it began, a small tugging. It wasn't painful, it was like a pulling, a warm safe pull as if someone was calling her. Throughout the day she kept feeling it pulling at her, calling her. It was weird, yet comforting. Each time the sensation tugged she touched the spot trying to understand. It was just another confusing thing happening today, another to add to the list of unknowns, yet it was reassuring. Somehow it made her feel safe, protected, loved and secure. As she walked up the stairs it got stronger as if someone calling her was close near her. Again, she raised her hand to the sensation and kept it there as if it was protecting her, letting her know everything was fine. She cherished the feeling, a comfort during this trying time.

She stood there in front of her wardrobe wondering if her clothes would match or if she would need to buy more. She hoped everything would work together. As she did not want to go shopping with all the hustle and bustle of the shopping centre. She heard quickening footsteps outside coming up the path and stopped, a pause and a loud knock. The sensation leapt in euphoria and forcefully pulled her downstairs. Throwing open the door, she hesitated a second before throwing herself at the stranger, into his strong muscular arms sobbing softly "Help me, help me understand. I don't understand."

CHAPTER 3

Annie had flung herself at this unknown man standing at her door who felt familiar and safe, someone she could trust, someone who would help. She couldn't explain why she felt this way. He hesitated before placing his arms around her hugging her close and spoke softly, "I will help you Elentari, I will help you." he said as he let out a long sigh of relief.

With her ear against his chest, she could hear his heart beating strong and fast, feeling safe and secure at the sound. She stepped back puzzled as he called her Elentari when her name was Annie. He was tall 6 foot 8 with strong muscular biceps and bulging pectorals. The feel of his stomach beneath his shirt was rock hard, a six-pack was hiding under his sleeveless shirt. His long brown hair with streaks of blonde was tied back and his crystal-clear blue eyes shone. His eyes were honest and rimmed with dark thick lashes, a warmth flowed from them. His face was unshaven and rugged. He was like a demigod who had come to save her.

"My name is Annie," she said, touching her chest where the sensation was, looking for something to comfort her as she began to wonder if she made a mistake. The sensation was very strong, she could feel her whole-body reverberating and was surprised when she felt it respond as he lifted his hand to his chest.

"Yes, that is me and our link. In this world, you may be called Annie but where you are from, where you were born, it is Elentari. My name is Rorien. Please let me in and I will explain." She nodded and led him in, unsure she was doing the right thing but he felt safe and he understood her sensation. He followed her upstairs and paused at the top, taking in the room. "This is big! Is it a meeting place?" He asked.

"No this is my apartment." Please don't hurt me she wanted to scream but he seemed safe, someone who would protect her. She could not explain this feeling she had for him, what it was about him which made her trust him, feel safe and secure. It was very unlike her to allow any male into her home, yet he was different, trustworthy and dependable. She wondered if she was going insane, allowing a total stranger into her home.

"Apartment?"

"Yes, where I live."

"Our apartments are called casa and nowhere near this big." Her casa smelt clean and fresh with a hint of honeysuckle flowers. The room was long with a kitchen bench and table at one end and couches at the other. The table sat eight and four stools were under the bench. The lounge was set in an L shape with two couches seating four and a small table filled the void between them. Against the wall was a short cupboard with a strange black thin box sitting on top. Two bookcases overflowing with books leant against the opposite wall. He observed she kept it neat and tidy with everything in place and minimal. He estimated his and Jasper's casas would be able to fit in her casa.

"Explain what is happening but first tell me how to stop the noise, please?" she begged

He chuckled, shaking his head "We all have that problem when it first arrives. You can close your ears. It's like how you close your eyes but with an imaginary door over your ears. Focus on your ears and imagine a door closing over them. You can shut out the noise to be like it was before or leave it open partially to hear better. How much noise you chose depends on how open the door is." He stepped towards her and gently took her ears in his hands, his heart beating faster as he touched her. Her beautiful scent filled his nostrils, a scent of many different kinds of flowers which didn't seem to be her true scent, it was like she had covered herself to hide her true self. "Concentrate on your ears feeling how my hands move over them." He moved them to fully close over her ears and opened them leaving his hands against her head. "Can you feel how my hands create a door?" She nodded. He slowly moved his hands away not wanting to, he wanted to keep touching her, holding her, wanted any excuse to hold her. "Try to use your imaginary door and feel the door close like my hands did."

She tried and nothing happened. "It didn't work," she said frustrated.

"It will take time, just keep practising. We are taught before we reach our awakening to close our senses off, all our senses."

"Awakening?"

"Yes, this is what is happening to you. You have started your awakening. We all start on our 20th birthday."

"My birthday is not until another month."

"Maybe in this world but where you were born, in my world, it is todia." He began to explain who she was and what had happened. He explained how he found her using their link.

"Link?" she touched her chest again.

"The link is special between two beings who are connected. It helps us find our link, anywhere anytime. This probably seems very strange to you. Trust the feeling, the link and let it guide you. I won't force you to do anything you are not comfortable with. I came to find you and will leave in seven dias, returning to my world. It is your decision if you return with me. I have no choice to stay any longer but you have a choice to come with me or stay. Oh, and you can touch our link without physically touching it."

"Dias?"

"Dias, as in sunrises and sunsets, that is a dia."

"Here we call that a day. Guessing there may be a lot of other different words we both need to learn." It was getting late and she started making dinner, turning on the lights. "What do you eat?" she looked at him, his head turned to the side with a quizzical look.

He was puzzled at how she could light the room so quickly. "Fruits, vegetables, meats, seeds, bread, grains things you can find growing mainly," He said as he tried to work out how she lit the room when there were no powers in this world. She had touched the thing on the wall before the room lit up and lights appeared, it made no sense to him.

"Mmm like us except I don't eat meat."

"Oh, ok," he said. He was more interested in how the room lit than what she ate. The lights were not lamps or candles, they were more like little suns stuck on the ceiling. His eyes kept looking, checking, searching and again, he found no answers. She noticed him looking at the lights as if trying to work out what they were.

"Do you have electricity in your world?" She grabbed her phone to turn the music on, Imagine Dragons rang out. She turned it down to a manageable level and continued to make dinner for them.

"Electricity?"

"The lights are electric, a power source to run things."

"We use candles and oil lamps, not electricity."

"Mmm." She moved to the music as she cooked, still attempting to close her ears, nothing was working, and she was getting frustrated at not being able to shut out all sounds. The fan, the buzzing of the induction stove, the rice boiling and stir fry sizzling, all enhanced and loud in her head. Try as she must, nothing was working to close out the sounds. "Tomorrow we will visit my parents to find out what happened. I need further answers."

The noise had come from nowhere and was another thing to puzzle him. He could see no beings playing instruments and couldn't understand where it came from. The sound was very different from anything in his world. It was music with many different instruments to create it. He liked how she moved gracefully to the music as she made their meal. She didn't have an angelic voice but he could tell she enjoyed singing along with the music.

Rorien watched her, taking her in. She was 5 foot 8 with a petite curvy frame, a thin waist and wide hips. Her hair was closely cropped and almost black. Her eyes were green with a yellow rim and flecked with red and blue, the most unusual eyes he had ever seen, it made her even more special. She wore a striped coloured dress which ended just below her knees and hugged every curve, the plunging neckline showing her cleavage, her large perky breasts. She was perfect, she was his link, he wanted her and he needed to find a way to ensure she would come back with him. Her world was more advanced than his and he wondered how he could convince her to leave with him and return to his world, a simpler world.

"You do have tea in your land, don't you?" she asked, putting the kettle on.

"Yes, there are many different teas we have. Dandelion, chamomile, lemongrass, peppermint."

"I hope you have black tea and not just infusions?" she said looking directly at him annoyed.

"Yes, we have black tea and green."

"Mmm good. That could have been a deal-breaker." He looked at her puzzled. "Deal breaker is…"

"I know what a deal breaker is. I wondered what deal it would break if there was no black tea in my lands."

"Me coming with you," she said quietly. He grinned, his eyes dancing with joy. She felt their link dance with joy. She touched it, surprised she could feel his joy, could sense feelings pass along it.

"Yes, feelings can pass along our link."

"Oh." She tried smiling along with the link or she hoped she did.

He smiled at her. "Yes, like that. Sometimes it just happens. Intense feelings pass along without having to do anything."

"Ok. So, at times you will know how I am feeling without me saying anything and I will know what you are feeling as well?"

"Yes. Our link is our connection. We can let each other know what we are feeling, pull me to you or you to me, find each other, lots of things. The link helps you find who you're linking to."

"Linking?"

"Linking is the completion of the link, who you will spend your life with. You have a linking vows ceremony and bite your link to leave your mark and let all know you are now linked."

"Mmm we call that marriage, without the biting bit."

Throughout dinner, they chattered about growing up and how their worlds differed. Even though his world had no electricity or industry, it seemed similar and sounded so peaceful and surreal. They lived with the basics, only taking what they need, supporting each other as one big happy family. She was beginning to like his world and was planning to visit especially if it meant spending more time with him. He made her heart race, made her feel special and she wanted to be with him as much as possible. She had never felt this way before, such strong feelings and had never kissed anyone. Her mother had always said that her body was hers and only hers, and it should be treated with respect and honour and to let no one take advantage of her. Now all she wanted was to kiss him.

She had cooked a rice dish which wasn't much different from his world. There were flavours in it he didn't understand and assumed it was the stuff from the glass jars she used. She had made water appear from the silver pipe by pulling the lever, another thing he didn't understand. The water in his world was collected in buckets from the rivers or via the handmade canals flowing through the cuedel from one river to the next. Every being collected their water to use and carted to their casa and here, water poured out like a waterfall and could be hot or cold. Her dishes were smoother and lighter than their clay or stone plates and bowls. They drank from clay or wooden cups not glass, glass was used to make jars for storing herbs and oils. The fork was something different, they used a spoon or their hands and a knife for cutting but never a fork. He kept watching her to make sure he was doing things correctly and so as not to make a fool of himself. He helped her clear up and wash the dishes before they moved to the couch.

Her heartbeat fast every time he looked at her. Those thick full sensual lips of his, she wanted nothing more than to kiss them, wanted him to take her in his strong arms and kiss her passionately. She wanted to feel those burly arms around her again, to smell his scent and melt against him. His wonderful scent was like a crisp winter's morning where the earth is covered in ice and the sun begins to shine, the first smell of the morning. She loved that smell and that was what he smelt like. She had met him only a few hours ago and already she was so smitten with him. She didn't understand how she could have such strong feelings for him after knowing him for such a short time, it was very unlike her.

As they moved to the couch after dinner, she picked up her stuffed dragon putting him in her lap. "What's that?" he asked

"Drachenstein of course. He is my stuffed dragon. Generally, kids have stuffed toys but he was too awesome not to keep. He is a great companion, always listening, never argues, always hugs me when I need it," she said, hugging Drachenstein tight. "This band playing now are Imagine Dragons, one of my fav bands. It would be awesome if dragons were real."

"Dragons were real in my world, except they died out many thousand anoks ago."

"Dragons are mythical and make-believe in this world."

The night grew late and he began to yawn. "Guess we should get some sleep. We have a long drive tomorrow." She rose and walked to the spare room as Rorien followed her. "This is my spare room. No male is allowed in my room which is there," her hand pointed down the hall. "Not even Dad ventures past the doorway." She stepped into the spare room, his room and into the walk-through robe. "Dad has changes of clothes here for when they visit. As he is larger than you and shorter, hopefully, trackys will work for now until we can stop tomorrow get you some clothes and help you fit in since you are here for a week, seven dias," she said, remembering his word for the day. She threw some clothes on the bed. "Through there is the bathroom and there are fresh towels in the cupboard," she said pointing through the robe to another door. She turned to him placing her hands on his chest looking up at him and said softly, "Good night Rorien. See you in the morning."

"Good night Elentari," he said as his stunning blue eyes stared into hers. It seemed strange to hear herself called a different name. She liked the sound of Elentari, it seemed mystical, regal even. She could hear his heart beating fast as was hers. She wanted him to kiss her but she wasn't sure she could trust herself not to grab him if she didn't move away. He turned away from her and felt him touch their link as he checked out the clothes, trying to distract himself. Their link was such a strange thing, a strange sensation to link them together and she wanted to know more about it. She walked slowly out backwards, watching him before heading to her room.

Rorien headed into the bathroom unsure of what to do. He opened the cupboard to find a few containers and a pile of towels. He closed the cupboard and looked at the pipe on the bench. He had seen how Elentari made the water appear and pulled the lever causing water to flow out. He had seen how she moved the lever to change the temperature and did the same, the water began to get hotter. He adjusted the lever to get the right temperature and washed his face using his cupped hands. He grabbed a small towel from the cupboard and washed himself.

Beside the bench was a strange chair with a lid. They had spoken about toilet habits and guessed that it was a toilet. It certainly was different from the open floor drains they used and communal bathhouses. He noticed another lever on the wall near the large tub and lifted it, cold water hit him from above. He quickly shut it off. He was surprised by the water falling from above him, like a waterfall, and assumed they bathed under it. Shrugging he dried himself and walked back to the bedroom. The bed was plain and simple with no wood carvings. He stripped off and climbed in naked, the cotton sheets feeling soft and smooth against his body and the mattress firm under him. He fell asleep quickly and slept soundly with the knowledge his Elentari was near him.

He woke as the sun began to rise and put on the clothes, she left out for him. The pants were very loose and kept falling down. He took them off and put his leather pants on. The top also loose-fitting but he could wear it. He stood in her bedroom doorway, softly calling her name, gently pushing on their link to wake her. Her window faced north and he could see the ocean out it and watched the sunlight hitting the waves as it peaked over the horizon. She rolled over towards him and lifted her head off the pillow. Her eyes squinted as she looked towards him. "Good morning Elentari. Shall we get moving?" he asked.

"What time is it?" she asked, reaching for her phone to check. Still coming to grips with her new name.

"It is sunrise."

Her phone showed 5:48. "This is too early. Usually, I get up much later," she grumbled as she rose from her bed, another thing she would need to get used to, early mornings. She walked towards the bathroom before stopping and turned towards him, hands on her hips "Head on out to the lounge, I will shower and be out soon." He nodded and left. She quickly showered, enjoying the feel of water droplets hitting her skin, the one sense she would gladly keep and would have happily stayed enjoying the sensation except she had company and a trip to make.

He had watched her rise from bed fully clothed, assuming the clothes were bedclothes as she wore a top which just covered her backside and they were different from her clothes from yesterday. Another thing which differed in their worlds. He understood he was not wanted by her stance, her hands-on-hips, and headed into the lounge. He noticed a room outside, facing north, with glass separating the lounge to the room outside. He inspected the glass trying to find a way out and found what seemed like a door but it did not budge as he pushed and pulled it. Stepping back, he inspected the area and noticed a rail on the floor which kept the door from moving as he pushed. Doors in his world only opened in or out and didn't slide. He slid the door and stepped into the outside room which had a view of the ocean. He watched the sky dance with colour as it was filled with glorious reds streaking across with a florid of oranges and the sound of the waves crashing on the beach below, travelling up the hillside through the crisp silent morning to his ears. The sunrise looked fantastic, as did the start to the dia, and he paused to enjoy the morning.

He heard the water stop and stepped back inside, entering the kitchen, he began looking to see what he could make for breakfast, opening the cupboard filled with food. There was too much to choose from and he was unsure what she ate. He turned the kettle on and got the teapot and tea out, choosing one from her many teas. There were heaps to choose from and he hoped he got the right one. To boil the kettle was so much easier here than his world where the kettle was placed on the fire to boil. He began to worry, if electricity stuff makes her life easy, how would he convince her to return with him? His world had nothing like this and what if she didn't like the idea of no electricity and won't return with him? He had to convince her to come to a world with no electricity.

She found him in the kitchen trying to work out how to make breakfast. "Sit down, I'll do it," she said as the kettle boiled. *How sweet, he is trying to help. I like that, a male who wants to look after me*, she thought as she smiled, grabbing her phone to turn the music on.

"How many teas do you need? There are heaps in there," he said. He sat at the bench watching her as she moved her body to the music. He liked the way she moved and some moves made him want to grab her and take her into his bed. She looked so inviting, so sexy.

"Many teas I need. I like tea and tend to buy them when I find a new blend. Last time I counted there were 37 different ones."

"That is almost one a dia for a mesik."

She placed the toast, butter, jam and tea in front of him. "Can you put these on the table and what is a mesik?" and turned to fetch the plates and cups.

"A mesik is 40 dias. An anok is 8 mesik or 320 dias."

She sat down and grabbed the teapot to pour. "Oh, a bit longer than our month. After breakfast, we will head off and stop partway to find you some clothes and have a cuppa. Did the pants not work?"

"No, they didn't, they kept falling down. Cuppa?"

"Cuppa," she said, holding up her teacup.

"Oh, have tea," he smiled and touched their link in a teasing way. She liked the feeling her link gave her.

She responded, touching it back in a teasing mood. He stroked the link making her feel fantastic and excited. It felt so good that she did not want him to stop. She cleared the table after breakfast with his help and, as they finished, she pulled hard on the link and he responded moving quickly towards her. She looked into his eyes as he stroked the link making her insides scream with desire.

"I am enjoying you playing on our link Elentari. I have been searching for you for nine anoks, touching our link and no one responding. It is nice to feel a being on the other end," he said as he stroked her hair.

Her heart cried at the thought of him pulling on the link wanting someone to answer and no one answered. It was she who didn't answer him. "Well, you can search no more. I am here and will respond when you touch. I like this special feeling between us that makes me feel safe, secure and protected. Even better knowing you are on the other end." She winked as she moved into him causing their bodies to firmly touch, her face lifted towards his face and she stared deeply into his eyes. He wrapped an arm around her waist holding her close to him as his fingers ran through her hair, staring into her eyes and stroking lovingly on the link. She almost melted to the floor, her legs were shaky and her heart pounding, longing for him to kiss her. Her hands were resting on his hips as they stood locked together. She could stay here all day in his arms, breathing him in, memorising him, letting him physical and mentally stroke her. She wanted him with every fibre of her body.

"We should go," he said, his voice breaking as he moved apart from her. He wanted her, desired her, his body screamed to have her but he would wait until they returned to his world to take her into his bed. Oh, how his body sang with joy at the thought of them linking and being together always. She was his and he was hers, his link, his Elentari.

"Mmm. Yes. We should." Elentari stood for a moment, waiting for her legs to strengthen. She wanted to stay here and have him hold her, spend every moment wrapped in those arms. "Before we go you should shave. Dad won't like an unshaven male visiting. How do you shave?"

"With a razor," he said

"Oh, I wasn't sure." She moved away from him and headed to his room. "Dad has stuff in the cupboard you can use." She entered the bathroom, opened the cupboard and knelt looking for the shaving items. "Here we are," she said as she placed shaving cream and a razor on the bench.

"Ok, we shave a little differently. What is this?" he asked, holding up the tin canister.

"Shaving cream." She opened the cap and pressed the top, foam forming on her hand. She smoothed it onto his face. His face felt rough yet she did not want to stop touching it, taking a little longer to spread the foam then necessary. "Now you shave," she said, handing him a razor. He took the razor looking at it puzzled.

"This is different. We have knife-like razors." He loved how she softly touched his face, smoothing the cream over it.

"Like this," she said, taking another razor and starting to shave as her Dad did.

"That I can do." He smiled and started shaving, keeping an eye on her as he did. She had moved to the tub and sat on the edge watching him. She looked so elegant and beautiful in her blue dress, the way the dress flowed over her and the way she sat leaning back with her hands behind her on the other side of the tub.

He finished shaving and bent over the basin to wash his face. As he stood, she reached up with a cloth and dried his face. She looked so perfect. Her touch was soft and loving as she gently ran her fingers over his clean-shaven face. He wanted to kiss those fingers, her hands, kiss his way along her arm to her lips.

"Ok, that is better. We should go now," she said, still caressing his face with her palm. His face felt so smooth and soft and she wanted to rub her cheeks against it. Instead with every ounce of strength, she walked out and downstairs to the car.

Rorien followed her, she turned away from the door he had entered the dia before and continued down a hallway and into another room. Inside was one of the metal creatures. He paused, a frown on his face wondering what they were doing. She noticed he stopped and turned to him.

"We are travelling by car," she said pointing to the metal creature, "as it is a 4-hour drive. We won't get there until nearly noon, high sun." She hoped the words made sense.

"Oh, how far is it?"

"Do you know what a kilometre is?"

"No."

"What do you measure distance in?"

"Well a cani is about this long," he said as he held his hands out about a meter apart.

"Mmm, that is about a meter in earth terms. A thousand of them is a kilometre."

"That is a stadi."

"We are travelling 400 stadi to visit my parents."

"That is about the distance from North to South in my lands where I live."

"Mmm," Elentari opened the door and eased herself onto the driver's seat. Rorien watched her and walked to the other side. He managed to open the other door and got in. "You need to put your seatbelt on," she moved her hand to reach hers and buckle it. Rorien followed suit and she helped him to buckle up.

He felt strange being tied into the seat, it didn't feel comfortable and he was worried. He was used to running or walking to get to where he wanted to go. It took 10 hori to run North to South in his lands and this metal creature could do it in 4 making it very fast.

Elentari pushed a button and the creature came to life. Rorien was startled as music blared through the car. "It is ok. The car is not alive, it has been created by us and requires us to make it move. It can't move by itself." She pushed the button on the sun visor to open the garage door, cringing at the sound, and drove out slowly, stopping at the end of the driveway. Rorien clung to the dash, his knuckles turning white from clinging so hard. Elentari reached over to touch his hands and stroked the link, hoping to ease him. "It's ok. I am a good driver and I won't put you in danger." He was stiff, staring directly in front of him, not breathing. "We will take it slow. This is very normal in this world." She felt him soften slightly. "Will you trust me?" she asked, still stroking the link and his arms.

"Yes," he moved his hand to hold hers, still very nervous and unsure. "Yes, I will trust you. You trusted me when you opened your door, I will trust you. How does it move without being pushed or pulled?" Rorien's heart was racing, fear and excitement flowing through his body at the prospect of a new experience. He guessed in the next seven dias, there would be many more new experiences. "I'm not sure as we have nothing like this in my world."

"Mmm If you were sitting on a chair what would you do with your hands?"

"Put them on my knees or beside me, I suppose. Never really thought about what to do with my hands when I sit. They just do whatever."

"Think of this as a chair, sit normally. Just relax, you will get used to it soon." He smiled and put his hands in his lap, clasping them tightly together. He was still unsure.

"Relax and breathe deeply. I will go slow, to begin with until you will get used to it. Are you ready?" He looked at her and nodded.

"Ok. Breathe deeply. Let's go," she gently moved the car out into the street, taking her time to allow Rorien to relax and calm. "Breath deep and slow, it will help."

He had begun to relax and got used to the car when they came over a hill and he could see many buildings scattered far and wide below them. Amongst them was an area of very tall buildings altogether. His eyes went wide and his mouth dropped. "What is this? Does every being live in the same spot?"

"This is the main city. Lots of people live here but not everyone lives here. Lots of these buildings are shops and offices as well."

He watched wide-eyed as they passed between extremely tall buildings, buildings almost as tall as a mountain. He was amazed at how many buildings could be together in one spot and how tall they were. He felt unsure and concerned as they passed between the buildings, hoping they wouldn't collapse. There was nothing like this in his world, all buildings and casas were only one story. These were so tall and large and he felt so small compared to them.

Rorien kept watching everything as the car sped past her world, asking her questions on what he saw. He was taking it all in. They had been travelling for a few hours when she pulled the car into a building.

There were many cars here and it was very long and wide. She stopped the car and turned towards him.

"This is a small shopping centre and will have what we need. We will find you some clothes and shoes, have some tea and continue. It's not far now," she said as she unclipped her seat belt and his. "You ok?"

He nodded watching her. She opened the door and got out, taking her bag with her. Rorien followed her and she entered a door which opened by itself. He stopped, watching it close by itself. Elentari turned back and walked towards the door. Again, it opened for her. He was frightened and curious as to how the door could open by itself as there were no powers in this world.

"These are called automatic doors and are designed to open as you approach, like an invisible person opening them for you. They run on electricity." He looked at her and back to the door before cautiously stepping through, his eyes constantly searching the door and turned to watch them close again, taking it in and scanning all around. They stepped onto a moving path and headed up.

"Escalator, electricity again," she said as she walked up. To Rorien, it was a strange feeling to be walking on moving ground and he was not sure he liked it. The escalator ended in a large, long open area with many humanoids running around and wide, open doors leading into rooms. Rorien had never seen such a large inside area before. He stopped, turning around to take it all in, scanning all around him as he watched the humanoids go about their business, wondering if it would hold every being from the cuedel.

"Come on," said Elentari, gesturing for him to follow as she pulled on the link, "hurry up." He smiled. She was learning quickly to use their link. They entered through a large open door into a room filled with clothes. He had not seen so many clothes before it was as if every being in the cuedel had put all their clothes in one massive big wardrobe.

"We're looking for some jeans and tops for him," Elentari said to another female.

"What style and size?" asked the female

"What would he look good in and suit him? No idea of size."

Elentari heard the assistant say to herself 'my bed'. This was a new discovery, the ability to hear others thoughts. She smiled and held their link. *He is mine, all mine as we are linked and you can't have him and he won't be in your bed*, she thought. She did like knowing he was her link and liked feeling it gave her. The assistant moved to the wall of jeans and took a few down.

"Try these on and see what fits best," she said, handing Rorien the jeans and leading him to the change room.

He closed the door of the small room and he was not sure what to do. Elentari had spoken to him about what to expect and to lock the door. He was glad for the info. He turned the lock on the door and stripped off his pants. He grabbed one of the jeans and put them on. It felt different from his leather and cotton pants. The first pair were a bit tight around his waist, he tried on another pair. They fitted much better. He liked them, not as restrictive as his leather and firmer than his cotton. He was certainly bringing these back with him, even if they would stand out. He stepped out of the dressing room. "These fit ok," he said as he heard both females suck in a breath. *I guess this looks good*, he thought to himself smiling as he watched the females faces, their eyes full of desire, scanning his body and both lost in thought.

Elentari sucked in a breath as he stepped out of the change room. The jeans showed off his tight backside, a yummy tight backside. *Oh, how I want to grab that*, she thought. Elentari smiled thinking how she was absolutely going to enjoy grabbing that backside. *Wow girl, you never think this way. Interesting feelings you are having.* "Can we have these and a black pair please."

The assistant snapped back to reality. She was staring at him dreaming of what she wanted to do. *I agree* Elentari said to herself answering the assistant's thoughts. *I want to do that too.* It seemed strange to know what others thought. She couldn't hear Rorien, maybe he had his mind closed off. "We need some t-shirts too please."

The assistant disappeared to gather clothes. Elentari stepped into Rorien, placing her hands on his shoulders as she rose on her tiptoes and she whispered in his ear "She wants you in her bed. She can't have you. You are mine and mine only, my link."

He looked at her and whispered "And you are mine and only mine. I shall need or want no other." His hand moved to stroke her hair, taking in her facial features and scent, a different flowery smell from yesterday distinct with lotus flowers. He wanted to taste her ruby red lips and leant in to kiss her as the assistant returned, he pulled away.

The assistant had three different shirts. "Which do you prefer?" Rorien chose one, removed his shirt exposing his rock-hard abs and buffed pecs. Both females gasped and licked their lips at his unbelievably gorgeous upper body. He put the new shirt on, covering his body, watching both females as their eyes wandered up and down, searching every muscle of his body.

"Needs to be bigger," he said, watching Elentari staring at him, making him feel sexy knowing she wanted him. He began to feel more assured she would return with him if she wanted him and maybe wouldn't care about electricity if she had him.

"Mmm, maybe. Try a few sizes bigger" said Elentari. The assistant handed him another size which fitted better. He wandered the shop picking out tops he liked and Elentari chose a few in the right size.

"We will take these and can he wear these out of the shop please?" she asked. The assistant took her time to remove the tag on his jeans. Elentari smiled knowing she was taking her time as the assistant wanted to check out his biteable butt and find any excuse to rub her hands on his body. Elentari felt the same. She never had such strong desires before maybe because she had not seen anyone so strong and gorgeous as Rorien.

She paid for the clothes and headed to the shoe shop with Rorien falling into step beside her. They found a pair of shoes for him and headed to the café for tea. She could hear the thoughts of those they passed, it was strange and certainly different and hard to get used to. She chose a table near the window and they sat down, Rorien sitting opposite her. "Do you eat cakes?" she asked.

"Yes, we do," said Rorien as the assistant came over to take their order, her eyes on Rorien looking him up and down. Elentari listened to her thoughts and to another female who wanted her link, desiring him. She ordered tea and cakes for them.

"It is not much further to mum and dad's place, about an hour, a hori away," she said, remembering his word for an hour. "We will stay tonight and tomorrow and head back in two days, dias. How has your trip been so far? Are the clothes ok?"

"I love these jeans, they are fantastic. I am taking them with me back to my world."

"Yeah jeans are good. How have the sights been?"

"There is much to see and much to learn. It has been exciting to see much of this world. The car trip, tall buildings, open spaces, small cuedels, large cuedels, heaps of things." Tea arrived as Rorien continued to express how he was enjoying the trip and all the exciting things he saw. Elentari enjoyed his excitement, taking him in. She hoped it would be the same for her if she returned with him. There was much to leave behind, her friends and family, and much to gain, a new world with new possibilities waited for her. He would be there with her also, his world and him.

CHAPTER 4

Rorien was amazed as they arrived at her parent's place. "This is even bigger than yours. Does every being live in large casas?" he asked, wondering just what was in the casa and why they needed so much room.

"Homes, casas, vary greatly, some with many bedrooms and bathrooms and some with just one bedroom and main room. Homes are what people want. You chose how many bedrooms and bathrooms you want."

"Oh. Why so many rooms?" he asked as he turned to face her as she turned towards him.

"Bedrooms for each child, spare rooms for guests, spaces to spread out in. We spend a lot of time in our casas and gardens."

"Oh."

"We spend time with family and friends for gatherings for birthdays, celebrations, footy and cricket matches, weddings, engagements, lots of different reasons."

"Oh. We do that at the parestala. They are large areas where we gather for celebrations, festivals, markets and supper."

"That's awesome, everyone coming together. Are you ready to go in and meet my parents?" she asked, a touch of concern on her voice. She had never brought a man home to meet her parents and this man, she had known for less than a day. No boys had ever come to her house, not even for her birthday parties, they didn't interest her.

He nodded and they headed to the house where she opened the front door and walked straight in without knocking, "Mum, Dad, where are you?"

"Kitchen dear," answered her mother and they headed into the kitchen "We didn't know you were coming. Why are you not at work?"

asked her mother puzzled. Her mother spied Rorien and her face changed to a frown as she nudged her husband whose nose was stuck in a newspaper. He looked up.

"Hello. Who is this man you bring home to meet us? You have not mentioned a man before. Who are you and what do you want?" Her father folded the paper forcefully as he put it down and glared at Rorien showing he was not pleased to have a strange unknown man in his home or an unknown man travelling with his daughter.

"It's ok Dad, this is Rorien. I came to find the answers. Was I adopted?" she asked abruptly as she stood behind a chair, her hands holding the back. She was not one to fluff around and preferred to get straight to the point and this was straight. Rorien stood quietly to her right.

Her mother looked away, fussing, trying to remove a fake stain on the table to avoid answering the question. Her dad's face was blank as he stared directly at her, not moving. "Was I adopted?" she asked again more forcefully, her eyes drilling into her fathers. Her mother began to sob and her dad lowered his head as he softly answered

"Yes."

"Can you tell me the story, please? I want to know and hopefully, I will understand," her voice softened.

"Who is this and why is he with you?" demanded her father.

"Story of my adoption first. It may help to explain who he is."

"Ok." Her father paused, "We were walking along the path through the hills when we heard a baby crying. We ran towards the sound and came across an older woman struggling on the ground with a baby in her arms. 'Please take Annie and look after her' she said. Your mother took the baby and tried to comfort you as you were screaming. I told the woman I was getting help and your mother nodded. I ran off and when I returned, the woman had vanished. Your mother was puzzled and alone with you. We searched the area for her but found no trace. When the police arrived, they too searched and could find no trace of her. We had no idea what happened to the woman. After lots of discussion and paperwork, we were able to bring you home as foster parents until the woman could be found. It was months later that the police closed the case and officially allowed the adoption process to begin. There was no evidence of you being born and the date we found you became your birthday," said her father. "How did you know?" he asked looking up at Annie.

Annie explained who Rorien was, his journey to finding her and being his link.

"It still doesn't explain who the woman was and why she left you here," said her dad.

"That may be something we will never know. The answer will reveal itself when it is needed," said Annie.

"Also leaves more questions unanswered, as in Rorien and his world."

Her mother nodded and said quietly "You were so little and wouldn't settle. I couldn't get you to stop crying. Nothing would comfort you, milk, songs, holding you, nothing. I kept holding you and talking to you hoping you would understand we were helping you. It seemed like you knew something was wrong. You kept pulling near your chest, trying to grasp something."

"That would have been Elentari pulling her attachment, trying to call her mother. The attachment keeps babes feeling safe and mothers use it to find their babe," said Rorien

"That explains why you kept pulling your chest, you wanted your mother. We had nothing for a baby and had to stop at the store to get some basics just to get us through the night. Lucky one of the staff had a car seat for you. We put you in a drawer on the floor for the night until we could shop properly for you. You were so little and just wouldn't stop crying" said her mother, lost in memories.

"It was fun ringing around all our friends for baby stuff and all were wanting to know what was going on. Everyone found something to bring for you, they only wanted to find out why we had a baby all of a sudden," said her father smiling at the memories.

"Yes, it was nice showing you off. It was amazing how much our friends gave us for you. They were so generous," said her mother

"Can you show me where you found me, please?"

"We will go tomorrow," said her mother softly, eyes downcast. "You were such a joy to have even if you wouldn't settle. I started to rub your chest when you pulled at it and eventually you stopped crying. I guess you began to realise I would take care of you."

"Rorien leaves next weekend and has asked me to come with him. I haven't made my decision yet. Why don't you come to stay with me before the portal opens? Come on Friday, which is seven days away" she said for Rorien's sake, "It will either be goodbye to Rorien or be our last goodbye, I haven't decided."

Rorien frowned in her direction. He questioned her on the link, confused at what she was doing as the doorway will have opened by then. She looked at him, 'later' she replied back along the link.

"We can come Friday. How long will you be staying here?" asked her mother, getting up to make lunch and fuss over everyone.

"I have today off and we head back on Sunday, back to work and uni on Monday." They began discussing things which had been happening lately, asking Rorien about his world and how he was finding this world. After lunch, they headed out to wander around the town, their house not far from a walking track along the river and into town. Her parents were accepting Rorien and seemed to like him. They happily explained their world to him, answering his questions and pointing out things to him, filling his curiosity.

The following morning Rorien woke and went to look for Elentari, following the music, he found her in the lounge room on her hands and knees. He leaned against the door frame with his, head sideways watching her quizzically. She looked up at him.

"Yoga," she said "this is the cat-cow pose. Yoga is great to build strength and flexibility. Come try." Rorien got on the floor beside Elentari and followed her moves as she moved from pose to pose which weren't difficult. Even with all his training and strength, yoga with gentle movements seemed to stretch his muscles and give them a workout.

"We are moving into the dragon poses. I like these." He was doing well for his first time. She decided to step it up and see how good he was. "This is crow pose," she said as she moved into position, hands-on mat, knees on her triceps and lifted her hips to the sky to balance on her hands. She watched him out of the corner of her eye. He began placing his hands on the floor, knees against his arms, lifting his hips to the sky and fell. Annie sat down and laughed. He scowled at her. "I wasn't expecting you to master it first up, most take time to hold it. I just wanted to see you fall over," she said smiling playfully as she tugged at their link.

He turned from her sending a growl down the link. She lunged at him tackling him to the floor and tumbled around, playing, fighting and wrestling with each other until he had her pinned beneath him. He stared into her eyes and moved to kiss her. Her heart was pounding.

"Time to make breakfast before mum and dad get up," she said, attempting to throw him off. She wanted him to kiss her, just not here with the possibility of her parents walking in while they were kissing and ruining the moment. She started making pancakes, instructing him what to get from the fridge and pantry to put on the table as she cooked. He set the table, as she poured the water for tea and made coffee for her dad. As she placed the pancakes and teapot on the table her mother entered.

"Breakfast is up," She said as her father came in behind her mother.

"I could have done that," her mother said.

"We were up and had finished yoga. It's not often you get spoilt from someone from another world, so sit and enjoy. We have a walk to do this morning before showing Rorien more sights." They ate breakfast discussing what they were going to do for the day, where to go and what to do with Rorien and what to show him.

Rorien helped her mother clear up breakfast as Annie got ready and they headed out with her father driving and Rorien in the front, driving outside of town to an area where Annie had walked and jogged the trails many times. She wondered which trail she was found on as they parked and her parents headed towards the path which followed the river up to the top of the waterfall. She loved sitting at the top of the waterfall watching the water tumble down over the rocks, seeing the water splash up as it hit the rocks below. It was soothing watching and listening to the roar of the water, especially after heavy rain when the power and force of the water increased. They had walked about 150 meters along the track when her parents stopped, her father wrapping his arm around her mother.

"We found the woman here as we were walking back from the waterfall. Your mother paced up and down the path from here to the car park, waiting for help, trying to comfort you and stop you crying. The woman was here," her father pointed to a spot just off the path, "the police thought she may have slipped down the slope into the water. Nobody was ever found and there were no leads to finding her, not even a car or pram to be found. I guess she must have returned to your world Rorien."

"It would make sense why you found no trace of her," said Rorien.

"I am glad you found me and am very grateful for you both." She could sense they were struggling with having to tell her and afraid of losing her. She had shut her ears and mind to give them their privacy. The ability to close them had finally happened during the car trip up to visit her parents and as much as she wanted to know what they were thinking, she left them to their thoughts. "This marks the spot where I was born in this world to Francis and Beth King." Annie placed a large smooth rock on the spot where the woman gave her to her mother. Her mother smiled for the first time since she had demanded answers, the small gesture brought a touch of happiness to both her parents.

The rest of the weekend was spent out exploring and showing Rorien the ways of this world. They took him to play mini-golf, bowling and to the movies. He quickly picked up mini-golf, struggled to knock down a pin in bowling and spent most of the movie glued to the screen, amazed and mystified. It wasn't until they were in the car and halfway back to her home that Rorien asked: "why did you invite them to come after the doorway opens?"

"If they know when we leave, they will try to stop me. I will step through seeing their pain, hearing them begging me to stay and all their sorrow. That will be my last memory of them. This way they believe they have a chance of stopping me and my last memories will be as you know them, this fun and amazing weekend. Their last memories will be of this weekend too. Which reminds me, best text work and see if I can take this week off."

"That makes sense, your parents. What is it you do for work and does this mean you are coming back with me?" excitement danced on his words.

"I work in a travel agent office. It's hard to explain as you have nothing similar to compare to. Plus, I attend uni, I can blow that off and yes, I am coming." She smiled at him and stroked their link lovingly. "I am happy with you, I feel safe, protected and loved. You bring me joy and I am pulled to you. If I stayed…" she trailed off as feelings of sadness and loss waved through her. She didn't want to think of what her life would be like without him here.

He felt the sadness along their link. *She is happy and safe with me yet she is not fully happy to be leaving*, he thought. He touched her hand to let her know he was there for her, she turned and smiled at him taking his hand in hers.

He sat back smiling, holding her hand. His link, his Elentari was coming back to his world with him, he felt so relaxed and calm. He looked at her lovingly. *For the first time in nine anoks, I am settled and complete, finally, I am with my Elentari*, he thought.

CHAPTER 5

For the next few days, he taught her to fight, to yield a sword, to make a bow and arrow and how to shoot it. He taught her skills she would need to know to fit in, to use her senses, grow them and hone them. She could pick up the sound of ants walking along and even spot them from afar. All their time was spent in the bush helping her to get ready for his world. In turn, she taught him yoga and tai chi.

Towards the end of the first day of training, she decided she had had enough, it was hard and her body was not used to fighting, swinging a sword or shooting arrows. Her muscles hurt and she knew she would be in pain tomorrow as her muscles weren't used to long, tiresome sessions. She sat down on the ground.

"Can we stop now? I am tired and my leg muscle hurts. I can't walk." She rubbed her calf pretending it hurt. Rorien came over to check her and she grabbed him tumbling him over. Training changed into playing, chasing each other, tackling and grabbing. She had him on the ground with her legs straddled over his waist attempting to pin his hands as Rorien flipped her over and had her pinned to the ground hovering above her. She looked at him and gazed into his eyes, wanting him to kiss her. She desired him and her body ached for him. She felt him stroke the link, saw the desire in his eyes as he moved his lips towards hers. She moved her hands to clasp them behind his head pulling him to her. His lips met hers, she opened to him inviting his mouth to explore hers. His tongue flicked against hers. She liked the taste of his lips, liked the way his tongue explored her mouth, liked how he kissed, bit and licked her lips. His kiss was deep and passionate, warm and loving. He moved his mouth down to her neck and she moved her head, opening her neck to him. He kissed, sucked and nipped her neck. She wanted more, her heart pounding, her body was screaming for more. His hand moved under her top, his lips moving back to hers, he raised himself from her and looked at her.

"What...how...I..." He looked puzzled, his hand on her bra. Elentari giggled.

"Most men have trouble with bras, can't undo them," she said, smiling, "Rorien, I never wanted someone to have me, to take me into their bed until I met you. You make my heart race and my body desires you. I always wanted to wait until my wedding day and want our linking dia to be the first time."

"It's ok, I can wait. After all, I waited nine anoks for you. Plus, I have no idea how to remove that thing, the moments over," he said, grinning as he sat up. She sat up and kissed him again. Their hearts were racing as they sat beside each other, his arm around her, allowing their breath to calm. This was torture to him, he wanted her but couldn't have her. His heart slowed and she turned to him.

"When will we get to have our linking dia?" she asked.

"When you return with me and settle into our ways, to where you are comfortable then we can set a dia to complete our link." He was using every ounce of strength to keep his distance. He desired her, wanted to take her in his bed, his loins craving to have her.

"Mmm. Ok." Elentari stood and walked away from Rorien, she gazed in the distance, off in thought. "Home and rest?" she asked as she turned to him.

"Yes, we can stop for todia," he said, starting to head towards home, "Come on. We will start again on the morrow and go for a run. When you come into your awakening, not only do our senses increase but so does our speed, agility and stamina."

"I tend to go for a run a few mornings each week before breakfast."

"We will go after breakfast. Once we've been for a run, we will continue with more training."

"Geez, bossyboots. Can you explain why I have to learn all this?"

"It's my routine, I train every dia and you can help me train. You don't have work or uni so what else are you going to do? Plus, it will help you when you return with me."

"How?"

"Stop all those males from trying to take you from me," he said, grabbing her in his arms grinning as he kissed her.

"Or maybe to stop you from constantly grabbing me." She grinned pulling away from him and running towards home but he quickly caught up to her.

"You'd better run faster than that if you don't want me to grab you," he said as he grabbed her, kissing her neck. She giggled trying to break free from him and he let her go. She stretched up, kissed him and continued to walk home as Rorien fell into step beside her, taking her hand and letting her be lost in her thoughts. He was off in his thoughts thinking of their future at least 900 anoks together.

On the morning of the doors return, Elentari wondered what she should take with her. They had been for a run and had breakfast. She had even called her mum to check what time they would come tomorrow. Now she was deciding what to pack in her big suitcase. She had been downloading all her songs to her hard drive as well as TV series and movies. Her laptop, hard drive and solar charger were in the suitcase. She thought about packing tea and decided that could cause issues in the new world, the possibility of an introduced species taking over, even though it should be right, she wasn't risking destroying a world just so she could have her favourite tea. Plus, there were too many to take. She wondered what clothes to pack and if she should take her toiletries. Still looking at her wardrobe working out what to do, Rorien appeared and leaned against the door frame looking quizzically at her.

"What you doing?"

"Trying to work out what I should take. Almost everything in my wardrobe, I have decided to pack and then decided against it. I don't know what you all wear, what females wear?" she asked in a desperate tone, her fists in a tight ball shaking them slightly in front of her and body tense.

"The females mainly wear dresses, sometimes skirts. If you allow me in, I'll work it out for you? This won't be your room anymore...unless you stay." He squinted looking sideways at her.

"I am coming with you. Come in and see what you can find." She sighed and nodded, softening her body as Rorien entered and took a big breath in.

"This is all your clothes!?" he said, his hand moving around the wardrobe, his eyes were wide and mouth open as he scanned the two sides of the wardrobe, shocked at how large it was.

"Yes, and this is after I cleared it out the other day...dia you arrived. It was filled on both sides. This is about half of what I owned. Why, is it not enough?" Her body stiffened slightly as her hands clenched at her sides and a worried look crossed her face.

"No, it's huge. I only have a few items to wear and could fit into these two drawers," he said as his hands grabbed two drawers.

"Oh. Is everyone the same with only a few sets of clothes, a few dresses to wear?" Her body softened as she began to shuffle clothes.

"Yes and no. We keep everything minimal, simple and what we need. I think Sarina has more than a few things. Don't know about female stuff."

"I need all this and more." Her arms stretched wide hugging her clothes hanging in the wardrobe, a slight smile in the corner of her mouth. He looked shocked until he realised, she was teasing and smiled. Life with her was never going to be boring.

"Pack the clothes you like the most. These could blend in and these I like. Guess the first thing we do is find you some clothes."

"Shopping spree! Yay!" she shouted, pumping her hands in the air and doing a little turn. He looked puzzled. "When we need to get new clothes, we spend time searching different shops and buying more than we need. Shops similar to where we got your jeans and tops. Sometimes it can take all day just to get a dress to go out in and you bring home another few outfits just in case."

"We don't have lots of shops for clothes. There are one or two shops to get material for sewing. Some shops have clothes they made and can make clothes for you but mainly the females spend time together sewing. Mothers sew for their link and themselves as well as their child, sewing clothes until their male child leaves or their female child can sew."

"Mmm. I can use the sewing machine but not very well. I suspect females don't have machines as you don't have electricity and they sew everything by hand. That is going to be a problem," said Elentari, a little concerned and worried how she would be able to provide clothes for both her and Rorien. "Your mother still makes your clothes?"

"No, my parents died about three and a half anoks ago, while I was spending every moment looking for you." His head hung down and shoulders slumped as he spoke about his parents, sorrow in his voice. Elentari put her arms around him to let him know she was there and leaned on him as he put his arms around her, placing his head on her shoulder and sighed. "I miss them. When I joined the Kings army, at 14 and I was living between the army and them. I moved completely at 17 and I spent little time with them. Mum was trying to speak to me but I was too busy consumed with the army and finding you." He lifted his head, tears welled in his eyes. She had no words to help him. "Sarina's been wonderful making sure I had enough, making me clothes," he said.

"Sarina is talented. Hopefully, I will be able to sew as well as her."

"You have a vika or else," he said, his face terse. She looked concerned at how she was to learn and keep him happy. He smiled at her. "It's ok, we can buy clothes and I have enough. You, what are you taking?" He moved away from her to study her clothing, his hands on his hips.

"Oh, you scared me. Pain." She said as she smiled and nudged him. He grabbed her from behind and swung her off the floor, holding her so she couldn't getaway. She was laughing and squirming as he bit her neck, biting and snarling as if he was going to eat her. She wriggled more, laughing hard. Her feet touched the floor, giving her grip to pull away from him, getting free from his arms and turning to face him.

"We have work to do. We can't be playing around when the door opens, we may miss it" she said trying hard to be serious without laughing.

"Oh really, no play?" He was grinning at her as he stepped towards her. She turned and ran out, laughing as he chased her through the unit until they collapsed on the couch laughing, kissing and holding onto each other.

"Yes, we have things to do before the door opens," her smile faded as she continued, "I am about to leave everything I own behind and step into a new world with nothing." He took her into his arms gently caressing her. "I am about to leave everything I know."

"You'll have me to build a life together with our furniture and casa. You will always have me," he said as he kissed her. She snuggled into him feeling safe.

"Mmm. I will have you. I like that idea, the idea of us building a life together." She sat wrapped in his arms breathing him in for a few minutes. "Back to it," she said, rising and heading to the closet. "These you think?" he nodded. She placed them in her case. "What else should I pack? Knickers and bras, I need them." She placed her knickers and bras in the case.

"Nope you are not taking these," he said, grabbing her bras out.

"Why not? They keep my boobs safe from wandering hands." She grinned

"And who's wandering hands do they need to be safe from?"

"Just yours." She grabbed them off him and placed them back in the bag. "You will just have to learn to undo them." He grinned and grabbed her, trying to undo her bra. She giggled and squirmed "Not now. Once we are linked you can try all you like."

"Really? You're going to make me wait?" he smirked, stroking her back and their link.

"Yes. Shopping, linking and then bra removal."

"Whatever. Sarina can help you with female stuff" he said, letting her go and studying her wardrobe. She finished packing and shut her case placing it near the couch as she sat down.

"When will the doorway appear?"

"I assume around the same time as I arrived, about the high sun," he said as he walked to the kitchen and grabbed the unopened packet of tea and put it in her case. "A little bit of home to help you settle in."

"But won't that be bad to take?"

"It'll be fine," he said shrugging.

Elentari looked at the clock. She loved her analogue clock her best friend Donna gave her, Winnie the Pooh and Piglet were holding hands looking at each other, two friends walking and facing the world together. Donna, she would miss most. They had been friends for over fifteen years, grown-up and travelled together, living at each other's house and inseparable to the extent their parents came to the conclusion they had twins and treated them as such. This was one adventure they would not do together and an event to end their time together. She wished she could explain to her in person, instead opting to write her a letter, one big long letter explaining it all, and had posted it during their morning run. Donna would get it tomorrow after she was gone and would have no way to talk her out of it. She had also created a photo book of all their times together with special messages throughout it for her which was due to be delivered in a few weeks, her last gift to her best friend.

It was nearing midday and her heart began to beat faster. She was feeling anxious, excited and nervous. She paced the floor, afraid she wouldn't like this new world and if she didn't, she had no way to return. *What am I doing? Leaving with a complete stranger to a distant land. Am I going insane?* she thought.

"It's ok Elentari, I am here and we'll do this together." He took her hands in his, looking at her with soft loving eyes and led her to the couch.

"I know this is a big adventure and one I don't think I can return from." Her words trailed off as a bright light appeared stretching into a door. Rorien turned to see what made her eyes widen and mouth drop.

"The doorway is here," he said standing up and holding his hand out for her. She looked at him and hesitantly took his hand, her heart racing and tears forming in the corner of her eyes. Her emotions were racing from concern to excitement, dread to courage, and so on. She grabbed her case as she stood, holding his hand tightly. He grabbed Drachenstein and guided her to the doorway. "Shall we do this together?"

"Yes, please. Don't let go of my hand?" she said, pleading and holding tight to his arm and body, her eyes concentrating on the doorway.

"I won't," he said, looking at her. "Don't plan to ever let you go. Shall we?" he said as she nodded and he led her through the doorway and into his world.

CHAPTER 6

Just as Rorien had explained, the door was bright and warm with no sound and void of gravity. She felt empty, an empty feeling that went right through her as if she didn't exist. Fear crept into her, not knowing where she was or which way to go and she clung to Rorien tighter as he moved them forward. They stepped into a small room that had been built into the rock with one window to light the room and a single lamp hung from the ceiling. There was little furniture and what was there was basic.

"Welcome to my casa, my home as you call it," said Rorien bowing to her, taking her case.

"You weren't wrong when you said my unit was huge. Is your bedroom through there?" she asked pointing to the partially opened door. His casa smelt heavily of him with an earthy undertone.

"Yes. This room and the bedroom, that is all."

Elentari wandered the room taking it all in, there wasn't much to explore as it was just a bit bigger than her large bedroom. There wasn't much furniture and what was there was plain, simple and basic, a couch for two and armchair, a small table with two chairs, a kitchen with a bench against the wall near a fireplace. She wondered how they lit the fire if they used matches or a flint? She opened the bedroom door to see a wooden bed with blankets strewn across it, drawers for clothes with a washbasin on top and no sign of a bathroom. *I wonder if they have bathhouses like in Turkey,* she thought hoping there was something as basin washing was not her style.

Rorien stood watching her as she moved around the small room and into his bedroom, her hands touching and running over everything, checking everything out. She showed no emotion on what she thought.

"Is it ok?" he asked quietly, scared it would not be enough and she would want or need more or even desire to return, not that he was sure she could. He was never concerned with how little he had or how small his casa was until now. He had not bothered with furnishing it beyond his needs as he spent little time here and now, he wished he had.

"Yes, it is. You said everything is minimal and you only have what you need. This is enough…for now," she said playfully tugging on the link. Their link was something different and an unusual way to communicate which she liked. Their way of being close without physically touching, able to talk without others hearing, knowing each other's feelings without asking, a special bond.

He was happy she was ok with everything and knew she was being kind. She reached up to kiss him and he held her in his arms, kissing her, not wanting to stop holding or being away from her. He enjoyed holding her, how she felt in his arms. He could stay like this forever. They were locked in a passionate embrace as the door swung open and Jasper, Sarina, Lorcan and Fendton walked in.

"You found her!" "She's here, you're back!" "Woohoo, the search is over!" "She came," they said in unison, hugging them and celebrating their return. Elentari was overwhelmed being hugged by strangers as if they had always known each other. Rorien reached for her, holding her to protect her as he gently pushed the others away. Even though he wanted to be alone with Elentari, he was happy his friends were here to meet them.

'I will protect you,' he said on the link.

"Elentari, meet Jasper and Sarina, Lorcan and Fendton. Friends, meet Elentari and not all at once," he said looking at them sideways.

He was taller than his friends and his friends were taller than her, she felt small surrounded by them and the room felt tiny with the six of them. Jasper was robust, powerfully built and sturdy. His dark eyes matched his jet-black curly hair and stood 6 foot tall, shorter than Rorien and Lorcan. Lorcan was a strapping male with a large chest which curved outwards, standing at 6 foot 4 with shoulder length dreadlock blond hair and green eyes.

Sarina took Elentari's hands in hers "It is nice to have a female in our group. Welcome to our world." She hugged Elentari. "I am here whenever you need." Sarina was 5 foot 10 with long wavy ash brown hair reaching the waist of her pear-shaped body. Her face was heart-shaped with soft hazel eyes and pencil-thin lips.

"Thanks," said Elentari moving back from Sarina and closer to Rorien. "This is a little overwhelming and so far, very different to what I am used to. This is all I've seen of this world and it is much different to what I know, much smaller and very basic," replied Elentari "Lucky I have Rorien to help me transition." She glanced lovingly at him, taking his hand and leaning into him, he wrapped his arm around her.

"On the morrow, you will meet the Master and he will ensure you settle in and help you with what is to happen." Sarina turned to Rorien. "The Master requested you both meet with him after breakfast. He suggested Elentari can stay with us in our spare room until she has her own casa."

Elentari turned to Rorien and her face looked frightened. She grabbed tightly to the link "What does she mean my own casa and staying with them? Can I not stay here?" she asked, her hands gripping him tightly, hoping it was a mistake and she could stay with Rorien. He gently rubbed her back and stroked her face.

"We're not fully linked and can't stay together. That is the law. You can live with your parents or your link after linking. Remember I said this when we were talking about the differences?"

"Yes, but I didn't...I hoped...it's just. This is so old fashioned." she sighed and rested her head against his chest, her body drooping. "Ok, I can do this. It won't be long until we can be together. I hope," she said, looking up at him pleading.

"The decision was once you are settled. So, settle quickly and we can be together," he said, his eyes squinting at her and mouth tight before he winked and his face softened.

"Tell us what happened," Fendton said with excitement in his voice. Fenton was short at 5 foot 9 and not as muscular as the others. He was athletic with curtain styled mousy hair and hazel eyes. There was a child-like innocence about him yet he looked lost.

"Before we do, let's get Elentari settled at our place," said Sarina. "Plus, we have more room." She began to shuffle them out as Rorien grabbed Drachenstein, passing him to Elentari and took her bags.

"You brought Drachenstein!" she said, hugging Drachenstein tight. "You are awesome." She kissed Rorien. "Thank-you."

"What is that?" asked Fendton

"This is Drachenstein, my pet dragon."

"Pet dragon? It's real?"

"No. It is a toy," she said handing him to Fendton so he could check it out. "Generally, children have stuffed toys but he was too awesome to leave."

They all headed off to Jasper and Sarina's casa, weaving their way through the cuedel. Casas were carved into the mountain and sparsely spaced. Each casa has their individual ornate façade and gardens. The stonework was exquisite and the stone lattice was fine and delicate, almost like lace. Even the stone pillars, columns and plinths were masterpieces with animals and flowers carved with intricate detail on them. Everywhere she looked, elaborately detailed stonework met her eye even the stone steps chiselled into the path had details etched in them. Nothing was ordinary or basic except for a few casas.

Oak, birch and fruit trees grew through the cuedel. Gardens were filled with food, herbs and flowers and were lavish with their designs. There were vertical growing gardens which used the casa walls and cliff face to cling to, herbs gardens growing under windows for ease of picking, wagon wheel gardens with spikes as pathways, each segment filled with vegetables, herbs or flowers, tiered gardens to create good use of the steep cliff to grow more. Even the garden stonework was chiselled with intricate detail. There was nothing she could see which was basic.

Jasper and Sarina's place was larger than Rorien's and still smaller than her old apartment. The entry divided the main room in half. The kitchen was on the left and had a cupboard against the wall near a fireplace and an island bench, a table seating four filling the rest of the space. To the right was the lounge with two blue couches and the floor had a beautiful blue rug with many shades of blue swirling through creating soft patterns flowing across it. It was calming, almost like flowing water. The rest of the furnishings matched in with different coloured blues. On the wall hung a painting of the ocean during a storm and a small tapestry of trees with humanoids playing under it and the stone carvings on the wall created a story. It was lavishly furnished and beautifully decorated.

"Ok, sit down I'll explain everything," Rorien said and began to explain all that happened since stepping through the door. Elentari sat beside Rorien, their bodies touching, holding hands and constantly watching each other.

"It was amazing and so different from here. They have these metal things called cars which you sit in and take you places. It's like a cart but much different, no pushing it or camels to pull it. Elentari took me to visit her parents in one. It's strange to sit and not move while the world passes by, travelling fast, way faster than we can run. The cars are like ants following each other on a black smooth path. Sometimes the path fits four cars side by side. You move them somehow as they can't move by themselves. Don't know-how. Elentari does and makes it go where she wants and uses the wheel to go in the direction she wanted. That's all I know."

His friend's eyes were wide and their faces fixed on him wanting to know more. Listening to him explain more about her world. They asked a few questions before Rorien continued, his arm wrapped around Elentari and her hand found his knee.

"We passed through cuedels and villades. Their main cuedel was massive with buildings so tall they were seven, eight even nine casas high, buildings over 30 cani tall! It had 20, 30 more tall buildings all beside each other with lots of shops and casas all inside. The shops are different with many shops under one roof in a shopping centre, like our markets but bigger and undercover and stacked on top of each other. Shops are bigger than casas and have a multitude of items. Some doors open by themselves as you approach like an invisible being opening the door for you. Escalators are moving floors taking you from story to story. It was weird to stand still and everything around you moved.

The group was hardly breathing, listening so intensely to Rorien. They asked more questions to Elentari and she answered before Rorien continued.

"Elentari's casa is two casas tall. Casas are big with lots of rooms, three, four even five bedrooms, can have two or more lounge areas, separate kitchens. Elentari has these silver pipes which water flows from. You pull the lever and water comes out. Showers are like waterfalls where the water comes from above and they bathe under them. There are different types of stoves, some have a small fire in them that lights when you turn the knob and others, are flat and heat up when you put the pot on."

Sarina got up to prepare food for them. "Elentari doesn't eat meat," said Rorien, rubbing her shoulder.

"Ok, thanks Rorien. No meat supper it is" replied Sarina.

"What else did you do?" asked Fendton, sitting forward in his chair eagerly waiting for more.

"Elentari took me mini-golfing, bowling and to the movies. Mini golf is an easy game to play with a straight stick with a bulge at the bottom which is used to hit a ball. The idea is to hit the ball into the hole at the other end of the path but the path is not always straight. There were tunnels, bridges, sharp corners and obstacles in the way. My first few tries I hit the ball way too hard and by the time we got to the 18th hole I was getting good. Each hole has a number of hits it should take you to get the ball into the hole and Elentari made almost every number, she is really good. Me, I was off on all of them, way over the required hits. Mini golf was the best fun and bowling not so much. Bowling involves rolling a ball down the lane, smooth path, to the other end and knocking down as many pins as you can. Pins are blocks of wood and there are 10 of them in a triangle. A few times Elentari knocked down all 10 which is called a strike. I was lucky to knock down four as my ball kept rolling off the lane and into the gutter, which is on the side of the lane, and missed all the pins."

"Something you are not good at! We need to make one here so I can laugh at you playing," said Jasper smirking as both Fendton and Lorcan laughed at the idea.

"It did make me laugh watching him miss and get frustrated. We could make a bowling alley," said Elentari, smiling as he squeezed his leg.

"No, we are not! No bowling alleys." Rorien pushed her away and waved his fist at her.

"But it brings so much joy to people who are good at it," she said, batting her eyes at him. He continued, ignoring their pleas.

"Movies are amazing. They have these big, massive windows called screens which show life on it. It is like sitting in the markets watching every being except they are not real. You follow a story about each being like just watching all the good bits of your life for a whole anok. It's strange to watch, hard to describe really. I was mesmerised by it that I did not move, so focused on the screen, I was almost lost in a trance."

"He did not move? For how long?" Lorcan asked Elentari, his head shaking.

"Movies run for two hours and he sat still for almost that long." She answered.

"We need them here. He never sits that still but then again neither do we. Too much to do so let's not bring them here."

"Done. No movies but bowling alleys," she said elbowing Rorien. "At movie theatres you need snacks. Rorien got to taste cheezels, popcorn and jaffas."

"What are cheezels, popcorn and jaffas?" asked Fendton.

"Cheezels are a fun snack. They are orange and round with a hole in the middle which you put your finger through like a ring and eat them off your fingers. A playful snack which is crispy and crunchy. Apparently, you cannot go to the movies without having popcorn. Popcorn is corn which is heated until it bursts, becoming large and light and they put salt or butter on it to flavour them. I preferred the salted ones better. Jaffas are a red-covered ball of chocolate with an orange flavour," said Rorien.

It grew late as the story of his adventure to her world finished. His friends were amazed at his time away and all the new things he had experienced. Fendton and Lorcan took their leave, while Rorien fussed over her making sure everything was ok.

"Are you going to be ok here?" he asked as he stood in front of her with his hands on her hips and her hands on his chest just below his shoulders.

"Yes, I will survive tonight without you…just," she said teasing, "I have Drachenstein to keep me company. Thank you for bringing him." She raised up and kissed him.

"Is the bed ok? Will you be warm enough?" he asked as his eyes looked towards her room.

"It will. Sarina has more blankets in the cupboard if I need. I will be fine," she said as she patted his chest.

"Are you sure? Can I get you anything?"

"Nothing. Sarina has provided me with all I need. When I awake, I will call you like this," she pulled hard on their link and he fell into her.

"Ok, make sure you do as soon as you wake. I will be here." He kissed her passionately, holding her tight.

"Ahem, about time to leave Rorien," said Jasper, "She will be here on the morrow. Now go." Jasper raised his hand and pointed to the door.

"Ok, ok, I'm going." He headed to the door pausing as he opened it. "Are you…"

"Go!" said Jasper, cutting him off and pointing to the door.

He loved how excited she was that he brought Drachenstein. *At least she has him to hug for the night,* he thought, *would prefer if it was me. Hopefully, something from her world will make her feel safe and hopefully not miss her world too much. If only I could hold her all night, trade spots with Drachenstein. It won't be long and she will be in my bed always as my link.* He sighed and climbed into his bed holding their link all night with the hope it would comfort her and she wouldn't feel alone.

She changed into her nightshirt and slipped into bed, sinking into the mattress. The mattress was made of feathers and felt like sleeping on pillows, and the bedding consisted of sheets and blankets. She curled up under the blankets and slept soundly feeling Rorien on their link. All night she held tightly to their link and to Drachenstein. She was most pleased he had thought to bring him, Drachenstein made her feel like she was still at home and not in some strange new world.

CHAPTER 7

When morning broke, she tugged Rorien to her as she quickly dressed and entered the main room as Rorien burst through the door. She raced to him flinging herself high into his arms and wrapping her legs tight around his waist.

"You miss me?" said Rorien, grinning and teasing her, kissing her.

"Not at all' she answered happily, kissing him. She released her legs, placing them on the ground "Did you miss me?"

"Nope" he grinned, passionately kissing her as Jasper and Sarina entered the room.

"Morning Rorien, Morning Elentari," said Jasper and Sarina together.

"Morning," they both said, still clinging to each other.

"Todia," said Sarina, beginning to prepare food for them, "you will meet the Master, Elentari, and he will introduce you to the other Masters. The Masters will introduce you to the King. The King has requested your presence, both of you. You will spend most of the morning with the Masters as they show you our ways. We are here to help you settle in and find your way once the Masters have finished."

"Thank you, I am very grateful for your help and glad for a friend. Does everyone meet the King?" she asked as she stood in the kitchen with Rorien standing behind her with his arms wrapped around her holding her tight and his chin resting on her head. Her arms were over his and her hands held the back of his hand.

"Not every being. As you were taken from these lands and have returned, he wanted to meet with you. You are all every being has been speaking about these last few dias. Every being in the community is waiting to hear if you returned and to see you. Every being."

"Mmm, I hope they don't all swamp me like you all did last night. I might have to return to my world."

"Don't you dare" glared Rorien, twisting her around to look at her and pulling her closer to him, holding her tighter. "You are going nowhere."

"She can't without the code and potion," said Jasper slapping Rorien across the head, "You big fool!"

"And if I did you would have to come with me." She battered her eyes at him "I am but a helpless female who needs a strong man to protect her." Sarina and Jasper looked at each other and roared with laughter.

"You are in trouble," said Jasper, slapping Rorien on his back taking his seat at the table. Sarina had everything on the table for breakfast. Lots of different fruits and cakes were laid out with a teapot sitting in the middle.

"Do you drink tea, Elentari?" asked Sarina

"At least 4 times a dia she has tea. It was a deal-breaker if there was no tea here," answered Rorien, holding Elentari's hand as they took their seat at the table.

"Yes, I do," she said, sticking her tongue at Rorien. "This looks delicious Sarina." During breakfast, they chatted about the different things her world ate and there was not much different except for cereals. No coco pops here and they hadn't heard of pancakes.

"We'd best go find the Master," said Rorien, rising as she finished her tea. "There are lots to do," he pulled out her chair, "and lots to see." She rose and followed him out the door.

"Thank you for breakfast and hospitality. It is most appreciated," she said to Sarina waving as they left. She took Rorien's hand as they weaved their way through the community. The paths were even and smooth, perfectly cut into the ground, winding around the landscape and were wide enough for two to walk side by side. Elentari held onto Rorien's hand with both of hers, as he pointed out things explaining them to her. The cuedel was built into the mountain and ran the whole way around the remnants of an old volcano plug. The top of the cuedel extended two stadis around the mountain and stretched a stadi down to the flats. The very top was 137 canis straight above the cuedel with ridged sides straight and bare, sides almost as if claws had scraped down them creating grooves. No one ventured to the top and she was curious as to why and what was at the top.

Four rivers ran down from the mountain to split the cuedel into four districts, East, West, North and South. The King's casa, the royal court and Masters casa were on the north side of the mountain. Half of the King's army lived on the east and the other half on the west. Rorien and his friends had casas on the east side. They crossed the river dividing the East and North districts. Four straight, wooden platform bridges with no guardrail, spanned over each river, one near the top, one near the bottom and two in the middle and nothing changed between the districts, the casas, gardens and landscape were similar.

"You are on the east side but the sun is rising in the west?" she said puzzled.

"The sun rises in the west and sets in the east. Doesn't it in your world?"

"No, it rises in the east and sets in the west. The high sun is in the north here too?"

"Yes." They approached the Master's casa and Rorien knocked.

"Come," said a voice inside. Rorien entered with Elentari following. The casa was messy and disorganised. Many books lined the walls and lay open on benches, jars filled with different herbs and powders sat on amongst the books and all around the casa. The sink was filled with dishes in various states of cleanliness. The Master was either a busy man with little time to keep his area tidy or a disorganised being. "Rorien you are back and you have brought Elentari with you. Good. Welcome Elentari," said The Master as he looked up at her from his chair at the table which was filled with open books, bowls and jars.

"Good morning Master. Yes, we have returned. Elentari, this is the Master of air."

"Good morning Master," said Elentari. The Master was old with a long grey beard almost reaching halfway down his chest with curly and long hair with all colour faded from it. His face was filled with creases and folds of skin so pronounced it was hard to see the real male. His forehead deeply ingrained with worry as if he carried all the woes of the cuedel.

"What is your age Elentari?" he asked looking at her with deep-set hardened eyes and bushy unkempt eyebrows.

"My birthday is next month in my world. It is the day I was found. I am 20 in that world," she answered. He was examining her, working her out and it was unsettling her.

"Come." The Master rose and walked out the door with Rorien and Elentari following, walKing in silence. She noticed casa adorned with silver and stonework more elaborate than most with gems worked into it. Knowing this was the Kings and Masters area she guessed they belong to the King. They entered a wooden double door with carvings and gems embedded on each. The frame was adorned with clouds at the top and mountains at the bottom, fire and flames were on the left and waves and water droplets on the right, a frame representing the four-element powers. The middle of the left door was a carving of a King sitting on his throne with beings bowing at his feet and on the right door was the queen sitting on her throne looking lovingly at the King with females curtseying at her feet.

Inside the long, large room, about 30 meters long and 8 meters wide were seven other Masters, all similar-looking, old with long hair and pronounced wrinkles. Even their robes were matching, plain simple flowing robes of one colour, each robe a different colour and a matching belt tied around their waist. The air Master wore a yellow robe. Elentari was a little confused as they walked the length of the room as to why there were eight Masters when there were only four powers. *I guess the answer will be revealed when needed,* she thought.

At the far end was another male sitting on an elegantly carved wooden chair with a high back and silver lace adorning it and red gems were set into it. The chair sat on a pomp, a raised stone platform with four steps leading up to it. His clothing was embellished with elaborate needlework and made of silk. As there was no one else here, she guessed he was the King. Behind him stood another male, arms by his side, eyes forward, not moving. He carried a sword and bow and she guessed he may be the King's personal bodyguard

"My majesty, my I introduce Elentari," the Master said as he bowed to the King holding a hand out towards Elentari.

Yes, I got that right, he is the King, she thought.

The King sat looking her over. She held her ground, standing straight with her hands clasped in front of her, her eyes watching him. He had an oval-shaped body, thick around the waist, and his salt and pepper hair hung around his shoulders. The lines on his forehead flowed like ripples on a lake with prominent crows' feet around his eyes. He may be the King but she was not going to feel small, it was hard enough for her having to be here without being belittled. Rorien stood on her right just behind her and she could just see him. She felt safe knowing he was there.

"You are Elentari?" he asked quietly. There was a gentleness about him, a hint of sadness in his voice.

"In my world, I was called Annie. When Rorien arrived on my doorstep, he informed me my birth name was Elentari. The name feels right like it is mine whereas Annie meant nothing to me. When I heard Rorien say Elentari, my whole-body responded," replied Elentari, her face showing no emotion.

"You have similar features as her, look very much like her," he turned towards the Masters standing in line on the left side of the King, "does she not look like her? Do you think it is her?" The Masters nodded like puppets on a string. The air Master turned to the King.

"As we know of no other who was taken and she is of age and her features match Elena's. It must be her. She has been found." said the air Master.

"Her mind is closed. I cannot search," said the Master in a white robe.

Elentari stood still listening and watching. Something was missing, something they were not telling her. She opened her mind to read their thoughts. Not much was forthcoming, the Masters were giving her a once over, picking her flaws and how she looked like her. What power she may hold. Picking on her physique to work out which power she would yield. She closed her mind, nothing of interest. She heard the entry door open and heard footsteps coming towards her, stopping a distance from them, just over halfway into the room. She knew they were Rorien's friends who had entered by the sound of their steps. She heard other footsteps enter behind them, another four had entered and they approached closer before halting. She kept herself straight and eyes forward. She would not be intimidated.

Rorien was delighted at the way she held her ground with the Masters and smirked wondering how they were coping with a being not trembling in their presence. Every being seemed to tremble when they first met the Masters, to meet the Masters and King together would have most collapsed on the floor. Here was his Elentari standing strong and tall, almost looking as their equal. He was most pleased and most proud at how his Elentari presented herself, held herself. Touching their link, he let her know she was doing great and he was there.

"Shall we see which power she yields, my majesty?" asked the air Master.

Great, I am to be tested. Nothing was said about being tested. How am I to yield something I know nothing of? Do they expect me to know this? she thought.

"Yes lets," said the King "Elentari these are the four Masters of the elements - air, water, fire and earth." Each Master took a step forward as he said their elements, bowed and stepped back, "and these are the four Masters of the spirit - sight, heal, shift and movement." Again, each Master stepped forward, bowed and returned. "The element Masters will show you how to yield each power. As we practice each movement from an early age, you may not find which power you yield todia." The King nodded to the element Masters. Each Master began to move his hands to yield each element showing how to bring the element under control.

"The hands move the way each element moves. Some moves will cross between elements, air and water flow gently and move similarly and moves to yield will cross," said the King

The moves are similar to tai chi, yoga and martial arts, Elentari thought. *The Masters are like Avatar, the Last Airbender except for each of their elements.* She smiled. *Maybe this isn't going to be so bad I do yoga every day and tai chi twice a week with Donna. This could be easy or an immense fail.*

"Follow the Masters and see which you yield. Which calls to you most?" asked the King.

"They all do, they all look interesting," answered Elentari. How would I know what calls to me? I am just finding out about all this she wanted to scream.

The King smiled. "Elena's, your mother, her power was water. My power is fire. Try them both."

The Masters showed her how to yield the powers and she was to try. Rorien's friends moved closer to him, standing a few feet behind him and he heard Jasper speak.

"Bets in on our power," said Jasper.

"Done." They all agreed.

"You lot are terrible. I hope she has a spirit power just so you all owe me," said Sarina, her nose turned up.

Elentari turned slightly to fully face the Masters, Rorien still behind her. "Master of fire and Master of water please show me." The Master of water in blue robes, had moved his hands to produce a ball of water suspended in mid-air, in another move, the water bubble exploded and the water-soaked back into the air. Elentari moved her hands the same as the water Master. A ball of water appeared. Again, her hands moved and it popped. *Oh man, that is way cool. I just produced a ball of water from nothing. Ok, let's try this fire one.*

"Pay up males!" stated Jasper with his hand out, "she yields water" Fendton took a coin to hand to Jasper.

"Catch." Rorien flipped a coin over his head hoping he would miss.

"Another water power in the group," said Jasper fist-pumping the air, doing a little victory dance. "Go water."

The Master of fire in red robes had moved his fingers to form flames, a wave of his hand and the flames died. Elentari continued copying the movements of the fire Master and flames appeared.

Even better, at least I will be able to light the fire to cook, she thought.

Lorcan kept quiet, he was not getting a coin out just yet, he was watching as she moved and her hands to yield fire.

"Half to me thanks" stated Lorcan, "she also yields fire."

"What!?" said Jasper and Fendton. Rorien took a few steps back towards his friends.

She heard everyone in the room gasp and saw Rorien step back towards his friends, away from her. She was puzzled by the reaction but continued.

What is going on? How can she yield two powers? This is not right. Who is she to be able to yield more than one? Rorien thought. He was confused and concerned. His Elentari held two powers? How can that be when no one holds more than one? What did that mean for him and for her, for them?

"Shh and watch. She is not finished," growled Sarina to the males.

Rorien was uncertain as he watched her approach the air and earth masters. *Why ask them, you can't yield them as well, it is unheard of,* he thought He didn't like this and was feeling disturbed and uncomfortable. Stop please stop, he wanted to yell.

"Master of Earth and Master of air show me please." The two Masters repeated their moves. The air Master moved his hands, causing a breeze to flow past her and the earth Master, in green robes, caused a floor stone to ripple up. *That would make laying the garden path easy, why couldn't I have that power when Dad paved the pergola*, she thought. She turned slightly towards the King and moved her hands causing a breeze to flow past him and a floor stone to ripple near his feet. The King was silent, still, his face showing no emotion. She could feel everyone in the room staring at her, knowing the Masters stood with mouths agape and eyes wide. Rorien let go of their link. She felt shock flow through the link before he let go. Still, she did not understand. Was it because she had not been practising from an early age?

He watched her yield air power, his power and then earth power and shock flowed through him as he realised, she could yield all four elements and he let go of the link. If she could yield all powers what did it mean for him? He was there to protect her, keep her safe, how could he be there for her if she could take care of herself? He was deflated.

"You yield all four elements. Let us see if you can yield the four spirit powers," stated the King. The four Masters stepped forward.

"My King, no one yields all four elements. Why is it she can?" the air Master questioned. The King waved his hand to dismiss the question and gestured for the spirit Masters to continue.

Oh, that is why everyone is shocked. No one yields all powers. I guess this is pretty cool that I can. She smiled feeling pleased with herself and relaxed. *This could be fun.*

"Yielding the spirit powers are different from the elements. With elements you use hand gestures, the spirit powers require your thoughts to yield," said the sight Master in white robes, "sight is the ability to see the past, see the future and read thoughts, movement allows you to move from one place to another in an instant, heal gives you the ability to heal others and shift gives you the ability to take on any living form."

"Sight I can yield," answered Elentari, opening her mind to read the Master's thoughts. "You are thinking of the number 17." She turned to the King, "My King, your thoughts are on me and how I remind you of her," she turned back to the Master, "shall I continue or is that enough?"

The spirit Masters were showing her their powers. Surely, she would not be able to yield these as well. He sank lower as she announced she had sight. He moved beside his friends, needing something familiar to comfort him.

"That is all." The Master stepped back and another stepped forward.

"Movement is where you visualise the place you wish to go to," the Master in black robes said and vanished. "Visualise." Elentari turned to the voice behind her. He had transported himself from one spot to another "Will your body there and see your body there."

"Visualise and will myself and see." Elentari closed her eyes. Rorien had moved away from her to his friends in the middle of the room. She had seen where he was when she turned to the Master. She visualised him in the room and herself beside him, willed to be beside him where she felt safe. That was easy, she always wanted to be beside him, able to smell him and feel his body heat. Her body went tingly and she heard the room gasp, she opened her eyes. Elentari was standing beside Rorien, right where she imagined, right where she wanted to be, safe and secure. *Wow, that is way cool* she thought. Again, she closed her eyes and visualised herself back where she started. She felt the tingly feeling and opened her eyes. She was back standing in front of the Masters. She smiled thinking about sneaky midnight visits to see Rorien, sneak in an extra good night kiss and how handy it could be, popping by to say hello.

Rorien wanted to scream when she appeared in front of him.

The Master nodded, stepped back and the Master in orange stepped forward.

"Heal is the ability to heal the injured. We all can heal small injuries quickly, larger injuries take time. This is where healers come in, using their touch to bind broken bones, knit wounds together and attach limbs which are almost cut right through. To heal, you visualise the wound healing, see in your mind a needle sewing the wound together, the blood flowing in the veins and staying there, bones linking, the healing and how the body heals. Let's start with you healing yourself to give you the idea." The Master removed a knife from his robes and held it out to Elentari. "Cut yourself and heal."

Elentari turned towards Rorien looking distressed. He shrugged. She could not feel him on the link yet she clung to it. This power was scaring her, healing herself without a doctor or first aid kit was insane. "So, just cut yourself and heal. No biggie," she said to herself, *except it is! For one, I can't cut myself.* She turned back to the Master and paused her mind racing. She straightened herself and said "Master, cut me please," and held out her hand. The Master nodded and sliced her hand. "Ow," she said, closing her hand and grabbing it with her other hand to stop the blood flow. She felt a prickling sensation and opened her hand. She could not see where the Master had cut her. She looked up with shock on her face unsure of what had just happened.

By the time she was talking to the heal Master, he had lost all desire for her. He ignored her when she looked for help in healing. She was not his linked, not what he had expected. All feelings and desire for her were lost. He was unsettled and troubled. What did this mean for him?

"You have self-healed. You can heal yourself when you come into your awakening. Now heal me," said the Master, cutting his hand deeply, cutting himself without warning and holding it out for her.

Elentari was not ready. Shock flowed through her and she was frightened. *How do you heal someone without help? He can heal himself, he has the ability*, she thought, *he won't die if you fail.* She took it gingerly in her right hand and closed her left hand over the wound to stop the blood flow as she normally would in her world.

"Just concentrate to stop the flow and sew it back together," said the Master. Elentari concentrated on the cut imagining the blood flow ceasing, feeling stupid and foolish, imagining a wound being healed. She pushed the negative thoughts aside and concentrated, feeling a prickling sensation in her hand, the same sensation as when she healed herself. She imagined a needle and thread sewing the wound together and it felt like a needle was in her fingers and it was sewing. She removed her hand and looked at the Master's hand, the wound was gone.

The Master nodded and stepped back. The last Master stepped forward in his purple robes.

"Have you found your animal guide form?" he asked.

"I am not sure what you mean."

"We all have an animal guide we can change into, that guides us, helps us. Each guide is individual to each being, a guide they need or represents them. Some are birds, lions, bears and each being has only one animal guide. Until you find your guide, we will not proceed."

Elentari turned to Rorien and his friends. "You all have a guide, what are they? Can you show me?" The thought of being able to change forms excited her. Each changed for her into their animal forms and stood before her, except Rorien who flew above in his hawk form. Jasper stretched tall in his bear form growling, Lorcan bared his teeth at her in his wolf form and Fendton looked cuddly in his cheetah form. Sarina stood as she was, she had not changed. "Wow," she said as they changed back. "That is so cool." Elentari turned to the King and asked: "What is your form?"

"I am an owl as was your mother" and with that, he changed and perched on the back of the throne. He looked wise and knowledgeable. He changed back and sat down, smoothing his robes. "Are you able to channel your animal guide?"

"No, nothing is forthcoming my lord," replied Elentari head bowed, "You looked wise and knowledgeable in your animal form, it suits you."

Rorien almost laughed when she couldn't summon her animal guide. A touch of vengeance he felt. The others were whispering together, he ignored them. He was not happy, he felt confused, agitated and wanted out of here except he was stuck. *At least my friends are here, hopefully, they can help keep her from me, distract her and keep her away*, he thought.

"What does it mean for her to yield seven of the eight powers?" asked Fendton to no one.

"Who knows. Maybe the Masters will have an answer," said Jasper

"Except they're all a bit taken back as well. They don't seem to have an answer either," said Sarina.

"Scholars then."

"Nope. They are also looking perplexed," said Lorcan "I like it. To yield more than one power would be great. Imagine the possibilities. How awesome is Elentari to yield seven?"

"She is amazing. Guess we are going to find out just how amazing she is," said Sarina.

"Depends on which ones. I'm not sure what other I'd like. Water is a good power. Why would I need another?" answered Jasper.

"Fire to warm the water is a good match," answered Lorcan.

"Listen, she is still discussing with the King," said Sarina.

"Thank you Elentari." The King paused watching her, smiling. He had a fatherly look about him.

"It seems you knew my mother well. You keep comparing me to her. Was she a relative?"

"No, she was not a relative. I did know her very well."

"How did you know her?"

"She was an amazing loving female. Always wanting to help those in need. Always giving and never taking. She was a friend you knew would always be there for you, no matter how small." He stopped lost in thought.

"Someday, dia will you tell me more about her?" He hadn't answered her question. She wondered why he wouldn't say how he knew her.

"Yes." He looked at her with much sadness in his eyes. Elentari could see he missed her but did not understand how after sixteen anoks he could still be mourning for her.

"Your majesty it seems you have something on your mind, something you are wanting to speak yet is not sure you should."

"Something is playing on my mind. I am not sure how you will take it."

"I have been through much in the past week, umm vika, and have managed to get through it all. I am standing here in front of you tall, strong and not backing away. The Masters have tested me and I have completed what has been asked. To yield these powers is something unheard of where I came from, yet I completed it without argument. To find out I can yield seven of the eight is frightening yet I still stand here without an issue. I see the Masters all in shock and unsure of what it means, even Rorien has stepped away from me. Yet I am still here.

Whatever it is you have to say please say it. There couldn't be much more that you could throw at me. Before you do, can you tell me who my father was? I assume he is no longer as no one has spoken of him."

"You know your mother's name was Elena, your father," he paused looking with concern on his face at her, his fingers nervously thumbing on the arm of the throne, "I knew your mother as she was my linked. Your father is me. You are the princess, the next to sit on the throne and rule all the lands." He was watching her, his eyes and face filled with worry as he anxiously shifted in his chair.

The answer was revealed, the question which plagued her mind since walking in was answered. The puzzle pieces all in place. Why she was summoned to the King, why she was requested to yield, why everyone was discussing her. All the questions now answered. She knew something was being kept from her and now she knew she was the princess. I am a princess!? *Wow, I was nothing in my world and here I am the next to sit on the throne.* She was unsure whether to be excited or to run screaming from the room. What did it mean for her to be a princess?

"I am the princess?" she asked quietly.

"Yes. Does that concern you?"

Rorien's surprise at his link being the King's daughter was mirrored on his friends' faces. "The King's daughter?" he said

"We were searching for the future Queen and not just Rorien's link?" asked Fendton.

"Makes sense," said Jasper, "why the Master was eager to help us find her."

"I am not sure. It would make sense why I was taken from this world. Someone had a vendetta against you or Elena, wanted to destroy you both or wanted to be next on the throne."

"Yes. Except why you were taken has not been revealed. No one has come forward or made any move. It is a mystery."

"Why not just kill me, why take me alive to another land?"

The Master of sight stepped forward. "When the first King of all the lands was crowned, it was written in the ancient text any who kill the one who sits on the throne or any who are to be crowned will be tainted. Their scent changes to the smell of death, to encircle them with a foul smell, so all will know they killed the crown."

"That explains why I was removed and not killed. Is that the same of all who sit on the throne? For the other kings who rule a land?"

"Yes, any who sit or are to sit cannot be killed. Any who scheme to have you killed and succeed will also be tainted. The only way a killer cannot be tainted is in war."

"So, for me to be killed by someone I have to go to war?"

"Yes. The Scholars can discuss this further with you."

"Make sense." She turned to the group and asked: "Did you all know?" Their faces told her they had no idea as they shook their heads.

"We all found out just then." *What does it matter, you don't need me, you yield seven of the eight powers* thought Rorien? He stood there listening to their conversation, trying to figure out a reason to escape all this but nothing would get him out of this mess.

"The journey to finding me was to make sure you were wanting me and not because I was the princess. The Masters were wise not to tell you. 'It's not the destination, it's the journey. Ralph Waldo Emerson quote.' The struggles you went through was to know you were committed to your link and finding her, how you handled everything and what lengths you would go to be with your link was what the Masters were testing you for. It would mean you would protect your link with your life and in turn protect the princess." She turned back to the Masters "Very wise of you." Walking towards the King she asked, "what shall I call you?"

"Most fathers are called Dad or Father."

"Father seems more of a title. To me there is no warmth in calling someone father, it is a title to explain who you are. I had a dad in my world and do not wish to have another dad. If it pleases you may I call you Papa, another word for dad in my world?"

"Papa? Mmm" said the King stroking his clean-shaven chin, his head raised and eyes looking upward, "Yes it pleases me. You may call me Papa," he said to her. "You shall call me My King, Father and Papa depending on which title is required."

"Thank you, Papa."

He looked lovingly at her, smiling for a moment before turning back to the Masters and straightening up. "To business, each element master will work with the Princess, allocating equal time to train her from morning to high sun. Air Master, Rorien will also train with you. The Princess will have lunch with me and the spirit Masters and Scholars shall spend time teaching and training the Princess until supper. After supper, the Princess shall spend time how she wishes. This shall last a mesik and we will discuss further what training and guidance the Princess requires," said the King.

"As you wish" answered the Master's bowing.

Elentari guessed the others who entered were the Scholars. She divided up the dia, which started at sunrise, 28 horis per dia, 8 horis in the morning, excluding breakfast, equates to one and a half horis per Master. An hori for lunch leaves seven horis with spirit Masters and Scholars. The morning was getting on and she was beginning to look for a cuppa. "Father, do you drink tea?"

"I do have tea on occasions and your mother liked tea. Do you like tea?"

"Yes, I have tea at least four times a dia," she said, turning to Rorien and smiling, "It was a deal-breaker if there was no tea in these lands." She teased Rorien on the link.

"It has been a long morning and it is a good time for a break before we continue. As the Princess would like tea, we shall have tea. Come Elentari." The King rose and held out his arm for Elentari. She took it and he led her through a door on the side of the hall. The male behind the King's chair followed close behind, the Masters, Scholars and last Rorien and his friends. The left wall when entering the hall had four doors and the right wall had two doors. They entered the door on the right wall at the throne end.

The room had a large table sitting in the middle, seating 20. Along the side wall were elaborate cabinets adorned with intricate wood carvings depicting a mountain scene with full trees in the foreground. The King sat in the chair at the end gesturing to Elentari to sit in the chair to his right. The chairs were also intricately carved with each seatback depicting a different scene. The King's chair was high backed with a carving of the King and queen dancing and her chair design was Pegasus playing amongst the clouds. The craftsmanship was exquisite. Even the stone wall chiselling was meticulous and produced a storyboard of eight different scenes complete with frames. The scenes were three-dimensional with very fine detail including creases in the clothes and features of the face.

The Masters all sat on the left side of the King, Rorien and his friends sat beside her and the Scholars filled the remaining seats. The King and Masters asked questions to Elentari about her world and to Rorien about his adventure in her world. The Scholars sat quietly, observing. When the table was cleared, the King stood.

"Time to continue the business," said the King, holding his arm for Elentari and returning to his throne. All followed and returned to their places in the hall.

Rorien was not pleased with having to sit beside her at the table having tea. When her hand reached under the table and rested on his leg he wanted to scream 'Move your hand' at her instead, he took her hand, holding it until he found a reason to let it go. Her cup was getting empty, he put her hand in her lap and taking the pot, poured her some more tea. He did not want to be here, anywhere but here. He was counting the horis until he could be rid of her.

CHAPTER 8

"As Elentari is the princess she will require a guard confidant. Elentari, you will choose a guard to take the oath. This is my guard confidant," he said gesturing to the male behind his throne "More confidant and advisor then guard. We have known each other since we were young. I trust him which is why I chose him."

"Father, as I am to train for a mesik with the Masters, may I choose my guard once training is over? It will give me time to find someone I trust and can advise me correctly and being with the Masters should be guard enough until I seek what I need."

"Good idea. When the mesik is over you shall announce your guard. On the morrow, Elentari will train with the Masters and Scholars for a mesik and then choose her guard. Business is finished. You are all dismissed," he said waving his hand at the Masters and Scholars to dismiss them. "Shall I show you to your casa, Elentari?"

"Yes Papa, I am excited to see where I am to live in these lands. A new home is exciting. I hope it has a large wardrobe. I am looking forward to filling it with new clothes," said the Princess excitedly.

"Rona, where is Elena's clothing? Will they fit Elentari?"

A female appeared, "My Lord, they are hanging in her wardrobe and should fit the princess. I will fetch them and a seamstress and bring them to her casa," she said, bowing before leaving.

"The seamstress will help you and fit the clothes for you. Once your training with the Masters is over, we shall look at working with the females and honing your skills."

"Which skills shall I be learning Father?"

"Sewing, embroidery, baking, weaving and such, the females shall teach you."

The King rose and held his arm for Elentari. She took it, turning to Rorien pulling on the link asking him to her. He fell in behind the King's guard with the others and followed them. Elentari again pulled on the link, he did not respond. Sadness filled her heart. She wanted him beside her where she felt safe. Maybe he has to stay behind as is the custom she told herself. Her father was chatting about royal duties as they approached her casa. The King entered the main room guiding Elentari in, his guard stood by the door.

Rorien ignored all the tugging she was doing on their link and stuck beside his friends. No matter what happened he kept being shoved to Elentari, always put beside her. Now he had to train every dia with her as well, he just wanted to be rid of her. He wondered if he could send her back but would need the potion to do so. He was stuck with no out. *Why did I have to find her? If I just gave up, I wouldn't be in this mess*, he thought. The excitement of his friends about her having every power he could not understand, it was not usual and strange and certainly not something to be excited about. He was in no mood for discussions and just wanted to be left alone.

As she stepped inside, she was surprised it smelled very fresh even with the earthy undertones and perfectly straight and smooth rock walls. She loved the walls with the way they showed all the layers of sediment build-up, the streaks and patterns of each different layer. The entry door separated the main room in two and two windows to let the light in sat either side of the door. The right side was furnished with two chocolate coloured two-seater couches and four matching single chairs with two lamps hanging from the ceiling. The room was large and would fit the group comfortably and was almost as big as her place back on Earth. The left side had a table seating eight with a lamp above, a bench for preparing food and cupboards on the wall beside the fire. Everything was ordinary with no extra furnishings, only the basics to live. Two other doors were leading from the room. She opened one to reveal a bed, set of drawers and cupboard and the other was furnished similarly. She decided on the room with the larger cupboard and larger drawers as her bedroom.

Maybe I can get another cupboard or drawers, maybe a nicer blanket for the bed. Raw cotton colour is a bit plain, she thought.

"The room has no extra furnishings. You can choose what you want. Cushions, mats, paintings, rugs, what you need and like," said Papa. "These were placed here to help you settle in. They can be exchanged to suit your tastes. We can organise for one of the stonemasons to line your walls with images you like."

"Thank-you Papa. This is enough for now," she said as she put her hand on the Kings arm. He placed his hand on hers and patted it.

The main door opened and in walked Rona and another female, which she assumed was the seamstress, both with arms laden with dresses. "Which room shall these be put in?" asked Rona, curtsying.

"Please hang them there," said Elentari, pointing to her room and Rona and the female walked into the room.

"Princess, may we see you in here to check the sizing?" asked the other female head bowed. Elentari turned to her friends

"Please make yourselves comfortable while Sarina and I try on clothes. Papa, are you staying?"

"Yes, we shall have lunch together and I shall take my leave after."

"Great. I shall try on some dresses and be out soon." She gestured to Sarina and they both entered her bedroom.

Of course, her casa would be large. At least this is what she is used to, similar to her apartment, thought Rorien. He hoped this would keep her occupied with Sarina finding furnishings and leave him alone. At least he now had a way to keep her away from him, just mention shopping with Sarina. She liked to shop in her world and would spend all day shopping, maybe that will be the way to keep her occupied and away from him. He found himself sitting beside the King as she tried on dresses and he kept silent letting the King and his friends talk, hoping no one would speak to him.

"This is Rita, the seamstress," said Rona.

"Welcome, Princess. I am at your service," said Rita curtsying. She took a dress from the closet and held it out for Elentari, "Please put this on so I can check sizing." The dress was fitted in the bodice with a square neckline and flowed out from the waist ending at the ankles. Many shades of red swirled through the dress looking like fire dancing across the fabric. Elentari removed her dress.

"What are you wearing?" asked Sarina with interest.

"These are underwear. The clothing you wear under your clothes hence the word underwear. Knickers to cover your female area and bra to cover breasts." Elentari said feeling a little exposed with the females curious about her undergarments and she moved her arms in front of her across her breasts.

"Interesting" stated Rita "what reason do you need a bra?"

"They are designed to support and elevate the breasts," she said, putting on the dress Rita held for her. The dress almost fitted perfectly with the waist a little big and the hips a bit tight and needed to be widened a little. "Wow, I am almost the same size as my mum. That will make it easy for you Rita. May need to widen the hip area a bit and tuck it in at the waist."

The seamstress began fiddling with the dress, turning Elentari around and measuring her. She stepped back. "This will do for now. I can take them in if you wish?"

"This is fine, I like it. Maybe fix the other dresses, please can you show me them?" Rona and Rita removed each dress to show Elentari. There were eight dresses and two coats.

"These are all that is left of your mothers. I can make you some more," said Rita

"I shall like that. I like the colour and patterns and all my clothes were mainly red based in my world."

"I can see what we can do, princess. What colours are you wanting?"

"Red, blue, green, all colours. I do love the colour."

"I can make dresses in all colours for you. Is there a style you like?"

"What do you think will suit me and a princess? I don't know what styles you have here. I have some clothes from my world which are at Sarina's place. I shall call for you when I have them and you can see what we wore. Maybe even give you some ideas for new styles here."

"Thank-you Princess. I am most interested to see clothing from your world and design you some dresses." Rita and Rona curtsied and took their leave.

"Let's join the males, shall we?" asked Sarina.

"Before we do," said Elentari taking Sarina's arm to stop her, "Is Rorien always this quiet?"

"No, he is never this quiet," said Sarina with a look of concern.

"Mmm, I hope it is just a passing phase and he is back to himself tomorrow. I don't like this shutting out thing he is doing." She let go of Sarina's arm.

"It will pass," Sarina said hoping she was right, "Shall we?" said Sarina, taking Elentari's arm and heading back to the males wanting to avoid the conversation. She was not sure Rorien would be ok. Before the yielding test, he never shut up and since Elentari revealed she held seven of the eight he had changed. He was different, withdrawn and distant. She wondered if he would be able to accept Elentari's gift and Elentari.

Her father turned towards them as they walked in. His face softened "This was your mother's favourite dress. She knew red was my favourite colour. It suits you." The males were sitting at the table, Rorien on the kings right, Jasper and Fendton on his left and Lorcan at the end facing the King.

"Thank-you Papa. It fits perfectly. I do like reds too."

Rorien couldn't deny it as much as he wanted her away from him, she had a good body and the dress showed off her curves and breasts. She did look good in it, it suited her.

There was a knock at the door. "Enter" answered her father. Females entered bearing trays brimming with food and placed them on the table before curtsying and leaving. "Lunchtime, let us eat."

Elentari and Sarina took their place at the table with the others. Elentari sat in the seat beside Rorien. Fendton moved a seat down to allow Sarina a place beside Jasper.

"The maids will bring you supper and food for the morning each night. Just leave everything on the bench and they will clean up after you. Every dia lunch will be with me. The Master shall collect you in the morning and take you where you are needed. Rorien will accompany you. Todia, your friends will show you around," the King said.

"Papa, I don't eat meat. Can you please make sure the maids know?"

"No meat?"

"None. I never have. Mum said I wouldn't eat it as a baby and never had a desire to try it."

"Mmm. Your mother Elena did not eat meat. I shall let them know." Once lunch was finished the King took his leave and the group moved to the lounge area. Elentari sat close to Rorien on the couch, Sarina and Jasper on the other couch with Lorcan and Fendton in the single chairs. Elentari turned to her friends.

"I am unsure about what happened todia. What do you all think about the yielding testing?" They all began talking at once, except Rorien, and Elentari laughed. "Maybe I should say one at a time please," she said, smiling at them and looking at Sarina.

"This has been a big morning for us all and you have conducted yourself amazingly. You certainly have shown you are a princess. I would have crumpled up into a little ball sobbing to be in front of every Master and the King." Sarina said.

"They were just males to me. I know them not and were no threat to me. I guess if I understood who they are, I may have crumbled. The King was the only being who I felt intimidated by. In my world, we have a Queen. It would be intimidating to be summoned to meet her with all the regulations and stipulations on how to act and behave."

"You yield the power of all four elements and three, maybe four spirit powers," said Jasper "That is unheard of. You are one special female."

"So, what does it mean?" asked Fendton.

"I have no idea. The answer will reveal itself when it is needed," she answered. "Has anyone yielded more than one power?"

"I think thousands of anoks ago, they yielded an element and a spirit power. Surely the Masters will know or the Scholars. Hopefully, they can explain why you have almost every power, what reason it is to need them all. It must feel strange." Lorcan said

Elentari saw the others nod in agreement. How could she be so lucky to have these amazing beings in her life? She looked to Rorien, he was quiet and withdrawn. She gently touched their link lovingly. He glanced at her and diverted his eyes again. She knew he was hurting and unsure, she had felt those feelings on the link before he closed himself to her.

"It does feel strange but then having one power would feel strange to me. There is nothing like this on earth. So, who ended up winning the bet?"

"You heard?" said Lorcan.

"You were only a few feet behind me. I heard." She rolled her eyes.

"We didn't decide," said Jasper

"Yeah, give me back my coin," said Fendton holding his hand out to Jasper.

"Fine. Here you go," Jasper flipped a coin high in the air and Fendton caught it.

"Maybe I should have them all. After all, I completed all tasks…except one," said Elentari

"Agree, Elentari should have all the coins," Sarina said, nodding to her. Four coins came flinging at her as the males grunted their disapproval.

"Now I have some money. Four coins to my name." laughed Elentari.

"This casa is perfect for you Elentari. I will enjoy visiting you and helping you furnish it," said Sarina. "There are lots we can do, the walls are a blank canvas with heaps of potential. What would you like carved on them?"

"I don't know. I did notice there are a lot of carvings which tell a story. Maybe one wall can be my story. A babe stolen from her crib, a woman handing me to my parents, Rorien and you all searching, my world, Rorien and I stepping through the door and a few blanks to fill in."

"That would be beautiful. What about the other walls?"

"We'll start with one and see what takes my interest. There may be paintings to add and I would like stars on the ceiling."

"Let's show you around," said Lorcan.

"Great idea. I have had enough of being indoors todia," she answered. "Lead the way Lorcan."

Lorcan headed out the door, the others following. He pointed out things to Elentari, explaining how things operated and worked within the cuedel. A normal dia consisted of duties in the morning and markets late in the dia to exchange goods and to share supper. They walked the whole way around the mountain through the middle of the cuedel. Scattered around amongst the trees were areas where beings gathered to socialise, a parestala, the main one for celebrations and linking vows. Each side of the mountain had one large main parestala, and a few smaller ones scattered throughout. Almost every month some sort of festival was celebrated, festivals for harvesting, preserving, oil extracting, wine-producing and jam making. It all sounded so exciting, gathering together to celebrate or create. She was looking forward to her first festival and she hoped it would be soon.

Elentari noticed the shops were mainly around the parestalas as they stopped on the west side for tea in a small shop. Rorien stood away from them, looking down the mountain. He kept finding ways to avoid being near her when they stopped to show her things, he would move away from her. She kept tugging on their link, kept asking if he was right but he ignored her. They took their time to wander around and answered all her questions as the afternoon was theirs to enjoy before the morrow when she would begin her training.

Why is he avoiding me? What have I done? She kept wondering.

Rorien hoped getting out would keep her from him. She kept on grabbing his arm as they walked. Will you leave me alone? He screamed at himself. Each time they stopped he would move away from her hoping she would move on. Instead, as they walked off, she would again link arms with him. There was no avoiding her. He just wanted to be alone to work out what to do. He was standing away from them during tea, staring down the mountain, looking at nothing in particular.

She was not normal, too different, too powerful yielding all the elements. He was always strong, capable and efficient in everything he did and now he was the minor one of their relationship. He just wanted to work out what to do and how to stop their link. He had not heard of anyone not completing their linking before. Maybe he would be the first as he didn't want to be linked with her anymore. How could he protect and provide for her when she could be very powerful? He was feeling insignificant and worthless in their relationship.

"So, who is paying for tea?" asked Elentari. "After all, I have very little coins and this is my first dia here. Surely one of you gentle males will pay for us helpless females." She smiled at Sarina.

"Yes, which of you gentle males will fix our tea?" Sarina said, playing along with her.

"Rorien's shout. He brought you here and took four anoks from us, he can shout," Jasper replied.

"Agreed," answered Lorcan.

"Rorien, your shout," said Fendton.

"Princess, there is no need to fix my services. It is an honour to meet you. I saw you when you were a babe and pined for you when you disappeared. It is fabulous to have you returned to us," said the shopkeeper.

"That is most kind of you. What is your name?"

"Asvik is my name, Princess."

"Thank-you Asvik. I look forward to seeing you again." Elentari bowed slightly to Asvik and took her leave, the others following. Elentari made a mental note to bring her something another time as thanks. What she could bring, she was unsure. The answer will reveal itself when it is needed, she thought.

"This could be a bonus being with you," said Fendton "Not having to pay for anything."

"It's not going to happen that often. I am not interested in using those around me. Except you of course. I shall make you my personal gofa."

"Gofa?"

"Yes. Go for this, go for that, a gofa."

"Oh yeah, you can be our personal Gofa," said Lorcan. "That would be great. Fendton, fetch me a drink. Fendton, I want food. I could get used to this."

"No way. You can get your things. I am not going to be your personal gofa," said Fendton to Lorcan. "Elentari do you want a gofa?" he asked as he turned to her, a bit concerned.

"No Fendton. I do not need a gofa. I was teasing."

"Oh. I was a little concerned." Elentari laughed, giving him a push. He pushed her back grinning at her.

Elentari liked the idea of a town who exchanged goods and services instead of coins like her new cuedel. Those who live here sell their wares to other cuedels and villades to gather coins for when they need it. It seemed a wonderful idea, offering help to those around you and even the other cuedels used coin or exchange.

They arrived back at her casa and she stood outside looking at the façade as the others entered. It was plain without embellishments and no garden or plants.

"What's up?" asked Lorcan, turning to her as he was about to enter her casa.

"It is very plain. I was wondering who lived here before me?" she said as he stepped up beside her and scanned the area.

"Many of these casas have been empty for many anoks. Yours may be one where no being has lived in for vekulos."

"Vekulos?"

"That is 1000 anoks."

"Oh. How do you employ a stonemason to carve embellishments?"

"Those that yield earth can carve stone and keep the paths around the cuedel maintained. Stonemasons are earth yielders who have honed their skill to finer details. You can find them throughout the cuedel. Fendton can carve a bit, he is not skilled in details. He could carve the stars on the ceiling you would like."

"Cool. I may have to ask him. Can you help me find some being to complete the façade?"

"Yes. What are you thinking?"

"Dragons curled around the column's tails at the bottom and heads at the top. One each side of the door to begin with."

"You do like dragons, don't you?"

"Yep."

"Ok. I will help you find a being. Let's head in and have supper. The morrow is going to be a big dia for you."

CHAPTER 9

For Rorien, the rest of the dia was agony. He just wanted to be anywhere else, even extreme training would be better than this. He spoke little following them around and keeping up the pretence. Back in his casa, he collapsed on his bed, letting out a long breath. How is this happening? I have spent nine anoks searching for her and now she is here, I want her gone. Why did she have to be the Princess, yield the powers? What did that mean? To yield almost every power?

When Elentari woke, she pulled Rorien to her but he did not respond. She asked him to come to have breakfast with her but he did not respond. She found some fruit, made a fruit salad and ate alone, feeling very lonely. Her sadness grew and she hoped he would open up to her soon. This coldness of his was making her wonder if she had made the right choice to come here. Should she return? She hoped she wouldn't need to approach the Master to help her get back, and hoped that she made the right choice. There was a knock at the door.

"Please enter," she called out. The Master of air stepped inside with Rorien behind him and her heart leapt at the sight of him. At least he would be with her todia, that pleased her.

"Good morning Princess," said the Master bowing.

"Good morning Master, good morning Rorien. It is great to see you," said Elentari rising from her chair, moving to kiss Rorien on his cheek.

"Time for training Princess," said the Master as he turned and walked out. Elentari took Rorien's arm and they followed the Master to one of the training areas to meet with the other three element Masters, the Masters were standing waiting for them.

"Good morning Princess, Rorien," said the Masters

"Good morning Masters" they both said.

"We will each run through different techniques for you to learn and yield. Each morning you are to meet us here to begin your training. I will train with you first, Master of water will train with you after, followed by Master of earth and Master of fire lastly. Once you have completed training, you will head to the royal hall to lunch with the King. Princess you and Rorien will train with me each morning and once we are complete, Rorien will return to his duties. Todia Rorien will spend the whole dia with you. Do you have any questions?" said the Master.

"My training is clear, thank-you. I do wish to know if you have apprentices?"

"Yes, we take on a new apprentice every 100 anoks. Apprentices start training when they reach their 100 anoks. We can each have seven apprentices and we are all in our 900 anoks. When we leave these lands, the oldest apprentice will become the Master and choose a new apprentice to train. There are Professors and teachers throughout the lands as well. Does this answer your question?"

"Yes, thank-you Master."

"We shall begin training."

Elentari trained with the Masters until high sun. Element yielding was physically straining, using muscular movement in her fingers, arms and body as well as mentally straining. It took mental focus as well as physical movement to build, shape and move each element. She learnt different movements to control the element, different hand gestures to build and shape the element and different actions to move the element. Each power was limited to her ability to move, hold and focus.

Rorien sat with the Masters when his training was completed and watched her train with the others. He mostly spoke to his Master and answered the Masters if they spoke to him. At high sun, the Master of fire walked them to the royal hall to lunch with the King.

"My King we have finished for the morning," said the Master bowing to the King. "The princess has shown great talent and she has great potential. She would easily top her class."

"Excellent. Well done Elentari. Have you enjoyed yourself?" grinned her father.

"Thank-you Papa. It was most enjoyable. I do love training with Rorien," she said turning to Rorien smiling and stroking their link.

"Come let's eat before your next sessions with the spirit Masters and Scholars," said the King moving towards the laden table. "Master of fire please join us."

"Papa I know my mother's name was Elena what is your name?"

"My name is Adtarian."

"Oh, is my name a combination of your names?"

"Yes, it is actually."

"Lucky I was a female. It certainly wouldn't suit a male." She smiled.

"If you were male it would have been Lenarian."

"Glad I was female. I like Elentari better. How old are you and when is your birthday?"

"I am 484 and my birthday is the 3rd day of the 3rd month."

"What is my actual birthday?"

"The 4th day of the 4th month. Tell me all about training." They discussed training over lunch, how the morning went and what was to come. Lunch was cleared and the Master of sight arrived.

"I shall take my leave my Lord and return to my duties, Princess until the morrow, Rorien," the Master of fire bowed and left.

"My King, Princess, Rorien," the Master of sight greeted them.

"Master," replied Elentari and Rorien.

"It is time for your next training sessions, Elentari. I shall meet you for supper in your casa," said her father rising from his chair and kissing her forehead.

"Until supper Papa," said Elentari as she and Rorien followed the Master to the royal gardens where the other spirit Masters were seated.

"Masters," said both Elentari and Rorien.

"Princess, Rorien," replied the Masters.

"Princess, we will run through teaching you each of our powers. As you are yet to find your animal guide, Master of shift will not be teaching you. Once you find your guide, he will test you to see if you yield the power of shift. When teaching is complete, you will head to the library to study and learn from the Scholars. Do you have any questions before we begin?"

"The teaching is clear. I am ready to start," she answered. The Masters of sight, heal and movement gave their teachings, helping her to use her mind to action each spirit power, building on the basics to delve further into the power, to build focus and imagery to complete each task. It was mentally straining and her brain hurt. Rorien sat watching, talking to the other Masters as she completed each of the teachings.

"Your teachings with the other spirit masters for todia are over," said Master of shift, "have you found your animal guide?"

"No, as much as I try, I am not finding my guide. All the animals I have brought to mind, have not been the animal I seek or need," replied Elentari.

"Very well, todias teaching is over. I shall walk with you to the library where I shall take my leave," replied the Master. Discussion on the teachings and what to expect filled their time as they walked to the library where the Master took his leave. They entered the library to find the four Scholars seated at a table in the middle of the library, open books filled the table. The library was large and wide, with a spacious open centre where tables and chairs were scattered around. The bookshelves lined the walls and filled towards the centre, the long shelves running parallel to the front wall. A passage ran down the centre of the library from the entrance and two more ran down the sides.

"Welcome Princess, welcome Rorien," said one scholar, "May I introduce the Scholars to you, Enoch, Sigmond and Erasmus. I am Cornel. We shall teach you the history of these lands and customs. We will go through the past kings and queens and major events. Do you have any questions?"

"No Cornel, the teaching is clear. I do wonder if you have apprentices?" asked Elentari.

"Yes, as the Masters have Apprentices, we also have apprentices. Are you ready to learn?" replied Cornel.

"Yes, I am ready to learn," said Elentari. The Scholars began to teach, giving her information and getting to her read, asking her to answer questions and getting her to explain her findings. She asked questions when it wasn't clear. Her head was swimming with information overload by the time class was over and was glad to be outside, walking alone with Rorien.

"My head hurts," she said to Rorien as they walked back to her casa, "there has been so much to learn, it is exhausting."

"It's been a big dia," replied Rorien.

"It is nice to be just with you, alone," she grabbed Rorien causing him to stop. "I miss just us," she said quietly, looking directly into his eyes. She raised herself onto her toes to kiss his lips. He responded, kissing her back. They continued in silence back to her casa, her arm wrapped around his, her head leaning on his arm. She hoped it meant he was not shutting her out as he was still so quiet and distant. This side of him she did not like.

Her father's guard was standing outside her casa with her father and friends inside sitting in the lounge waiting for them to arrive. "What a nice surprise after a long exhausting dia, my father and friends here to greet and feed me. Most awesome," she smiled giving her father a kiss noticing the table was laden with food.

"How did your dia go?" asked Fendton wide-eyed and eager to hear all about it. Elentari loved his childish ways. He was two mesik older than her but younger in his ways.

"Other than long and exhausting, it was most exciting and interesting. Please come sit and eat. I shall fill you in over supper." They all ate as they listened to her dia, asking her questions and her father took his leave after supper.

"I shall see you for lunch on the morrow. Sleep well daughter, you have made me proud todia," he kissed her forehead and left.

Her friends stayed longer to catch up more on her dia and as the conversation began to slow, she asked: "The library where we were, was that the library where the ancient texts stairwell is?"

"Yes," said Rorien.

"Will you take me there somedia to see where you spent most of your spare time searching for me? It seems so romantic, the beginning of my story to move to this land. Where my link searched for his link, searched for me." She looked at him, her eyes pleading for him to show her.

"Some dia we can."

"Hopefully soon?"

"Yeah."

"Us too?" asked Fendton.

"Yes, I want you all to show me. You are all part of my beginning in this world and will be there at the end, I hope." She answered

"I will," said Sarina, "I enjoy having you as a friend and hope we always will."

"Yes, we will," said Elentari as she smiled. She was grateful for the friendship Roriens friends showed her and very thankful for a female who she clicked instantly with. This was one concern she had had before deciding to come here, unable to make friends quickly, but she did not need to worry, everything was turning out fantastic except Rorien.

CHAPTER 10

It had been two vikas since her training and teachings began. Training with Rorien was extending both their abilities. They practised working together and against each other. He was outclassing her which was no surprise. It was great training with him and it was like back on earth where he was tender and caring towards her. She loved how he made her feel protected.

She was learning a lot about yielding the powers and knew much history when they visited the ancient texts. She was excited to be seeing the out room and passages where Rorien spent many horis searching for her. Her heart was racing with the prospect of seeing the texts as they stood at the bookcases which guarded the staircase. Rorien placed his hand between the bookcases and opened the door, descending the stairs, Lorcan lit the candles. It was as they described it, many books lined the walls and tables filled the room.

"This is the table we worked from," said Fendton standing behind the chair. "We started in this passage and moved along to this one than this one and lastly here. This is the passage where we found your map," pointed Fendton. Elentari noticed symbols etched above the passage entrances.

"Yes, I found your map in this one," said Sarina.

Lorcan used his firepower to light the candles hanging from the ceiling down the passage. "This does come in handy," he said, grinning. Elentari smiled as she followed Sarina down the passage.

"The markings above the door, what are they?" she asked.

"That is the ancient text. Before this language became the main one, there was an original language, a minor language which the Masters mainly used and a few beings. Only the Masters and Scholars use it now," said Jasper. They stopped at the spot where her map was found.

107

"This spot changed Rorien's journey to you, from map hunting to code hunting," said Sarina. Jasper stepped behind Sarin taking her in his arms. Elentari noticed her name was written on the stone floor where they were standing.

"My name is written on the stone. Did you put it there?" she turned, directing her question to Rorien who was leaning against the books.

"Yes, I did. The spot my journey changed, I wanted to make sure I would always know where I found you."

"I love it," she purred on their link as she reached up to kiss him. "The spot of my beginning. There are so many books. Are all the passages this long?"

"Yes, they are all this long and all filled ceiling to floor with books" groaned Lorcan rolling his eyes as he collapsed against the books.

"We didn't find the end of the passages. The books stop before they reach the end and there's still more empty shelves," said Jasper.

"Let's get out of here. These passages give me nightmares of the long boring nights searching," said Lorcan grinning at Rorien teasing him.

"You wouldn't understand he-who-has-not-found-his-link" Rorien teased back, shoving Lorcan as they started walking back.

"You have not found your link?" asked Elentari, falling in to step with him.

"No, I started pulling on my link when I began helping Rorien but nothing." He leaned into Elentari and whispered, "she responded the dia you arrived. Ssh" he winked at her.

Elentari smiled excitely at him. "Let's talk later. I want to help you find her," she whispered back.

Rorien used his air power to blow out all the candles down the passage as they left. Elentari began looking at the books around the out room. "Do any of you know what all the books are about?" she asked, taking a book down.

"No, we just searched for maps and left the books. Some of the books we can't read anyway, they are in the ancient language. Wonder what they are about?" said Jasper.

They stood looking at the books waiting for an answer to come, all except Elentari who removed a book and was flicking through. "This one has information on past kings," She said as she flipped through the pages scanning her eyes over them. They all gathered around her to read her book, none of them game enough to touch any of the books without permission. These were the ancient texts, the forbidden library, hidden and only for Masters and the ancient library hadn't been entered by any being they knew and were afraid to touch anything without permission.

"We should leave, it is not right to be here," said Sarina. They all nodded their agreement except Elentari.

"If you want, we shall go," she said sighing, placing the book back and following them out. Each headed back to their own casas except Elentari who headed off to find her father to ask if he could summon all the Masters. She explained her reasoning and he agreed to meet with them before training.

All the Masters arrived almost together to the royal hall where the King and Princess waited, all puzzled as to why they were summoned on such short notice.

"Thank you Masters for meeting with us. The princess informs me her training has extended her enough," said the King.

"The princess has much potential and has surpassed many apprentices and has surpassed many of our expectations. There is more we can teach her if you wish," answered the Master of sight.

"Have any of the Masters heard if you can combine powers?" she asked.

"I know of no one who has," answered the Master of sight as the Masters shook their heads. "We tend to yield on our own. In war, we fight by ourselves and never together."

"The books in the ancient library, are they the same as the ones you all keep in your casa?"

"They are partial texts from the ancient books which previous Masters needed. They have been passed down from Master to Master."

"The ancient texts, could they hold more knowledge?"

"Very much so. The air Masters kept the ancient library known, passed the information to the next Master which is how I knew where to look. There is a book on their meetings and many vekulos have passed since they all gathered in the ancient library, they believed they had what they needed and no new information had been gained so they closed the library. The books in the normal library are parts of the ancient library," answered the air Master.

"Todias training will take place in the ancient library with the apprentices, send for the apprentices. They are to cease their activities and meet us in the library," said the King "Let us find new information to share. Maybe we can find a way to blend powers."

"Great idea Father. Have you seen the ancient texts?"

"No. This will be exciting to see where Rorien found you. Shall we?" the King rose holding his arm for Elentari, heading towards the library as the Masters headed off to find the apprentices.

The King and Elentari stood silently in the centre of the library, facing the door, as the apprentices filed erratically into the library, all unsure as to why they were summoned by the King and Masters. Concern showed on their faces and hushed whispers crept throughout the library as the King and Princess quietly waited for all to arrive.

"Todia is a special dia," said the air Master to the apprentices, "todia we are entering an ancient library where the air Masters are the keepers. This library has long been forgotten and the air Masters kept the entrance known to keep vital and precious information from being lost. This library here are parts of the ancient texts," said the Master, his hand out gesturing to the books. The Master walked through the library to the rear wall with all following him and opened the ancient door. The apprentices gasped, stretching and moving in an attempt to see what lay beyond. Their faces full of curiosity and hushed whispers again crept around as faces looked to those around them all wanting to know the answer to what the Masters had for them. All were eager to see what lay beyond the wall and what secrets it held. The Master descended the stairs, the King and Elentari followed with the other Masters behind them and the apprentices in the rear, still whispering to each other.

The hushed tones grew too excited voices as all began looking around, talking to each other and wondering what was happening. So many amazed faces were discussing how fantastic the ancient library was, pointing excitedly to things discovered and eager to explore. Elentari led the King down the fire passage lighting the hanging candles with her firepower.

"Nice work Elentari."

"Thanks, Papa, this fire stuff does come in handy."

"It is a good power to yield."

They heard the air Master speak, "Please find a seat and we will proceed," and continued ignoring his request.

"Here is where Sarina found my map and Rorien wrote my name on the stone floor to know the spot his journey changed. My name etched in the stone to always know where he found me. It's kind of romantic."

"I am glad he found you. You have brought me such joy these last few vikas and it is wonderful to get to know you. You were so little when you were taken, we didn't get to know you at all. Does Rorien bring you joy?"

"Yes Papa, he does, I do love him dearly," she said shifting on her feet.

"Has he asked if you will complete the link?" he placed a hand on her arm.

"No. He is uncertain with everything I can do, he has lost his reason for being with me. My abilities have squashed his male ego and he is lost. I do not know how to make him understand I need him," she said looking up at her father searching his face for answers

"Mmm. We will have to change that," he patted her arm.

"I hope we can. Shall we head back to the out room?" Elentari took the King's arm and as they passed the candles, she used her air power to extinguish them.

"You are liking your powers?" the King turned his head sideways to look at her.

"Yes, they do come in handy and are quite fun, like a new toy, and makes life easy." She smiled.

"I remember when I first started yielding, I also thought it was a new toy and had a lot of fun testing fire. I burnt the doors to the royal hall!" said the King with a smirk on his lips as he shook his head.

"Really? Oh, my how bad of you…and how funny." She giggled at the thought of the royal doors on fire.

"I didn't think so at the time, now when I walk through, I chuckle. The doors were replaced but if you look closely to the bottom left corner you will see in very small writing, 'Do not burn'. A little joke my father had added for me." His eyes were scanning the shelves. "There are so many books here. You were right to encourage the Masters to come back, there must be thousands of hidden secrets we could utilise. I wonder what mysteries await us amongst these books?"

"We shall find out. All the masters and apprentices will be spending much time finding and unlocking secrets. Maybe even more ways to yield the powers. How exciting if they could find a way to yield more than one at a time. At least it will give me a reason for being able to yield them all. Maybe we may even find out if others could yield more than one power," said Elentari excited thinking about what hidden secrets would be revealed.

"The possibilities are endless." Smiled the King as they entered the out room. The tables were filled and the Masters and Apprentices were busy scanning books and excitedly discussing findings. The air was filled with excitement and chatter.

"My King, Princess would you like to join us?" asked the Master of air.

"I shall take my leave. These books are here for you to seek knowledge, to enjoy unlocking new knowledge. Also, speak to the Scholars and let them help you," said the King

"Yes, my King" bowed the Master.

"I too shall take my leave," said Elentari as she continued with her father, his guard stepping in behind them as they started up the stairs.

"Papa since the Masters are busy and I have excelled, can I begin to learn from the females and to train in combat? Rorien was showing me how to use a sword and shoot an arrow back on my world, it would be nice to continue to learn them."

"Yes, to continue your training in combat would be wise. I shall summon the females to meet with us in the morning for tea and inform the Masters your training is complete for now. To the training ground to find you a trainer," said the King guiding her to the main training ground in search of a trainer. The King pointed out the Generals, Sergeants and drill leaders, different moves and abilities, those of talent and those who needed work. There was much for the eyes to see throughout the area with different training drills, some with swords, some with bow and others with yielding, hand to hand combat, fitness drills and mental exercises. The smell of hot sweaty bodies and dusty ground filled the nostrils as the clang of swords met, orders being yelled, the whack of a fist meeting the body, feet pounding on the ground and many other various noises could be heard.

"Is there anyone who stands out to you?"

"A few do. The sergeant over there has caught my attention as well as this general and he too," said Elentari pointing to each one.

"Please fetch these males and include him," said the King to his guard, "I like him as well," he said to her.

"Many different drills are being performed."

"Yes, and there are many others, these are but a few. My favourite was that drill over there," said the King pointing.

"Mmm, they are all so aggressive and active."

"My Lord, the males you requested," said the Kings guard

"Your majesty," said the males bowing.

"This is Princess Elentari, and you have caught her attention. She is requiring a trainer to help her hone her skills with a bow and sword. It is requested you meet with her in the morning to begin her training. The choice to train with one or with you all will be her decision and shall be decided after the first training. Do you have any questions?"

"It will be an honour to train the princess. Where shall we train?" asked one male.

"Father, may we train in the royal training arena?" Elentari asked. "It will be away from others and private."

"Excellent idea. On the morrow, meet in the royal training arena for practice."

"Thank you for your time, I shall see you in the training area," said the princess as she took her father's arm and took their leave, his guard following behind.

"I shall be able to come past and see you train, maybe even raise a sword with you. It has been a very long time since I picked up a sword or even a bow, it will be good to have a swing," said the King

"Maybe even have a go at your favourite drill," she smiled before becoming serious, "Papa, may I spend some time exploring the lands? Allow those who live in these lands meet their princess, future Queen? I have a desire to head east for some reason."

"When you choose a guard in two vikas, you may go then. Until that time, you will train in combat and learn the crafts of the females."

"Thank-you Papa," said Elentari excitedly, whatever reason was pulling her east she was soon to find out. The answer will reveal itself when it is needed. "It will be nice to see the rest of our land and how they live."

For the next two vikas, Elentari trained in combat and met with the females. Her father had come by a few times to watch her training and trained with her. He realised how out of practice he was and how he had let himself go and began his fitness training again. She was enjoying learning how to use a sword, how it felt in her hand as she swished it through the air, loosening her wrist. Learning how to cut properly by pointing her elbow towards the target, pushing the pommel until her arm was straight before using her wrist to engage the point of her sword to the target. She always thought wielding a sword would be more of a swinging the bat motion but the action reminded her of throwing a frisbee. She learnt about the balance point of swords and how the weight, length and shape can affect the balance, and the effort and force of swords.

Her sword was designed for her to use little effort to hold and with the correct technique she needed little force to use. The hilt, the combination of pommel, handle, and guard of her sword was beautifully designed to fit her hand perfectly. The guard with ornate back, knuckle bow, loop guard and quillon, each with ancient text etched into the silver. The pommel is a perfect counterweight to the blade with tiny details etched into the silver and opal at the end as the tang button and she handle bound in leather. When she wielded her sword, it felt like an extension of her arm.

With the females, she learnt the art of candle making, basket weaving, knitting, pottery and baking. The crafts of candle making, basket weaving and pottery she enjoyed and sewing she disliked and would much prefer to go to the shop. She hated doing the tiny little stitches to sew her garment together and needlework was tiresome, taking a long time for patterns to form. Baking was yummy, getting to sample so many different baked goods. Whisking was not fun by hand until she figured a way to use her air power to whisk and began to enjoy whisking egg whites. Even using wood ovens wasn't so bad once she got used to it. Cooking over the fire was another interesting task to grasp and she managed it with much guidance.

The Scholars were still meeting with her and were excited with a new lease on life. Their newly found knowledge and information in the ancient texts gave them joy which they thoroughly enjoyed sharing with her. Their studies had moved to the ancient library and finding a table to study from was proving difficult with Apprentices and Masters all in there as well. Every being was thrilled with finding new knowledge and the ancient library was never quiet or empty, she had never heard so much chatter in a library before and sounded more like a schoolyard.

It had been a mesik since she began her training and learning. On the morrow, she was to pick her guard and had already decided who her guard would be on the first dia. She wanted to make sure her words were right when she requested her proposal hoping it could be. Her animal guide had not revealed itself and no animal she thought of was right, it was like her animal guide did not exist. She couldn't understand why it would not reveal itself or what was it that made it stay hidden. Her mind wandered to all animals which meant something to her, attempting to find what she missed when it hit her. She channelled her animal and it worked. Everything pointed to this animal, all the signs, all the things, everything pointed to this one animal. How could she not have realised this was her and it did suit her. She was amazed at how beautiful her guide was and was admiring herself as she heard her friends' approach and changed back, wanting to keep it quiet until it was required.

"Elentari, have you decided your guard?" asked Fendton before he was through the door.

"Yes, and on the morrow, the answer will be revealed," Elentari said smiling, not giving away her plan.

"No fun," said Fendton slumping onto a chair.

"How have you found this past mesik?" asked Jasper sitting on the arm of the chair.

"Long, hard, tiresome and at times boring. The Scholars nearly put me to sleep in the early dias. Since the ancient library reopened, they have become more interesting and even have given me basics in the ancient language. I dislike sewing, it is the worst and I miss going to the shops to buy clothes instead of sewing them. At times I miss my comforts from my world but my highlight had been training with you all, very glad the Masters agreed to it. Training with you has been the most fun. Hope you all enjoyed training with me and learnt a little something too."

"Training with you was good. We have become quite the team," said Jasper, "Thank-you for asking the master to allow me to train with you, I have had my skills extended. The best bit has been continuing in secret to blend powers, that has been thrilling. Love how you have combined my water with other elements. Don't know why the Masters haven't thought about blending before."

"Same here. Fire play has been awesome and I've learnt heaps," said Lorcan as he lounged on the armchair with a leg dangling over the arm.

"Yeah, fire is the best power." Elentari flicked her fingers to yield fire playing with it across her fingers. Lorcan followed suit as they watched each other before throwing their fire to meet between them. The two flames spiralled upwards twisting and turning around each other before exploding into fireworks. "Heaps of fun." They both laughed.

"Another fun one is this." She yielded a water ball. Jasper followed her and threw their water ball to meet in the middle of them. Their balls twirled and danced around each other floating to the ceiling before exploding and forming snowflakes. "Snow is awesome, I like snow."

"The northern land has snow," said Fendton, his face looking upwards as his hands stretched out to catch the snowflakes.

"Then I shall have to visit the northern land to play in the snow. Will you join me?"

"Yeah. I've never left this land and to go over the ocean will be fun," he said looking at her.

"Then we shall. How about Lorcan and Jasper try this." Elentari created a water ball in one hand and flames in the other and floated them into the middle of the room where they twisted and twirled around each other before exploding into fireworks and snow.

"Cool. Ready Jasper?" said Lorcan.

"I'm ready, just nod." Both yielded and Lorcan nodded, their elements met and spiralled around each other before exploding.

"I have noticed you haven't turned your music on," said Rorien changing the subject, standing away from the group.

"I haven't cooked or been driving, the main times I turn it on. Why, do you miss the noise?"

"No, you like moving to the music and wondered why."

"You can play music from your world?" asked Fendton.

"Yes. I brought my computer so I would have something if I needed it. With all the training and learning I haven't missed my world. This still feels like a holiday."

"Holiday?"

"Holiday is a break from what you do every dia. It's a change in routine. When Rorien came through the doorway, he took a holiday. Where's Sarina?"

"She had some extra things to do with the females. I walked Rorien here, you know, for protection. He is no good at fighting." Jasper threw a water ball at Rorien and Rorien yielded his air to splash it against the wall. He grabbed Jasper in a headlock, messing his hair.

"Need protection, do I? From who? You?" The two fought together laughing before Jasper broke away.

"Fighting like that you will," grinned Jasper. "It has been fun but I must go. Until the morrow."

"Wait up," said Lorcan following him out.

Elentari and Rorien looked towards Fendton watching him. He looked up to see them both watching. "Maybe I should go too," he grumbled, sensing he was not wanted.

"So soon? It was nice seeing you until the morrow" replied Elentari giving him a hug and shuffling him out the door. She sat in the chair opposite Rorien. "What's wrong? To begin with, when I arrived, you couldn't leave me alone. Then you shut me out almost completely. Now at times, you are distant towards me and other times you will be so caring and loving. When you found me you were caring, loving, wanting me and now…I don't know. What is it?"

"Nothing," he said, eyes turned downcast.

"Then why is it that you are different? Have I not settled into this world? Remember you said once you are settled, that was the decision." Her eyes were focused on him.

"Yes, you've settled in and taken on the challenges thrown at you." He looked up at her.

"And?"

"And what? There is nothing," he turned away from her.

"You have given me the answers I need and the means to return to my world. Good night Rorien," she said as she stood and walked to the bedroom using her air power to extinguish the lights in the room and slammed the bedroom door. She slid down the door to the floor in tears as she heard Rorien leave.

CHAPTER 11

He awoke before the sunrise, washed and dressed before heading to the Master's casa, wanting answers. Elentari called him, he ignored her and knocked on the Master's door.

"Enter," he stepped in and slumped on a chair.

"Not the first time you have done that," said the Master "What troubles you this time?"

"Why does she yield almost every power? Who is she? I wish I never started trying to find her," sighed Rorien.

"I do not know. She is the Princess, future Queen of all the lands. Without finding her you would never know what she means to you. We must go." Rorien followed the Master to Elentari's casa and on to training.

He enjoyed his training this morning, he got to knock her down a few times. He was careful not to arouse suspicion and hurt her. The good thing out of all this was getting private lessons with the Masters and he would be able to grow his power, that excited him, fast-tracking. Lessons began with the basics, he had forgotten the basics as they came naturally, and it felt strange to go back. Even though it was easy he still had to concentrate.

Once air training finished, he sat beside the Masters and watched her train. The Masters were mainly discussing training and how to train with her, where to start and how far to extend her. He had little to add. Occasionally he would question them to understand but mainly he listened. Another benefit of having to spend time with her, he got all the Masters to himself.

"Masters, why does she yield almost every power and what does it mean?" he asked.

"We do not know. It is puzzling us as well," replied the fire Master. "We spent time together yesterdia to discuss the reason for her abilities. We have no answers."

"The answer will reveal itself when it is needed," said Rorien "that is what Elentari would say."

"It may puzzle us, to her it must be frightening. She will need you to help her through, guide her and give her understanding."

He nodded. *I'm sure she is going to do quite fine without me*, thought Rorien.

"What do you believe about her ability, Rorien?" asked the fire Master.

"It is strange. I wonder why she needs to yield all and her purpose." That was no lie, he did wonder why she had to yield them all. *Other than crush my maleness.*

"You are not alone in those thoughts. Other than the obvious, future Queen of all the lands, all are wondering what her purpose is. With your link being the princess, has that changed your views?"

"I spent nine anoks finding my link. I was surprised to know she was the princess but didn't care. She was my link."

"When she becomes Queen, she may choose any male to rule as King beside her. All Queens have always chosen their link to rule with them. Would it worry you not to be King?"

"No." He didn't want to be with her and didn't care for the future. He continued to watch her train while listening to the Masters.

To Rorien, it was strange to have a meal with the fire Master and his King. Another benefit of her, he was getting special treatment and it felt nice having extra attention. Todia was a good dia for him and he would enjoy the rest of the dia even if he had to be near her.

He spoke to the spirit Masters, asking questions about their power and their lives, taking an interest in their answers. Masters devoted their lives to teaching and were linked with their linked supporting and assisting with works, keeping jars filled and finding texts for them. Every one of the Masters linked had passed. The spirit Masters had no answers for Elentari's abilities either and it seemed no being understood her purpose.

The Scholars reminded him of knowledge once lost, it was good to refresh his memory and be top of the class. It had been a while since he was taught the history of this world and he could ask all those questions which plagued him. The Scholars delight in answering all questions enjoying sharing knowledge. Rorien enjoyed the attention, making sure to benefit from it, getting the most from the personal tutoring.

His routine changed, personal training first up with Elentari and onto his duties before dinner with his friends in her casa. Another perk of her, he got to eat with his friends every night. Normally there were always other things to do, whether it was one of them eating with family or performing duties or eating with others in the parestala and it was not often they all ate together. This he could get used to, enjoying spending time with his friends. He was becoming much stronger in his power and in his ability to yield air becoming equal with the younger apprentices. Training changed to yielding against the Apprentices to extend them both and challenge them.

It had been two vikas when Rorien decided to show her the ancient library. He felt important to show her the ancient texts, a sacred place and his special place where for four anoks he spent most of his time. It was like a second home with the many horis he spent here searching and only a handful of beings knew about it. He had only shown the library to those who were close to him and special to him and now he had to show her as he knew he could not avoid it. Rorien placed his hand between the bookcases, opening the door and descended the stairs. Lorcan lit the candles as Fendton and Sarina showed Elentari the library, walking the passage to where her map was found.

"My name is written on the stone. Did you put it there?" Elentari asked him.

"Yes. The spot my journey changed, I wanted to make sure I would always know where I found you." *Now I want to erase it. I wish I had not started this journey*, he thought.

"I love it," she purred on their link as she reached up to kiss him. "The spot of my beginning."

Please stop touching and kissing me, just leave me alone he yelled to himself, his body tense. He used his power to blow out the candles as they left the passage. She was studying the books and removed one. This got his back up and anger rose in his throat, these were the ancient texts that only the Master's touch. He wanted her to put it back and not touch them, feeling calm when they left and the library was sealed again. That part of his life was now closed and he did not need to enter it anymore.

Life changed after that night. On the morrow, he found a note from the Master saying class would be cancelled and it confused him. He didn't understand what was wrong until he found the Masters had returned to the ancient library to his special place. He felt used by her, his special, hidden hideaway was being overrun and it was her fault. She had encouraged the Masters to return and it was never empty with them always in the library coming and going all dia and night. How dare she use him like that and not know the ancient library was his place. She has tainted it, abused it and ruined it. He disliked her even more and took delight in knowing he didn't have to train with her every dia.

Routine changed back to his normal routine before he brought her home. He no longer had personal training or scholar lessons but he still got to have supper with his friends for which he was glad that didn't change.

On the morrow, she was to announce her guard and he hoped she didn't pick him for if she did, he would not be able to leave her side and would be stuck with her every moment of every dia. Rorien couldn't bear the thought of having to spend every waking moment with her. She had ruined his life yielding most powers and she was still his link. *Of all the females around, I get the one who needs no being to help her. Why me? Her and Fendton are close both in age and friendship, hopefully, she will pick Fendton,* he thought.

She sat in the chair opposite him. "What is wrong? To begin with when I arrived you shut me out almost completely. Now at the times you are distant towards me and then you will be so caring and loving. When you found me you were caring, loving, wanting me and now I don't know. What is it?"

"Nothing," he said, eyes turned downcast. *Be careful of your thoughts, she can hear if she wants.*

"Then why is it that you are different? Have I not settled into this world? Remember you said once you are settled, that was the decision," her eyes were focused on him.

"Yes, you've settled in and have taken on the challenges thrown at you." He looked up at her. *Clear your thoughts, don't let her hear. Close your mind.*

"And?"

"And what? There is nothing." He turned away from her. *Clear thoughts have clear thoughts. Keep your mind closed.*

"You have given me the answers I need and the means to return." With that, she stood, "Good night Rorien," and walked into the bedroom using her air power to extinguish the candles in the room and slam the door.

He was sitting in darkness, stunned at her words wondering what had just happened and if she was leaving. Confusion set in as the events did not happen as he wanted, he was going to tell her to leave him alone and instead, he was leaving completely. Again, he felt belittled and insignificant. He left and headed to Lorcan's casa, looking for a drink.

"What's up? Looks like your world's about to end?" said Lorcan handing him a mug of beer.

"Nothing and possibly" he replied into his mug sitting at the table.

"Spill," said Lorcan standing opposite him.

"No, I just want a drink and maybe a sounding board while I work it out," Rorien said as he looked up.

"She's worth it, you know. We all see you are struggling with her abilities. It's written all over you and has been since that dia. You know she still needs you." Lorcan said as he took a seat.

"Not how most females need a male. She can protect me, you and every other being in this community. She doesn't need me. She said so and is going to return." His eyes returned to his ale.

"What? She can't, she is the future Queen! How can she? If she leaves it's because of you. You drove her away. We all gave you four anoks helping you find her and now you're going to let her go?" Both Lorcan's hands were flat on the table as he rose straight in his chair leaning forward slightly.

"Don't blame me. It's her decision to go. We gave her all the information when we showed her the library and she can read our minds, remember." Rorien said, staring at Lorcan.

"Yes, but she did say she wouldn't use that on us and she would ask first. Remember, she learns very fast. She can find what she needs without us." Lorcan sat back, his hands on the edge of the table.

"Even without reading us she can read the Masters and has access to them. She found the way and I expect, on the morrow, she will leave." Rorien dropped his head.

"She can't, we won't let her. Complete the link with her or do something to keep her here. We can't lose her. She is part of our group, our friend. She can't leave." Lorcan stood up and started to pace.

"I don't want to complete the link, don't want her that way anymore. She is not my link."

"Yes, she is. She is who you spend nine anoks looking for." Lorcan slammed his fists on the table. "Dragged us into your search to find her and she was all you wanted. You enjoyed spending time with her in her world. It only changed when her abilities came forth. She is still the same, still loves you, still desires you and you are all she looks for." Lorcan stood looking at Rorien. "Remember your journey to bring her home. That first night she was here, you could not keep your hands or eyes from her. You both were constantly touching and watching at each other, it was almost sickening. You were protective and loving towards her. She is still the same, she has not changed."

"So, who do you think she will choose for her guard?" Rorien's eyes moved around the room avoiding Lorcan's.

"You would be the obvious choice. Except, expect Fendton may get a mention. Hey, don't try to change the subject. You're not getting off that easy. You know everything she does is for those around her. Did you know she asked for us to train with her?" Lorcan sat back down.

"It was worth a try. I thought that too with her and Fendton getting along really well."

"They're like brother and sister, with her being the big protective sister even if she is younger. Again, stop avoiding the subject of her returning. She is still the same person you first met. Forgot about her abilities and focus on the person, on her."

"More of a mother figure. He did lose him when he was a babe and he never had a female to watch over him."

"You are still avoiding what is right in front of you. She needs you. How can you not see it? Everything she does or questions she asks you. It's only you she wants. How can you not see that?" Lorcan was shaking his head. "Or that everything she does is to help those around her. She does nothing for herself. Wake up and open your eyes. She is the best thing that ever happened to us, all of us, every being in the cuedel. The stars on her ceiling, she asked Fendton to carve for her. Did you notice the new statues outside her casa? That was from Fendton making her a shower and bath. She got him to make us all a shower and a bath for Sarina and the stonemasons carved us statues of our animal guide from the blocks. She could do it if she wanted but she always chooses to let others. She makes us feel special and needed. If you took notice, you would see." Lorcan's hands were flying about in frustration as he talked.

"So, what!?"

"Don't 'so what' me. She needs you. Focus on who she is and not what she can do."

"How? I can't protect her?"

"It isn't protection she is wanting and if she was in danger, she's not the type to fight."

"Whatever."

"It's late, you need to work out what is going on. Are you going to let her leave and destroy your friends, destroy every being in the cuedel or what? Remember spending all the anoks looking for her and how happy she made you feel. Get out and find a way to keep her before I punch some sense into you." Lorcan's arm pointed to the door.

"Fine, I'm going." Rorien walked the long way back to his casa, the whole way around the mountain, trying to work out what to do. What he was feeling and what he had felt. His mind was fighting against itself, past with the present, life in her world against life here, who he imagined her to be against who she was. He seemed to always be in conflict, answers never in his grasp. He had finally settled and now he was back in turmoil. On the morrow he will know…he hoped.

CHAPTER 12

During her mesik of training, the olive harvest and festival happened. She was excited to be experiencing her first harvest and festival. The dia began with a long line of beings flowing from the cuedel to the field. The field was a hive of activity, buzzing with chatter with beings racing here and there, moving items around, setting up and assisting those to pick. There were carts placed all around waiting to be filled with olives as beings found a spot to pick. They found a place amongst the trees to begin picking.

"Ok what do we do?" asked Elentari

"Take this basket, hang it over your shoulders and pick the olives. Once the basket is full empty it in the cart. That easy," said Fendton, handing her a basket. There were two handles with straps attached which slung over your arm and head to criss-cross over the chest and back.

"That easy," she replied, taking the basket and putting her head and arm through one strap and head and arm through the other. "Ok, pick and empty. How do you get the ones up the top?" she asked as she began picking, adjusting the basket to sit better on her body.

"Ladders are around somewhere," Fendton said as he began picking.

"The whole cuedel comes out to help, does the King?" asked Elentari as she slowly picked.

"He hasn't attended any harvest or festival that I have been here," said Jasper as his hands raced across the olives picking them quickly.

"Mmm. I think that should change. Next festival I will have him come by. He should be here at least encouraging those if he doesn't help. Appearances are important."

"Good luck. Bets on you can't get him here," smirked jasper.

"Do you always bet on things?"

"Only when I know I will win," said Jasper without a pause in picking.

"Then this is one you will not win. May as well pay now. How long does it take to fully finish harvesting?" said Elentari, stopping to watch every being.

"We're here all dia, Elentari. On the morrow, we begin processing oil. Others will stay here to complete the harvest," said Lorcan glancing at her as he picked.

The group chatted as they picked, taking breaks as they tired. It seemed to Elentari she was not built to harvest and seemed to spend more time having a break than picking. It seemed to take ages to pick a full basket.

Surely there is an easier way to pick. I can yield all the elements surely one should help. Rorien seems to be doing well, picking lots of baskets. He has air, maybe that can help. She thought as she watched Rorien pick and use his power to assist him. Watching his hands, she followed his movements. Her second basket took half the time. *That is much easier, much better.*

"Did you have harvesting in your world?" asked Sarina pausing to wonder.

"Not really like this. We do harvest but we have machines to do our harvesting and pickers are hired to pick. Farmers own the crops and pay beings to help him. No special dia gathering together helping each other."

"What about processing?" she asked as she began again.

"We have factories to do that. Factories are tall and long metal casas with machines to do the work. Again, a being owns the factory and hires others to help and pays them to operate the machines."

"Oh. So, you don't gather for festivals?" she asked, pausing for a moment.

"We do have festivals, mostly you pay to attend. Food and drink costs, you have to pay a coin to have anything to eat or drink. If we did this in my world, we would have to pay to take the olives with us. This way is much better." The dia continued and they stopped for lunch.

Carts came around with water and food for them and Sarina laid a rug on the ground and filled it with food for them. They sat and ate together taking a nice well-earned break. The males went back to picking while Sarina and Elentari cleaned up.

"Mmm, I have an idea. Fendton, Lorcan, Jasper grab a corner." Elentari picked up a corner of the rug, the males following. Their faces showed uncertainty at what she was doing. "Stand under the tree with the blanket and pull it but not too tight." The males stretched the rug. "Stop. That will do. Rorien can you use your airpower to shake the olives, please?" Rorien looked at her from the ladder, standing his ground staring her down. "Please can you shake the tree and drop the olives in the blanket?" he shrugged and used his air to shake the tree and just as she hoped they landed on the blanket.

"Woohoo! This is much easier!" yelled Fendton. Jasper and Lorcan were smiling and nodding in agreement.

"Thanks, Rorien. A few fell on the ground. Maybe if I use my air, I can push them to the blanket. Rorien how would I do that?" she asked him.

"Try this." Rorien moved his hands and she copied.

"Sarina, can you take my corner and let's go again." Sarina took the corner and they moved around the tree. Rorien used his power to drop the olives and Elentari pushed the falling olives to the centre of the blanket.

"This is much better and not so back-breaking," said Jasper. "Great teamwork all. Let's empty this load and keep going. We will have this done in no time."

They continued harvesting using airpower, making their way from tree to tree. She noticed a few other groups watching and saw them doing the same.

"Looks like your idea is catching," said Jasper, his head nodding in the direction of the group beside them.

"If it makes harvest easier and quicker, I am most happy it is catching on. I am surprised it has not been thought of before," she said watching the other group.

"I guess we never thought to change our ways. We enjoy coming together and helping each other," said Lorcan

"This is much better and easier. What idea will you come up with next harvest?" said Jasper

Elentari shrugged. "Guess we will know when the next harvest arrives. Who takes the carts to the processing area?" asked Elentari.

"The males all help to take them to the processing area which is over that way," said Sarina, "and females head up to organise supper."

"So, we are back down here on the morrow for the processing side?" said Elentari as her shoulders sagged a little with the prospect of more work.

"Yes," said Sarina, straightening up.

They continued to harvest until mid-after high sun. All during the dia, beings stopped by to speak to the Princess asking her how she was and how she was enjoying the harvest and just to say hello as they passed by. Elentari chatted with them asking about themselves and what they do. She enjoyed how the community was accepting her. Asvik stopped to bring her tea and say hello. She was most thankful for her generosity and tea. The dia was the most enjoyable and came to an end as the females began to head back to prepare supper for all with Sarina and Elentari joining them.

Supper and festivities continued late into the night. She had lost Rorien after they left the fields and even Jasper and Fendton did not know what happened to either Rorien or Lorcan. Both had headed off as the carts were being taken to the processing area and that was the last they saw of them.

The parestala was full of beings dancing and singing and general frivolity. She enjoyed dancing with Fendton and was polite enough to dance with every male who asked her. Fendton taught her a few moves and stayed close by watching out for her.

"Thanks for walking me home, Fendton. It has been a great night."

"I enjoyed myself. You are fun to be with Elentari."

"As are you Fendton. I am exhausted and don't want to get up early on the morrow. Wonder if I would be missed if I skipped processing?"

"I will miss you and I'm sure others will notice you are not there," he said putting a hand on her arm.

"Yeah, the Princess would be noticed if she isn't there. I may be late as I have a bet to win." She grinned.

"Oh. Thanks for letting me know. I might be able to get one back," he said with an attitude.

They had crossed over into the north area when Elentari noticed something moving on the ground.

"What's that?" she asked, stepping cautiously towards the movement.

"I don't know. Be careful," said Fendton, grabbing her arm to hold her back.

"It is an animal of some sort, struggling," she said shaking him off.

"Oh, it's a turtle. It must have got stuck in the sewers," said Fendton moving towards it. They were standing over it watching it as Elentari bent down and picked it up.

"Oh, you smell bad, little turtle. Let's get you washed up and back to the creek," said Elentari as she carried the turtle to the creek. "Are there a lot of turtles around?"

"No, they are generally down on the flats, not normally this far up the mountain."

"If we put it back in the creek will it be ok?" asked Elentari with concern.

"It'll be fine. Check on the morrow and see if it needs any help. Umm, I think we may be too late, he is looking a little floppy."

"Oh, that is not good." Elentari used her air power creating airflow to breathe air into its mouth as if blowing through a straw. The turtle began to move and Elentari used water power to clean the turtle and checked him overusing her healing power. "He is all clean and breathing again and nothing is injured...that I could sense. Not sure how turtles are meant to feel but I could not find any major issues," she said "How did you mutate your shell, little one? This bulge is not normal, what did you do to yourself?" she questioned the turtle.

"You can use healing power on the animals?" asked a surprised Fendton, he thought it could only be used on beings.

"Yes and no. There is nothing to say I can't and nothing to say I can. I just decided to see what happened. I am concerned about his bulge and his tail is split like he has two tails."

"Oh, it does look strange, a bit mutated."

"Here you go, Vince. Nice clean water for you to swim home in. I will come by on the morrow to see if you are alright," she said bending down and placing the turtle in the water.

"Vince?"

"I named the turtle Vince," she said, standing up. Fendton smiled and continued walking her back to her place. "I will see you on the morrow Fendton." She kissed his cheek and entered her casa, collapsing into bed where she slept soundly.

After breakfast, she went to find her father and caught him as he was about to enter the royal hall. "Papa, come with me to the processing area and say hello to your subjects. It will be good for them to see you out and about taking an interest in them instead of royal duties." Elentari pleaded with the King, holding onto his arm.

"I don't like attending festivals. Your mother stopped when we lost you. I stopped attending anoks before that, I got too busy with being King and with more important things to attend," he said softly.

"I am back and believe it would be great for every being to see you. As King, you should be taking an interest in every being who lives within your lands. They are to follow your rules and regulations, at least see how they live to enable you to make correct choices. Are they not important too?"

"The Masters help with rules and know what they need. Yes, they are important."

"Then show them they are important and don't be so stubborn. Why not show how important they are by seeing them as they attend their dia duties? Plus, the Masters are puppets on a string with them, not game to argue with you. They are afraid you will remove their title from them," she said, removing her hand from his arm and folding her arms across her chest.

"How do you know that the Masters are afraid of me?" asked the King puzzled.

She looked sideways at the King as her hands fell to her sides. "Remember, I can read minds and I read theirs. At least do it for me, take me down to the festival and say hello to my friends and then come back. It will give you an idea of how every being has accepted me and how I fit in with the community." Her hand gently touched his arm.

"Are you always going to make me do things for you?" sighed the King as his body relaxed.

"No Papa, not always, just most times" she grinned.

"I will walk you down and return. That is all." His mouth was drawn tight as he raised a finger at her.

"That is enough. Thank-you Papa," she kissed his cheek and took his arm as they headed off.

"You are too good to every being, Elentari. You are going to make a great Queen," he said patting her arm.

"I don't expect to sit on that chair for at least 500 anoks. I want to see more of our lands and explore before taking the crown."

"Until then you will still be performing royal duties and helping with ruling," said the King looking at her.

"I am going to be a Queen who protects instead of ruling," she said puffing out her chest and holding her head high.

"Really? Is that how you will rule my kingdom is it?" he grinned at her.

"By then it will be my kingdom and I can sit how I see fit," she said with a smug look on her face.

They joined the procession down to the processing area. A long line of beings heading up and down the path and all who passed them said hello. She replied to those she knew with their names.

"You have gotten to know a lot around here in a short time." Her father was surprised at how many beings she knew.

"Yes Papa, I have. I make sure I meet at least four new beings every dia. So, in a mesik, I will know 160 beings well. I know I won't know every being but they know I am trying to get to know them all. They feel special when I speak to them and give hope to others that they may meet me."

"Mmm, wise of you."

"Look Papa," she pointed towards the processing area. It was bustling with activity with so much going on, it was hard to know where to begin to look. Elentari's eyes found a cart and she watched beings remove olives from the cart and transferred them into a large circular stone mill with blades on a vertical axis. Operated by airpower, the wooden blades whirl with such velocity and power turning the grindstones to create a paste. The paste is transferred to large mixers and mixed for near an hori before placed on disks and pressed. The last step was separating the liquids by decantation and the left-over dried paste is taken away to be made into bricks for the fires.

"How exciting is this Papa?" she said, her voice brimming with excitement. "Come on, I found Rorien." She grabbed the King and dragged him towards Rorien and her friends.

"Hello," said the King as they approached. Jasper turned to Elentari with a look of shock on his face as she held her hand out and he placed a coin in it.

"My King, it is nice of you to attend," said Sarina, bowing slightly.

"The Princess required an escort and was unable to find any being. Hence my attendance. When she has a guard, she won't need me or drag me places." He smiled.

"I will always drag you places," she said.

"Will you be staying long?" asked Sarina.

"I do have a business to attend to," he saw Elentari glare at him, "which can wait for a bit before I return. What is it you are doing?"

"We are pressing the paste to extract the liquid. The paste is spread on the disks and the disks stacked on the press. Once all the discs are stacked, a heavy, stone disk is placed on top to compact them down. Fendton can compact them down with his earth power. Would you like to spread the paste, my King?" asked Sarina as she stood up holding the bucket out for the King.

"I shall watch for a bit. Thank-you Sarina." Sarina bowed and continued. Elentari grabbed a bucket of paste, emptied it on the disk and spread it out. The King watched them before his eyes wandered around watching the beings as they completed their tasks and picked up a bucket.

"Make sure the layer is the same thickness all over, my King," said Sarina. The King nodded and when they stopped for lunch, the King took his leave.

"You are unbelievable! I lost big todia because of you," said Jasper, his hands on his hips glaring at her.

"Whatever do you mean Jasper?" her face full of innocence.

"You know damn well what I mean. Not only did I owe you but Fendton," Jasper pointed to Fendton, "I owe as well. How he knew you would bring the King todia…" his expression changed from annoyance to realisation, "you told him last night didn't you?" His fist in a ball waving at her.

"Fendton walked me home, that is all. If he guessed I would bring father to see me settling into the community…" she said winking at Fendton.

"Last time I bet against you," growled Jasper as he returned to spreading the paste.

"Stop whinging and spread the paste," said Sarina, "If you are going to bet, then be ready to lose."

CHAPTER 13

Rorien woke as the sun rose. He still did not have an answer and decided a run would help clear his head and focus. He ran around the top of the community, the middle of the community and around the bottom of the community and he was none the wiser on what he should do, how he felt or where to go from here. The very moment he saw her he knew she was for him, wanted her, needed her and a vika later he almost hated her. He was confused as to how one can go from love to hate in such a short time. He bathed and dressed before heading to the royal hall still in turmoil as to his decision. *She is a good person, always kind and thoughtful. She was always loving towards me, so why am I doing this? Why can't I love her or let her go?*

He walked into the royal hall to find the King sitting on his throne discussing Elentari and her training with the Masters, trainers and Scholars. He listened to their thoughts on what type of being she is, how they saw her as a Queen, her strengths, how her training and abilities grew. Everything they said was true, she was honest, kind, and protected the small being, always helping others and building them up. The Masters and trainers found her wonderful and a great benefit to the community. So why could he not fully love her? What was it he was missing? He wanted to love her, she was his link, what was it that would not let him commit to her fully? What was it that was stopping him? For nine anoks he wanted her and now she was here with him, he wanted her gone. His friends had meandered in and stood with him, Fendton entering as the King was finishing up his discussions.

"What's happening?" asked Fendton.

"The King has finished his discussions and we are waiting on Elentari," answered Sarina as Elentari walked into the hall, "here she is now," she said as her head turned to watch Elentari walk in.

"This is exciting. I wonder who she picks?" said Fendton, his hands rubbing together.

"Ssh and listen. You won't know if you don't listen," said Darina raising a finger to her lips.

The front of the royal hall was crowded with the eight Masters, their apprentices, the Scholars, trainers and her friends all standing around. The King sat on his throne with his guard standing behind him as always. Todia she would announce her choice in guard and she hoped the King would agree to her decision. She could find no information on if it was possible to do. The Master of shift would ask her if she had found her spirit guide and she was unsure if to reveal it or keep it hidden. It was unusual and again she could find no information on this guide. There was much uncertainty.

"Princess, it has been a mesik since you began training and lessons. The Masters have said you have excelled, the Scholars are pleased with your learning, the trainers are also pleased. You have brought joy to the Masters and Scholars opening the ancient library, they have found many new ways and information. As stated, when the mesik was over, you are to choose your guard to take the oath. Have you decided?" the King spoke.

"I have my King," she said standing in front of the throne with her hands clasped in front of her and eyes focused forward.

"Have you asked them?" questioned the King.

"No, my King." She had not changed her stance.

"Is the chosen guard in this room?"

"Yes, my King." She still did not move.

"You are hesitating. What is it my child?" asked the King rubbing his hands on the arms of the throne.

"My King, I am conflicted. I have been pondering how to ask what has been playing on my mind. This request is not usual and I wanted to make sure the words I spoke would be right," she said, relaxing her body slightly.

"You are not usual, Princess. Your request will reflect you. Please ask," said the King leaning forward in his chair.

"May we discuss this in private?" she asked as her hands fell to her sides.

"Ok," the King raised his hand to dismiss all.

"Can we leave father and let the others stay here. We can walk the royal gardens," she said, turning slightly to the main entrance.

"A much better idea. Shall we?" the King stood holding his arm out for Elentari to take as they wandered out to the gardens. "What is it that conflicts you my daughter?" he asked as they stepped out of the royal hall.

Those left behind in the hall looked at each other with confusion on their faces. The Masters stood watching the door hoping for an answer, their brows furrowed in puzzlement. The trainers began discussing to themselves and the apprentices spoke in hushed tones carefully moving around each other in the hope one would know something. The Scholars each took out a notebook and began scribing.

"What is she talking about?" asked Fendton quietly, his eyes searching his friends' faces.

"Leaving" answered Lorcan with his head bowed.

"She can't leave us, Rorien, do something. She can't leave," said Fendton begging Rorien, grabbing his arms tightly and shaking him.

"It is not my decision" he answered, shoving Fendton off.

"If you weren't a prick towards her, cold and distant, she wouldn't want to leave," yelled Fendton as tears welled in his eyes.

"It is ok Fendton. It is ok., Sarina said, taking him into her arms, tears in her eyes, trying to find comfort for herself as well as Fendton, feeling just as lost and upset as he. Fendton clung to her, his arms wrapped around her waist and head on her shoulder.

"She wouldn't leave, would she?" he whispered into her shoulder.

"Only she knows that Fendton," she said with her cheek on his head.

Jasper stood beside her and put his arm around her shoulders, leaning his head against hers. Lorcan stood behind Fendton with his hand resting on his shoulder. Rorien stood alone, head down and shoulders slumped. Sadness passed along their link, both from him and from her.

"Rorien has pushed her away and given her no reason to stay. Why would she want to stay when she came here for him and now what she came for doesn't want her. She has the means and way to return to her world." Lorcan was glaring at Rorien.

Leave me alone. I have enough turmoil and confusion without you adding weight to my shoulders, thought Rorien.

The King and Princess quietly returned and the King returned to his throne as the Princess moved closer to the pomp, standing at the stairs and in front of the Masters, trainers and Scholars, her way of avoiding all contact and questions. The hall quietened and all eyes faced the King darting from him to the Princess and back, searching for answers.

"I have discussed matters with the Princess. Masters, Scholars, have any of you come across any text which will either allow or cause an issue for the Princess to return to her other world?" asked the King.

The whole room was reeling with the news of her wanting to return to her world, they were speechless. No one spoke, no one moved, they just stood there with their mouths agape. Elentari stood straight and tall, looking directly in front of her, not moving. Rorien's head sunk lower, his shoulders dropped a little more and his heart cried. He had his answer, he did love her and now it was too late.

"Masters do you have an answer for me?" glared the King his voice raised. He did not like to ask twice.

"We…there…it is…she…" the Master of air was speechless unable to string words together. The Apprentices whispered amongst themselves, shifting on their feet. The trainers stood quietly not moving as did the Scholars.

"There is none we have found, my King, which will support her return or cause any issue if she did return" answered the Master of sight.

"You will search the ancient texts and find an answer. Until you find an answer, the Princess will stay."

Rorien lifted his head and the heaviness in his heart lifted slightly, a small smile slowly appeared on his lips. *I have a chance to change her mind. Hopefully, they won't find anything quickly,* he thought.

"Yes, my King," answered the sight Master.

"This will mean the princess requires a guard until the time arises for her return. Princess, please announce your guard" said the King turning his eyes to her.

"I have researched the past kings and queens of late and their guard. Each chose their guard to complement their power. When in combat, they would have two powers to use against their enemy. As you have said, I am unusual, I yield all four elements and three of the four spirits, it is difficult to find a guard to compliment me. My request is to have four guards, who each yield a different element," answered the Princess, her body tall and eyes forward.

"Mmm, that is a most unusual request. Masters, Scholars, is there any reason the Princess may not have more than one guard?" asked the King rubbing his chin.

"There is no law which says you can only have one guard or how many. Past kings and queens have only chosen one. It has always been a choice," said Master of sight.

"Then I shall allow it. Princess whom do you choose as your guards?"

"Of earth, I choose Fendton." Elentari turned her head slightly to the left before returning to her stance.

"Fendton, do you accept the honour?" asked the King.

"Yes, I accept," he said as he took his spot behind her to her left. He was ecstatic to be chosen and his smile was wide.

"Of fire, I choose Lorcan." Again she turned her head slightly to her left.

"Lorcan, do you accept the honour?" asked the King. Lorcan was already standing behind her on her left.

"Yes, I accept." Of course I accept he yelled to himself, how can I not want to be her guard. He smiled, stopping himself from doing a little happy dance.

"Of water I choose Jasper." This time she turned her head slightly to her right.

Jasper was standing behind her on her right. "Yes, I accept" he answered before the King could ask the question.

"My last guard is difficult to choose. There are two who would do well, one who WILL protect me without a doubt and one who will fit better with the other guards," she paused. "I have trained with Seneca, who yields the power of the air, and he has proven himself worthy but he does not know my other guards well. These chosen guards have worked together, trained together and spent time together, they know each other well," she paused. "The wise option would be to choose a being who knows them well and can work with them. For this reason, I choose, against every fibre of my being...Rorien."

"That is most wise of you. Rorien, do you accept the honour?" said the King nodding.

Rorien paused before moving forward and taking his spot behind her on her right, "I accept." He was dancing on the inside knowing he would be with her every moment and had the chance to prove to her that he did love her.

"Will each Master prepare for the oath. You will each conduct the oath for each guard who yields your power, in order of the Princess' choice," said the King scanning the element Masters.

The Master of earth stepped forward. Fendton and Elentari held out their left hands to the master. The Master cut them both, Fendton took Elentari's hand in his, their blood mingling together. The Master recited the ancient oath.

"By the ancient oath you are my guard," said Elentari looking directly at Fendton, her face void of emotion.

"I am your guard by the ancient oath" replied Fendton looking directly at Elentari without emotion.

They each healed their wound before letting go, both grinning at each other. She could feel a sensation in her chest. It was different to the link yet similar. She touched it. Fendton also raised his hand and touched his chest and she felt his touch. She had another she could communicate with this time via a blood oath, it was weird but she liked it.

The Master of fire stepped forward. Lorcan and Elentari held out their left hands. The Master cut them both, Lorcan took Elentari's hand in his, their blood circulating together. The Master recited the ancient oath.

"By the ancient oath you are my guard," said Elentari without emotion, looking directly at Lorcan.

"I am your guard by the ancient oath" answered Lorcan looking directly at Elentari and without emotion.

They each healed their wound before letting go, smiling at each other. She reached up to touch her new sensation, her Lorcan oath and he responded.

The Master of water stepped forward. Jasper and Elentari held out their right hands. The Master cut them both, Jasper linked Elentari's hand in his, their blood pooling together. The Master recited the ancient oath.

"By the ancient oath you are my guard," said Elentari looking directly at Jasper.

"I am your guard by the ancient oath" answered Jasper looking directly at Elentari.

They each healed their wound before letting go and both glanced towards Sarina. She was beaming. Elentari touched her new oath and Jasper responded. She was liking this, her new attachments, her guard oaths.

The Master of air stepped forward.

"My King, as Rorien is my link, is the oath able to be taken on the link instead of with blood?" she asked, turning to the King.

"Masters?" asked the King.

"There is no information on whether it can be done" answered the air Master.

"Shall we see if it works? If it does not work, the blood link can be used," stated the King.

"As you wish, my King," the air Master turned to Rorien and Elentari, "please take hold of your links." The Master recited the ancient oath with changes for the link and not blood.

"By the ancient oath on our link, you are my guard," said Elentari glaring directly at Rorien.

"I am your guard by the ancient oath taken via our link" answered Rorien remorsefully looking at Elentari.

On their link, she sneered '*You may be my guard but you are first my link. Our link is greater than being a princess' guard. First is the link, second is a guard.*

'*As you wish*' he replied on the link, his head bowed, '*I am your link first.*'

'*Then act it.*'

'*I will. I am sorry. I was not thinking clearly. Can I explain later.*'

'*Yes.*' She did like being able to speak to him without others knowing.

"It is done, the Princess has her guard by the ancient oath. Your oath is to the Princess, the future Queen of all the lands. The princess is to be protected with your life. You are to honour her, respect her, trust her and always be honest to her." Spoke the King

"Yes, my King." They answered by bowing their heads.

The Master of shift did not ask her if she had found her animal guide and she was not going to speak. She had decided to keep her secret quiet until she could find further information on her animal guide.

"As the oaths are fulfilled, business is complete. Princess, todia spend with your oath bearers. On the morrow, your routine will change. Oath bearers you are to move your things to casas near the Princess. Spend the dia moving and guard her with your life." The King dismissed them with a wave of his hand.

"Well I guess it is moving dia," she said, taking Rorien's arm as they stepped out of the royal hall. "Firstly, we should know our place within our oath. Lorcan, you take front left with Rorien front right. Fendton rear left and Jasper rear right." They moved into formation and continued. "At all times in public, you must show no emotion and be on guard. I will let you know when you may relax and how relaxed you may be via the oath." She loosened the oaths. "Appearances are important and as you are the guard of the future queen of all the lands, you need to act above all. Understood?"

"Understood." They all answered.

"Sarina please walk with me. It does not feel right for you to be lagging behind."

"Thank-you. It does feel strange by myself. I guess I will need to get used to it," she said, stepping beside the Princess.

"We all have a new role to get used to. Todia we get to move into a new casa. Shall we see which one you prefer?" Elentari led them to inspect each of the casas surrounding hers and to choose one. All casas had two bedrooms with a large multipurpose room and each was furnished. Sarina and Jasper chose the casa to her right, Lorcan took the casa to the left and Fendton took one below as it was closer to the middle path around the cuedel and quicker to get home at night. Rorien took a casa above hers.

"At least we won't have to move furniture. Unless you chose to bring something."

"I do like my blue couch. Can we bring it Jasper?" asked Sarina.

"I think all the males can manage to bring your lounge suite to your new rooms. These can be moved to your old casa," answered Elentari. "Males to work please." The males began to move the furniture. "I like this, making them do all the work. A perk of being the princess. Plus, it gives their male ego a boost." She whispered to Sarina.

"This is fun," giggled Sarina. The females packed up Sarina and Jasper's belongings into baskets, leaving the males to move them into their new casa. "I like being closer to you. It is going to save the long trek home."

"Yes, it will be nicer to be closer. We can have breakfast together every morning as well as supper," said Elentari.

By high sun, they stopped for lunch. Fendton, Lorcan and Rorien had moved all their items into their new casa, neither of them had much, a basket of clothes was about all for them. All items from Sarina's had been moved and yet to be unpacked.

"What shall we do after lunch?" questioned Elentari. Rorien was sitting beside her, his hand holding hers and she was happy.

"We are your guard. We do what you want." Smirked Lorcan.

"Really? I can make you do whatever I want, can I? Are you sure you want to run with that Lorcan?" smiled Elentari.

"Maybe not. Who knows what mean things you will have me do? After all, you made me move a couch. Do you know how heavy that was?" said Lorcan rubbing his biceps.

"Not heavy for me. Sarina was it heavy for you?" asked Elentari to Sarina.

"No. Very light and easy to move actual answered Sarina.

"I believe us males are in big trouble when you two are together," said Jasper rolling his eyes and causing the group to erupt in laughter.

"You and Jasper have some unpacking to do. Spend the rest of the dia together and enjoy being together. On the morrow, we start a new routine. Breakfast here," said Elentari.

"Thank-you Elentari," said Jasper.

"Lorcan and Fendton, what do you wish to do?"

"To head over to the market for a drink with the males" answered Lorcan.

"Then go. Be back here on the morrow for breakfast. Fendton?"

"Are you going to leave?" Fenton asked quietly, sorrow filling his eyes.

"Fendton, until the Masters find an answer I am staying. If things change between this morning and when they have an answer only time will tell," she said holding his arms.

"I don't want you to go," he said quietly as his head fell forward onto hers.

"I am not going anywhere for a while so enjoy the time we have together," she hugged him. "Why don't you go and do something you enjoy, have some fun?" she moved back holding his hands.

"Ok. Promise you won't go anywhere?" he asked looking into her eyes.

"I will not promise you something I cannot guarantee. Who knows what our future holds? I promise I will be here on the morrow for breakfast."

"You know what our future holds, you can see the future."

"I see only what is revealed and that can change with events. Now go have fun. I will see you on the morrow for breakfast." She kissed his cheek, spun him around and pushed him out the door.

"You have me alone. What is it?" asked Rorien.

"That is what I want to know." She sat on the couch patting the seat for him to sit with her. He obliged. "Tell me what happened? You let go of our link when the Masters trialled me. When I needed you, you ignored me and left me alone. Why?"

"I was confused and scared. What did you need me for? Who were you? What purpose did you serve? What purpose did I have? I didn't want to be anywhere near you. I just kept getting more questions and no answers. I'm sorry I left you," he said sadness in his voice and his eyes. He was holding their link pleading for forgiveness.

"How do you think I felt? That dia was massive for me. It was frightening and the only safe thing I had rejected me. I was frightened and alone in a world I knew nothing of."

"I am sorry. I didn't think. I…" he slumped forward tears in his eyes.

"I have no answers either. I know not my purpose or yours other than you are my link. I want to be with you." He looked up at her. She moved closer to him to hold him. "Todia is a new start. You are my link and guard. What has happened is behind us. Can we move on together?" she asked with her hand on his.

"Ok. We do this together. Together we work out our purpose and role in this world. I missed holding you. I was stupid to let you go." He moved to kiss her and she kissed him back.

"I missed us, you holding me, making me feel safe. I love you Rorien. You are my link and I am yours, only yours." She kissed him. They spent the rest of dia together holding each other and making up for lost time until the maids entered with food.

"Will the others join us?" Rorien asked.

"I can summon them. Do you want them here?"

"Yes and no. I want you to myself and I want to spend time with them too," he said rubbing her back.

"I've summoned them, the decision is made. Wonder how..." the door opened and Jasper and Sarina entered, "Never mind, that quick."

"You summon us?" said Jasper bowing.

"It is supper time. No guard duty, just friendship."

"Where are Lorcan and Fendton?" asked Sarina searching the casa.

"I let them head off for the dia. Not sure how long they will be." Lorcan burst through the door with Fendton two steps behind.

"You summoned us?" said Lorcan panting with his hands resting on his knees as he caught his breath.

"Yes, it's supper time. Where were you?"

Southsidee," said Fenton, inhaling deeply as he straightened up.

"At least I know how long it takes for you to get to me if I need it. Come sit. Fendton, it will be awhile. Things have changed." Fendton looked surprised and slowly smiled.

"Are you always going to summon us when you feel like it?" asked Jasper as he sat down at the table.

"No. Todia was the exception. I wanted to make sure it worked and how long it would take to respond. I don't plan to use it to create puppets. You all are individuals and have your personalities. If I want gofa guards I would have chosen others. I chose you all as I know you and have trained with you. I know your ways and little quirks. It makes it easy to predict you and you to predict me."

"Fair enough. Let's eat."

"Oh, and Fendton, can you please make sure you carve showers for you all and Sarina a bath?"

"Already on it," smiled Fendton

It had been two vikas since the oaths and routines had changed. Her dia was divided into five, one part devoted to spending with one of her guards individually and one part with them all. When not attending guard duties, they continued with their normal duties.

First up was breakfast together before training with Seneca. Their skills with sword and bow were being enhanced and they were learning to fight together, getting to know each other's movements and predict the outcome to complement each other. Elentari's swordsmanship had expanded. Her movements were elegant and lavish hitting the target every time. Her bow was not as accurate and she was lucky to hit any of the inner rings.

After training was a trip to the ancient library with Lorcan as her guard. They both enjoyed the Scholar's teachings, being able to search the texts themselves and learning the ancient language. Royal duties followed with Jasper and lunch with her father. Time with the females and Fendton was first up after royal duties. Fendton was not happy to be allocated to female duties and would stand back and show very obviously his eagerness not to be here. Of course, the males took great delight in ribbing him every dia about female tasks. Eventually, he gave in and started learning to weave a basket, giving him something to do.

The last part of her day was royal duties with Rorien before supper all together in her casa or in one of the parestalas. Her father came by at least twice a vika to sup with her. She made sure to be seen around the community and to walk the whole community twice a day. She chatted with those she met along the way, helped where she could and made sure those who lived here knew the Princess was there for them.

Tonight, she decided to attempt cooking and dug out her computer, finding a playlist to cook too. Rorien sat watching her, smiling as she began to move to the music and prepare food. Supper was nearly prepared and she was filling the table as each of their friends came in, searching for answers with the noise they heard. She smiled at them and continued dancing, singing and setting the table.

"I loved watching her cook. She always dances to the music while cooking or driving or whatever," said Rorien to each of them as they came in and sat at the table, listening and watching her.

Selena Gomez singing Wolves began playing. As the chorus rang out, Lorcan changed into his wolf animal form and pranced with her as she pretended to run. She smiled and changed into a wolf to race around the lounge with Lorcan close behind.

"What!?" screamed Fendton. "No not a wolf, anything but that," he said shaking his head in his hands.

She changed back and turned the music off. "That is not my animal spirit. I can shift and have been practising in secret since the oaths without the Master. He does not know I found my animal guide. No one did until now. Only you all know," she said her finger pointing to each of them.

"What is your animal?"

"Well…it is very unusual…I don't…it is scary, sort of…I'm not sure if anyone…" she sighed and rolled her head.

"I have an unusual animal form," said Sarina.

"Will you show me?" she asked and Sarina changed into her animal spirit, a rhinoceros. She changed back.

"How cool. Rhinos are animals that can push through a pack with force. You do need a bit of force to deal with this lot," said Elentari smiling at Sarina pointing to the males.

"I don't understand why I need my animal."

"Hey, I don't know why I need every power or what I am meant to do. Together we will find answers. At least I know who to turn to if I need a path through a group." Elentari placed a hand on her friend. Sarina smiled, feeling better about her spirit guide.

"So, what's your animal?" asked Fendton

"Any guesses?"

"Drachenstein," said Rorien. Elentari looked surprised.

"Yes. How did you know and when did you realise?" she asked.

"All the signs point to it and didn't know until now. About a mesik ago, I had an idea. Plus, since we have been constantly on our link…" he smiled at her. Since the oath day, the two of them were always chatting via the link. Their way of constantly being together without physically being together and both could hold two conversations at once, one verbally and one on the link.

"Is it ok? It's not too weird?" Along the link, she said '*I forget I am constantly talking to you and not keeping anything from you.*'

"For you, no. You are most unusual and anything normal would be weird. Dragon suits you, a fire breathing angry female." Rorien smirked. On the link, he said '*Don't keep anything from me. I like knowing everything.*'

"Oh really? Fire breathing angry female? Do you want to see my wrath?" she answered smiling. '*Back at you.*'

"I bet one day we will see your anger in full and hope I am not on the receiving end," said Jasper.

"Will you show us?" asked Fendton.

"You are always so inquisitive. Ok, but I warn you it is frightening to begin with. I scare myself when I get really angry," she said.

"No, your animal, not your anger, said Fenton rolling his eyes.

"I know, I was playing," she said laughing, "are you ready?" they nodded and she changed.

All stepped back, shocked, eyes wide and mouths wide open. She was a four-legged, bat-winged scaly lizard which filled the room. Her thin membranous wings as brilliant as stained glass sprouted from her sides, the iridescent surface constantly changing colour against the light. Her head, the shape of a horse, long and narrow with two twisted long horns protruding from her head, her nose long with two thick rounded nostrils and four tendrils on her chin. Her muscular legs each had four digits which ended in sharp, hooked, ebony coloured talons, capable of ripping the toughest hide to shreds. Her long, thorny tail ending in a fan-like tip, capable as a weapon. Her delicate scales, not much thicker than a thumbnail were mesmerising as they shimmered in the light. It was hypnotic watching the coloured streaks shoot along her body changing the scales colour constantly.

Fendton reached forward to touch her. She turned her head to snap her sharp teeth capable of ripping through metal at him. He quickly recoiled as she changed back laughing.

"Wow. That is awesome." Fendton said.

"Let's eat, I am starving. All that dancing makes me hungry," she said as they began filling their plates with her first cooked meal.

"This looks sensational Elentari. Your first meal and you have outdone yourself," said Sarina

"Thanks. I hope it is alright. Cooking here is so different than back home."

"You did marvellously," said Rorien, kissing her.

"Eat up as on the morrow we are heading east. Sarina, you will be ok while we are away, won't you?"

"Yes. I will be ok. It will be nice to have some time to myself and I have trained with the heal Master. Thanks for organising private lessons. Go enjoy and find out what pulls you East."

"Since you are linked to my guard, it is wise to have your power extended. Never know when I will need a healer for this lot," she smirked, thumbing at the males.

Elentari had been drawn to the east since she arrived and she did not know why. It would take them at least 5 horis travelling on foot to the far east, the fastest they could run was about 40km/h and that was without carrying anything.

Each of her guards was carrying a pack with food and clothes for themselves and her. They carried their swords and knives. Her pack was filled with food, a blanket and changes of clothes. They set off east, going at her pace, Lorcan in lead, Rorien beside her and Fendton and Jasper behind, in their guard formation as decided.

They were travelling slowly as Elentari was in no hurry and wanted to take in the land around them, enjoying the sights and bushland. Surrounding Thoroneath were farms on the flats, circling their cuedel and acting as a boundary for the royal lands. The mountain range ran around the edge of the flats encircling the farms and cuedel acting as an outer border. The path through the mountains was smooth and weaved around and through with tunnels cut into the earth giving a flatter and easier access through steep-sided mountains. A large grain field with fruit trees and vegetable patches lining the boundaries could be seen as they came out of the mountains.

"This is another of the farms," said Jasper. "Those from villades around here come to farm these fields and is where most of their food comes from." It was two hori from their cuedel travelling at speed.

"How many farms are there?" asked Elentari

"Our food comes from the farms which surround Thoroneath and you saw during the olive harvest. There are many smaller farms near villades, large grain farms with vegetables and fruits, similar to this, scattered throughout."

"Mmm, do villades come together to harvest like at the olive festival?"

"Yes. Every being will harvest together like us and have festivals like us."

As they continued to the far side of the farm, Elentari stopped to greet the farmers and ask them about themselves. She touched their hearts and searched their minds. All had hearts of light and warmth and spoke the truth to her. Yielding the mind power made her job as Princess much easier, she could confirm those she met were true. Those outside her cuedel did not realise she was the Princess and she did not mind. She introduced herself as Elentari to get to know the real beings she was meeting, as princess they would not open up as much.

They stopped along the path for tea instead of in a village, two horis from the last cuedel in the east, Rhunduin. Jasper using his water power to fill the kettle and Lorcan using his firepower to boil it. Elentari noticed the bush hushed as they stopped. She noticed and sensed they were being watched. She kept silent watching the bush, searching and waiting. The males chatting amongst themselves.

"You know we never did have that chat" whispered Lorcan to her as they began their journey again. Jasper and Rorien were talking in front with Fendton lagging.

"Which one? Link one?" she whispered, still watching the bush.

"Yes. My link pulled me east and is still pulling me east."

"This is good. We are both on a mission in the same direction, you for your link and me yet to know why," she said, turning to him smiling.

"The answer will reveal itself when needed," he grinned. She shook her head at him.

"Don't use my words against me, your pain. But thanks, appreciated." They continued chatting together, Lorcan pointing out the different plants and trees to her, including a 'red thing on a stick' plant, her name for it. She had seen this amazing red flower which sat above the long thin leaves on a tall straight stem. The flower had large outer petals protecting the soft fuzzy candy floss inner petals and whisker-like tentacles cascaded down forming a veil. It was a strange but beautiful flower.

They were close to Rhunduin when Elentari headed off the path and began collecting firewood moving further into the bush. The males followed unsure what she was doing.

"What are you doing?" asked Rorien both out loud and on the link.

"Collecting wood for the fire. Otherwise, the night may get cold." On the link she said *'I am not sure. Something is guiding me here. The answer...'*

'will be revealed' he finished her sentence on their link.

"We are but an hori away from Rhunduin," he said out loud hoping the answer will reveal itself quickly. He knew this area was not a safe place.

"And on the morrow, we will be there. Tonight, we'll stay here."

"This is not a place a princess sleeps," said Fendton concern in his voice as his eyes darted around the bush.

"Then tonight I am Elentari, a female from Thoroneath on her way to Rhunduin and not the princes," she said forcefully.

"But it can be dangerous," said Fendton

"Lucky I have you four to protect me. Fendton, I appreciate your concern and trying to protect me. When I make up my mind and we are in public YOU WILL NOT question me, accept and deal with it. Is that clear?"

"Yes," he said, head bowed.

"When it is just us, it is ok to inform me of the dangers. Remember Rorien is my link and he would not allow me to come into danger." *'You won't will you?'*

'I will always keep you safe.'

"Ok. I just…"

"It's ok Fendton. I know" she rubbed his arm with her free hand.

As they came to a clearing, she put down the firewood and Lorcan started the fire while Fendton organised supper and Jasper made tea. Elentari sat against a log talking and playing with Rorien on their link. He moved to sit with her, wrapping an arm around her and she leaned into him. Her eyes were on the bush, watching and waiting. He looked to where she was looking, trying to figure out what she was seeing. He felt warmth fill the clearing and he realised she was using her firepower to warm the clearing, knowing the fire was not large enough warm. He wondered why she needed a fire if she was going to use her power and asked her on the link.

She rose and moved into the bush where she had been watching. "Please come sit by the fire and get warm. We welcome you to join us" she said. "It is ok, I will not hurt you and there is plenty of space to sit. Come." There was movement behind the tree, a face appeared. "You look cold, come seek warmth by the fire," she said holding her hand out for the being to take. The face looked at her, to the fire and the males. "It is ok. They are my friends and we will not harm you. Please come warm yourself by the fire." She moved her hand to wave the being to come. "Come warm yourself. It is ok."

Out from behind the tree stepped a small faun, shivering, wet and cold. The faun was hesitant, not sure of her or her friends but wanted to warm herself.

"Come you are freezing and the fire is warm. Quickly." Elentari could feel her guard stiffen.

'What are you doing?' asked Rorien on their link

'Helping a wet cold child get warm' she replied.

The faun took a step forward watching Elentari. Slowly she walked to the fire, her eyes darting for one to another. Elentari stood beside her.

"Fendton, please get a cup of tea for our new friend to warm her. You must be freezing, all wet. What happened?" she bent down level with the faun.

"I…I…was playing…near the creek and fell in. My mum will be angry with me. She told me not to go there." Sobbed the faun, her arms folded trying to warm herself.

"It is ok, child. Here, have some tea, it will warm your insides. Stay by the fire and dry off. Your mum can wait, she will not want you sick." Elentari stoked the faun's hair. "My name is Elentari. What is your name?" She knew she could dry her quickly with her powers yet that would not bring them together.

"My name is Peana," she said holding the tea in her hands to warm them.

"It is nice to meet you Peana. Do you live near here?" Elentari had partially dried Peana's hair with her firepower.

"Yes, we live near the creek," Peana said, as she sipped the tea.

Elentari heard Peana's name being called. "Your mother is looking for you. Shall I call her for you?"

"Yes," Peana answered quietly afraid of what was to come.

"She is here" yelled Elentari, turning towards where she heard the mother calling. "It will be ok," she said quietly to Peana, her hand on Peana's back. "Peana is here by the fire." She yelled out. A faun came running from the bush followed by a male faun.

"Peana, where have you been?" said her mother racing to her, wrapping her arms around her daughter all stressed and frantic.

"She was hiding in the bush when I found her, wet and cold. I asked her to come to warm herself and get dry by the fire" said Elentari. "She was scared she would be in trouble for playing near the creak and falling in."

"Who are you?" demanded the male faun.

"I am Elentari, a friend. Please enjoy the warmth of the fire as your daughter dries off."

"You are the enemy! Come now Peana!" male was staring at her fuming from the edge of the clearing gesturing for his daughter to come to him.

"No daddy. Elentari is helping me," said Peana, taking Elentari's hand.

"They are the enemy! They hurt our kind! Now come!" the male faun said, forcefully gesturing for Peana to follow.

"I do not understand. How did we hurt your kind?" asked Elentari.

"Your kind killed our kind in the brother war. You did not help us and left us to die," spat the male.

"The war that was thousands of anoks ago, before you or I were born? The one where Eleanor's sons fought for the crown?"

"Yes, that war," he said glaring at her.

"That was our forefathers' war, seven kings ago. What they did was not right, it was a very big mistake and the past cannot be changed, only the future. I only offered your daughter warmth so she would not catch a cold." She rubbed Peana's back looking down at her smiling.

"She is quite wet and will catch a cold if we do not let her dry. Let us stay till she dries." said her mother, placing a hand on the male's arm.

"When she is dry, we leave." Anger filled his eyes as he folded his arms and stood stiffly watching them from the forest edge.

"I do not know what happened in the war. Are you able to explain?" asked Elentari to the male faun.

"Gornack was the younger child and wanted the crown. He entrapped the fauns to fight for him. We did not want to fight, yet he tortured us if we did not obey him. When the war came, there were fauns on both sides. The fauns on Leelan's side chose to fight and did not know there were fauns in Gornack's army. They begged not to fight when they saw us but it was too late. Neither brother would back down. When the war was over, we asked for help from King Leelan and he turned his back on us. We had nothing and lost many. Gornack escaped but he forced many fauns as his slaves. We found out about the faun slaves and asked King Leelan for help to free our families, he refused. You all turned on us." His hands were pointing to them all.

"That is horrible. King Leelan was wrong and I am not like them. I believe every being should be treated equally and a King should help his subjects if they ask. The Kings or Queens should protect all kinds and not just rule, protect those who dwell in their lands as well as govern."

"We have not spoken to any of your kind since. There have been fights between us and you over the anoks. Neither trusts the other. Your kind has given us no reason to trust you." He snarled.

"I do not expect you to trust me todia. Time will tell if you can and my actions will show you. What are your names?"

"That is none of your business. We leave when Peana is dry." The male faun said, folding his arms again.

"I am Rhen and this is Duggit," said the female faun sighing, shaking her head.

"It is nice to meet you both. My name is Elentari," Elentari said, dipping her head. "This is Lorcan, Jasper, Fendton and Rorien. We are heading to Rhunduin," she said as she pointed to each.

"Thank-you Elentari for helping Peana and allowing her to warm by your fire," said Rhen.

"I had to help. I would not want such a sweet child to be sick because of a stupid war so many years ago and male egos refusing to budge" smiled Elentari

"Yes, males can be a bother when the ego is bruised," said Rhen looking at her sideways.

"Even worse when it is crushed!" The females laughed and continued to chat. Elentari asked Rhen about their kind and their ways, showing them kindness, offering them food and tea. Peana dried completely and Rhen said nothing staying longer to get to know Elentari.

"It is getting late and dark. Please stay and sleep by the fire for the night where it is warm" requested Elentari.

"It is dark and late, we will stay. But we go first light" stated Duggit, still very hesitant. Peana skipped around showing her delight.

"Thank-you Duggit," said Rhen.

"You will be safe with us, Duggit. While we are here, the males will protect you, protect us all. Each of the males can swing a sword and is advanced in element yielding."

"Thank-you but I do not trust you."

"Trust has to be earnt. I hope I will earn your trust. You are such a nice family and I have enjoyed your company." Elentari grabbed the blanket from her pack, "Here, I have a blanket for you if you like," she said as she handed it to Rhen.

"Thank-you." She took it and settled Peana down to sleep, laying down beside her.

Her guard all found a spot to sleep. Fendton handed her the blanket from his pack before settling himself down. Rorien lay beside her. Duggit remained standing, keeping watch over his family. Watching her and her guard, still hesitant to let his guard down. She fell asleep not knowing if Duggit slept down or not.

CHAPTER 15

Elentari had heard Duggit quietly arousing the fauns before first light and leading them off. She ordered her guard stay quiet and rose when they left. After breakfast, they headed into Rhunduin and wandered around the cuedel so Elentari could see the differences between their cuedel and here. The casa was wood cabins and more like the old towns back on her world. It was centred around a square parestala with shops lining the edges. The parestala was abuzz with activity, with beings rushing here and there, groups conducting business and children playing. Elentari noticed a child playing by herself and watched her. There was something about her, something familiar which she could not place. Her guard spread out to keep a watch out. Her guard on watch, she smiled at the thought. She liked having a guard and how they complimented each other. She had chosen well.

She touched each being's heart and searched their minds finding out what sort of beings lived here. Many were unfaithful to their link and there were a few who were ones to avoid, those with dark hearts. She did not want to know what their minds spoke. Many had light hearts and good about them.

The child noticed Elentari. "Hello, you don't live here do you?" the child asked, skipping towards her.

"No, I don't. I live on the mountain at Thoroneath. What is your name?" She opened her senses, the child smelt familiar.

"Rewa. I haven't been to the mountain. I haven't been anywhere," she said, hopping about, skipping and jumping.

"I have only been here and the mountain. Where is your mother?" There was something about the child but Elentari didn't understand how she seemed familiar.

"I'm allowed to play in the square, she lets me," she said, spinning around. Rewa kept talking, telling Elentari all sorts of things, playing and constantly moving about.

"You are a very active child, Rewa. How old are you?"

"I am 3 and a half anoks," she said proudly "I'm a big female," she said, swinging her hips side to side, proud of her age.

"Rewa, leave the female alone," yelled a voice. Elentari looked up to see a female walking swiftly towards them.

"She is no bother. I have enjoyed her chatter and watching her play. She is very active."

"She is constantly on the move and draining" sighed the female shaking her head.

"You are her mother?" Not only was the female's scent nothing like Rewa's, but her looks were also very different. Elentari knew she was not her birth mother as parents and children have the same scent and theirs were very different. It was then she knew who Rewa was but was unsure as to why.

"Yes," the female said, taking Rewa's hand.

"If it is ok with you, she can stay. I do not mind, especially if it helps you out for a while."

"Thank you your kindness. We shall go," she said leading Rewa away.

Elentari watched them leave, trying to work out how she could speak to the mother to find out Rewa's story and why she was not her daughter. She knew who her brother was but didn't know how he did not know he had a sister.

"What are you thinking?" asked Lorcan, sneaking up beside her and watching the mother and child walk away.

"How I can speak to that mother again and find out the child's story. Have you pulled on your link?" asked Elentari, turning her gaze to Lorcan.

"I have now." Grinned Lorcan

"Let's go find her then" smiled Elentari. She took his arm as he led her away from the square and through the alleyways towards the docks.

He stopped as they entered the docks. Elentari let go of his arm and turned towards him.

"She is near," he whispered, turning to face her, a look of uncertainty on his face.

"Then go find her, go find your link. I will be here." Jasper stepped up beside her nodding at Lorcan to go. He smiled and left, walking swiftly away as the two of them watched him.

"You know who that child is, don't you?" said Jasper, still watching Lorcan.

"Yes, I take it you do too," she said her eyes on Lorcan.

"He doesn't."

"No, he doesn't and most won't unless he opens his senses." They watched as Lorcan approached a female, watched as she recognised him, watched as they hugged and watched them walk to the end of the dock and sit.

"Shall we leave?" asked Jasper, turning to her.

"There is a shop over there with tea. Shall we?" asked Elentari, taking his arm.

"You and tea," he said, shaking his head as a little laugh escaped his lips.

The shop owner was a lovely old female and Elentari guessed she was in her 800's. They ordered tea and cakes to have outside and Elentari handed over a coin. It was far too much for what they ordered. "I shall be back for more tea. Hopefully, this will pay for all we need before we leave. If it is not enough, please let me know." The female nodded and Rorien and Fenton joined them.

Lorcan came back, she dismissed him to do as he pleased. She was more interested in finding out about Rewa, who she was and finding out her story without him knowing. Rewa was the reason she was pulled east and she needed to find out why. They stayed by the docks till after lunch before heading back to the square where she found Rewa playing. Rewa spotted her and came racing up full of laughter and smiles, she was such a joy to be around. Elentari was pleased to see her here and hoped her mother would return soon so she could find answers.

As Rewa's mother came looking for her, Elentari sent Rorien and Fendton to find a room. Elentari struck up a conversation and they sat chatting while watching Rewa play. She wondered how you ask a being if their child is theirs, waiting for the right time to ask and the right words to speak. She had to know her story and find out for him. It grew late and still Elentari was none the wiser. She was getting anxious as they said their goodbyes and was frustrated at not being able to find the right time to ask.

Breakfast was on the docks at the tea shop before they headed to the square to find Rewa playing. Rewa's mother came before tea to find her and gave Elentari a way to keep talking. She had to know who she was and why her brother didn't know her

"I was about to go for tea when you arrived, would you like to join me? There is a beautiful tea shop on the docks with lovely tea and delicious cakes. I am paying" said Elentari.

"Thank-you tea would be lovely." Elentari and Roswen took Rewa's hands as they headed to tea while the males followed unseen. Rewa was enjoying her cake, cream covered her mouth and nose, and Elentari got her more. She was loving having Rewa around and did not want to head home until she had answers. She called Jasper on the oath.

"Rewa, would you like a shoulder ride? Jasper will give you one, if you like," said Elentari as Roswen wiped the cream from Rewa's face.

Rewa's eyes grew wide with excitement "Yes please!" she squealed rushing to him. He picked her up and headed off with her squealing with delight on his shoulders.

"I have wanted to ask you something since I met you but don't know-how," said Elentari looking directly into Roswen's eyes. "It has plagued me since I scented you and do not know how to approach the subject kindly."

"She is not mine but I have cared for her since her birth. I do not know her mother," answered Roswen shaking her head.

"I know her brother but he does not know he has a sister," she said as Jasper returned with Rewa and Lorcan and his link came in sight. "We leave on the morrow, could we meet up later?"

"Yes. If you explain who her family is, I will explain how I came to be her mother," said Roswen, taking Rewa's hand.

"Yes, I will. Goodbye Roswen and Rewa," said Elentari waving.

"Bye Elentari. I will miss you" said Rewa waving frantically to her as her mother led her away.

Lorcan introduced his link. "Elentari, this is Awnrie my link. Awnrie meet Elentari, the future queen."

"That is how you introduce me, future queen? So much for friendship." She rolled her eyes. "Hi Awnrie, it is nice to meet you." She bent her head in greeting.

"My majesty, it is a pleasure to meet you," said Awnrie curtsying.

"Please not so formal," she said, shaking her hand. "This is why I prefer my friends to introduce me as a friend and not as a future queen." She turned to Lorcan. "Lorcan, we will leave on the morrow and head home."

"Lorcan said he had to return soon. I had hoped it would not be so soon," said Awnrie, holding Lorcan's arm tighter.

"You can come to visit us and you have all dia with him. I have some unfinished business here, tea and cake for one." She smiled "When we return, why not come back with us and spend time with Lorcan. You can stay at my casa. Lorcan's casa is beside me, he won't be far."

"I have not left this cuedel," she said "It would be nice to see other places. I will let you know before you return."

"I am about to head into the square to do some shopping. What plans do you two have?"

"Spending as much time as possible with Awnrie if that's ok?" asked Lorcan, not taking his eyes off Awnrie.

"Go have fun. Meet here for breakfast and we shall leave after," she said waving her hand to dismiss them.

"Thanks," Lorcan leant in and kissed her cheek before heading off holding onto Awnrie.

"They look happy," said Jasper watching them walk off all giggly and clinging to each other.

"Yes, they do. Hopefully, she returns with us, on the morrow we will know. Let's shop." Elentari rose, linked arms with Jasper and headed back to the square.

Rorien fell into step with them and she took his arm as Jasper fell back. "How did you know the faun would be there yesterdia?" he asked. His feelings for her were growing stronger, similar to when they first met. He liked being with her, being near her and their secret conversations.

"I didn't. I felt pulled to the clearing but did not know why. Opening my senses, I could hear and see what I needed to know. You should try it sometime." she said as she glanced sideways at him.

"Yeah, yeah. Did you mean what you said about being a Queen who protects?" he asked as his eyes staring out in front of them.

"Yes."

"You yield eight powers, why rule as one who protects, when you can rule with power?" he asked, stopping to look at her, his face puzzled.

"How do you know me, see me?" she asked gently, turning to face him.

"You are kind, considerate, watching out for others, happy to ask and learn about others. You tend to put others first. Like Lorcan and finding his link. You could have made him stay with you as your guard yet you gave him time to be with his link." He was looking at her with admiration.

"Do you see me as ruling with power?"

"No, protecting is more you. You have a quality about you which beings are drawn to. They want to help you and love you. Ruling would be too harsh for you."

"Yes. I let Lorcan go to strengthen his link and get to know her. The link is very special as you explained to me and needs to be strengthened. That is why I let him go," she said as she lovingly stroked their link and he responded. She put her hands on Rorien's chest. "Rorien, I love you and desire for us to complete our link. You are my link and you make me feel safe and protected. I need you to keep me safe and protected, to save me when I need it. I may yield these powers but I still need you. You are my link, my protector, my everything. I love you," she said as she stared into his eyes. He wrapped his arms around her pulling her into him as he bent down to kiss her, making her feel alive and vivacious.

"I want you but I'm not ready to complete our link. You are amazing but I'm unsure," he said stroking her hair.

"I know. You have a lot to work out, male ego squashed and all." She smiled, stroking him with her airpower, teasing him on their link. He kissed her again as his airpower stoked her.

"Where are you heading?" he asked, pulling away from her.

"Shopping of course," she said merrily dragging him towards the square.

"Of course. What are you looking for?" he asked, shaking his head.

"Nothing. I am just finding out who every being is, getting to know them by touching their hearts and searching their minds. There are many who are not faithful to their link and some very shady characters. They are different to those we live with." She slowed down to a stroll.

"Where will we start first?" he asked as he scanned the shops around the square.

"Let's walk and see what takes my interest." They continued in silence holding hands as they meandered past the shops until Elentari stopped.

"What is it?" he asked looking at the shop window searching for what she saw.

"This necklace is beautiful. It has the gems for each element power and the silverwork is so elegant. I wonder if the jeweller can add the spirit gems to it?" she asked leaning against the window.

"Wait here." Rorien entered the shop as Elentari stood waiting outside watching him and listening.

"The necklace in the window can you add the spirit gems to it?" Rorien asked the shopkeeper, a hand on the counter and the other point to the window.

"Yes. When do you need it?" replied the jeweller.

"Can you have it completed on the morrow?" he asked, turning to face the keeper.

"Yes," said the keeper nodding.

"Can you make a ring to match by the morrow?" he whispered to the jeweller, dropping his voice so Elentari could not hear him.

"Yes."

"We shall return on the morrow as the female outside wishes to purchase the necklace," he said in his normal voice before dropping his voice, "I shall take the ring as a gift for her." Rorien left the shop. "He can have it on the morrow for you," he smiled.

"Oh thank-you," she jumped up wrapping her arms around his neck kissing him before taking his hand and continuing their stroll around the square before she stopped at a dress shop.

"I shall be a moment or two," she said, kissing his cheek and entering.

"Hello, may I help you?" asked the shop assistant. Elentari touched her heart and searched her mind to find her heart was light.

"I am looking for nothing in particular, hoping something will catch my eye," she answered, scanning the shop.

"I have a new dress which was finished this morning and maybe your size." The assistant moved behind the counter and produced a beautiful green dress which flowed to the floor. The sweetheart neckline was embroidered with flowers and leaves linked by a black line. The cuffs of the three-quarter length sleeves were embroidered the same. Each of the flowers a different colour with all eight colours of the powers exhibited on the dress. Around the waist was a band embroidered with large flowers and leaves linked together with black thread.

"Oh my, it is beautiful. May I?" she asked as her hands reached out to touch the dress.

"Here." The assistant moved to the changing area, a curtain at the rear of the shop and Elentari tried on the dress. She stepped out to view it better.

"It is beautiful and fits me perfectly like it was made for me. Does it look alright?" she asked, turning and moving around to feel how the dress flowed.

"It is perfect and suits you well." said the assistant watching the dress move.

"I would like to take it please." Elentari returned to the change room and handed the dress to the assistant to wrap.

"Thank-you. Did you make this?" asked Elentari as she handed the assistant coin and took the dress.

"No, my mother makes them."

"She is most talented. Please thank her for me," said Elentari as she left the shop.

"You have more clothes?" groaned Rorien.

"Yes. I can never have enough dresses and this dress will match my necklace. Where is a shoe shop?" she said teasing as he took the package from her.

"There's one on the other side." He pointed across the square. She looked puzzled at him, surprised he knew where the shoes were. "You have to complete the outfit." He smiled.

"You are learning." She said smiling as she kissed him.

"Come on. Let's find shoes to match for you," he said, taking her hand and leading her across the square to the shoe shop.

"You will be sorry if I find shoes. Remember you lot are carrying my things."

"Then you are only allowed one pair," he said. Elentari saw the perfect pair in the window as they approached as did Rorien. "I am going to regret this, aren't I?" he moaned.

"Yes," she said entering the shop and coming out later with another package which she handed him.

"I'll take these back to the room and find you here somewhere," he said moving off.

"Just pull the link. It will guide you or even ask me where I am," she smiled.

"You never cease to amaze me," he said over his shoulder.

Elentari found a spot in the square to watch all the happenings going on and Rorien returned finding a place out of sight to watch over her, just as Jasper and Fendton were. It wasn't long before Rewa appeared and came racing over to her.

"Elentari!" Rewa screamed with her arms out wide. Elentari lifted Rewa high into the air before hugging her close.

"Hello, beautiful girl. I missed you. Have you been good?" she asked, putting Rewa down.

"Yes, I helped mummy," she said, skipping around. "We baked and I helped mix the cake."

"Mummy must be very grateful for your help," said Elentari as she sat back down to watch Rewa play.

"Yes," said Rewa as she kept playing around her and chatting about all the things she had been doing. She spoke about the beings she saw in the square and the happenings going on, the fights and those who were kissing another who was not their link. She saw lots and missed nothing. Rewa talked about all the games she played and how good she was at balancing on the wall.

"Hello Elentari," said Roswen

"Hello again Roswen," said Elentari, "Rewa said she has been helping you bake."

"Yes, she has. She is very good at mixing," said Roswen looking lovingly at Rewa.

"Shall we have tea?" asked Elentari, waiting patiently for Roswen to bring up Rewa's past, her insides were screaming and tearing at her wanting the answer but she waited calmly.

"Please mummy, can we? Please?" begged Rewa pulling at her mother's skirt.

"Yes, we can," Roswen said as they headed off to the tea shop. Rewa, Roswen, Rorien and Elentari sat together at one table while Jasper and Fendton sat nearby. The docks were alive with fisher males returning from their dia of fishing. Baskets of fish were being unloaded from the boats and off to the market. Nets being washed down and hung to dry, holes patched and frayed ropes mended. The shop owner brought out food and tea for them all and a special cake for Rewa. Her eyes lit up and her smile widened.

"Thank-you," said Elentari.

"My pleasure, my Majesty" answered the shop owner as she curtseyed. Roswen looked puzzled and went to speak.

"You are very special, Rewa, you have your cake," said Rorien, changing the subject before Roswen could ask the question, knowing Elentari preferred those to treat her as a friend before treating her like a princess. They opened up more if they believed she was the same as them and he knew Elentari wanted information from Roswen but didn't know what it was as she hadn't revealed it to him.

"I like cakes. This is my favourite" said Rewa hoeing into the cake, cream and icing covering her hands and face.

"Would you like to see the boats?" asked Rorien as Rewa finished eating.

"Yes, please." She clapped her hands in delight, her eyes lighting up. Roswen cleaned Rewa up and Rorien took her hand and headed off to see the boats.

"Will you tell me her story?" asked Elentari. She spoke to Rorien along their link asking him to open his senses and seek answers.

"My link and I are in our 450's and have no children. We were heading back from the village over when we heard a cry, a groan. A little off the path we could see a being on the ground struggling. We saw the female was heavy with a babe and she had been cut so badly she should have been dead. Her linked was further into the bush and dead. He too had been slashed but his wounds much worse than hers. She was unable to string words together. She kept saying something like 'Rewa' and 'Rorien'. I thought she was calling her link. I tried to comfort her, knowing she would die, too weak to give birth. My linked cut her stomach and removed her babe. We named her Rewa thinking that was what they wanted to name her. Her mother died before she could hold her. We buried them together in the bush and have cared for Rewa ever since. She has brought us great joy." Sighed Roswen watching Rewa as she came running up.

"We saw lots of fishes and I got to hold a live one!" said a very excited Rewa. "Can we go back again?" she asked tugging on Rorien's arm.

"What about Jasper gives you a shoulder ride again, would you like that?" asked Elentari, her eyes shifting from Rewa to Rorien.

"Ooh yes please," she said running to Jasper. He picked her up, throwing her high in the air before placing her on his shoulders and trotting off, her laughter filling the docks as she bounced up and down.

"Rorien, have you noticed anything about Rewa?" asked Elentari quietly as she gently stroked their link, placing a hand on his as he sat down.

"Yes. I didn't notice it before. How is she my sister and when did you know?" His head was bent over.

"When we met her the first time. Roswen has explained how she found your parents and Rewa. She doesn't know, Rorien, Rewa does not know." Elentari said gently rubbing his hand.

"I haven't told her. There was never a reason to. Now that you are here…I am not sure. I want her to know but…but I…it's" Roswen's head moved all about as she spoke, uncertain and scared.

"It's ok, Roswen. When you are ready, you can tell her. We are not here to take her with us. To be responsible for her is frightening. I'm not ready to be a mother or look after another. She is yours and your decision. Plus, Rorien has only just found out he is a big brother," said Elentari, her hand on Roswen's hand.

"Thank-you. She brings me such joy and happiness and I don't want to lose her. I am finding it difficult to tell her." Roswen grasped Elentari's hand and looked at her.

"She brings joy and happiness to every being. She is very special," said Elentari as they heard Jasper and Rewa returning, turning to watch them and taking a sip of her tea.

"It is time to go Rewa," said Roswen standing and hugging Rewa.

"Ooh but I want to stay" pouted Rewa, her hands thrusting down against her sides in a fist.

"We leave on the morrow. I shall come to find you before we leave," said Elentari as she bent down and whispered in her ear, "and bring you a cake."

"Ok." Rewa's eyes shone as she took her mother's hand and skipped off.

"So, he knows?" said Jasper watching Rewa leave with his back to her.

"Yes, I do. Thanks to Elentari. That must have been what Mum was trying to tell me. How come they were hurt? Who would want to do that to them? And why were they so far from their casa?" he asked with a look of bewilderment on his face.

"I guess she was. I don't know and where did they live?" asked Elentari.

"They lived in the west and never went far from their cuedel. They wouldn't even visit me in Thoroneath. It doesn't make sense." said Rorien shaking his head.

"Yet again we have more questions without answers. I will be glad for the dia when we have a question and the answer is given. I guess our life is going to be one unanswered question after another." Sighed Elentari.

"I will be glad to have even one question answered," said Rorien

"Where to now?" asked Fendton

"What would you two like to do? How about you both go and have some fun?" said Elentari looking up at them from her seat.

"I saw an inn around the square, wanna go for a drink?" asked Jasper, nudging Fendton.

"Alright, let's go," nodded Fendton.

"What shall we do?" asked Rorien as they watched them leave.

"Let's head back to the room. My head is racing with information and I just want to stop," said Elentari as she put her hands on the back of her neck and tilted her head back turning it side to side to release the tension.

"You alright?" he asked, concerned for her as he rubbed her back.

"Yes. I am most fine being with you," she said as she kissed him. Her eye caught something in a shop further along. She was looking towards the shop, her forehead furrowed trying to work what the shop was.

"What is it?" he asked looking in the direction she was looking.

"I don't know. Let's find out." She grabbed his hand heading towards the shop. "It's chocolate! Oh, my. You have chocolate, real chocolate!" Her excitement was displayed in the way she was jiggling about.

"Yes. Did I not mention that?"

"No, and I haven't found any back home. I need chocolate" she said wide-eyed like a little child in a candy store.

"Hello may I help you?" said the male shop assistant.

"Yes, I need all the chocolate. All. Of. It," she said arms wide hugging the chocolate counter.

"Can we have a basket of mixed chocolates please?" said Rorien "I think one will be enough Elentari."

"But it's chocolate. It's almost as good as having tea." She pouted, her eyes blinking excessively at Rorien.

"If you have time, I can show you how we make chocolate. I am about to pour a batch," said the shop assistant.

"Ooo, can we please Rorien?" she begged excitedly.

"Ok," he said. They followed the assistant through the shop.

"These have been plucked, opened, fermented, dried and are ready for making chocolate," said the shop assistant grabbing a fist full of cocoa beans and turning his hand to watch the cocoa beans fall back into the tub. "We then grind and heat them to make a liquid," he said standing at a vat stirring the chocolate liquid with a spoon. "We then add the ingredients and pour into moulds."

"Is this ready for the moulds?" asked Elentari full of curiosity.

"Yes. Here, take a jug, fill with chocolate and pour," he said, handing Elentari a jug. Elentari grabbed a jug, filled it with chocolate and poured it into the mould. She continued to fill the moulds as Rorien watched, chatting to the assistant as he guided her and encouraged her, thoroughly enjoying herself.

"Once you can no longer fill the jug, we lift the vat and pour," he said as he scraped down the sides of the vat.

"I shall leave that for you to do. I am not sure I am steady enough to pour from the vat." Elentari put the jug down and stepped back near Rorien to watch the assistant finish.

"You have chocolate on your breasts," Rorien whispered in her ear, using his finger to wipe it off. She looked down as he wiped her breast.

"I have chocolate boobs, have I?" she whispered back a smile on her face.

"Prefer to use my lips to remove it," he said, sucking the chocolate off his finger.

"Ssh. We are with another," she giggled.

"And now the chocolate will set and be ready on the morrow," said the assistant

"Ready for me to buy some more before we leave," said Elentari teasing Rorien.

"Thank you for allowing us to help. She has enjoyed it." Rorien said as he paid for the chocolate, giving him a little extra. Elentari took a chocolate from the basket to eat as they headed to their rooms.

As she entered her room, she grabbed Rorien and pulled him close to her kissing him. His tongue explored her mouth as he dropped the basket to the floor. She could feel his maleness hard against her, could feel his desire for her. He picked her up, moved to the bed, laying her down gently beneath him, still lip-locked. He wanted her, wanted to take her into his bed. His lips moved down her neck biting and sucking. She kissed his neck in response, biting him. "This is where I will make my mark," she said biting him again. He moaned and moved his lips to her breast, cleaning the chocolate remnants from them.

"This chocolate tastes good," he said as his lips moved back to her mouth, flicking his tongue against hers, his loins yearning with desire. "You are beautiful and amazing. I love you Elentari." He kissed her, his hand moved down to her thigh, pulling her to him and she wrapped her leg over him.

"I love you Rorien. I want you but..."

"I know. Our link vows dia." He kissed her neck, biting her. "I should go before we get too far." She nodded not wanting him to leave. She longed for him, wanted him, not wanting to let him go. He untangled himself from her, rose and headed to the door and turned to her as he opened it, "Sleep well." He stroked the link, '*I love you.*'

'*and I you*' she answered back on their link blowing him a kiss as he closed her door.

CHAPTER 16

"Good morning Princess. I will have your tea and breakfast soon."

"Thank-you. We will have an extra, possibly two. Also, can you please pack some cakes for us to take back with us. It is a long journey to Thoroneath and it will make it all the better with your delicious cakes. If you have two packets of your wonderful tea, can you also pack it too? Do you have enough coins?"

"I shall and yes Princess, I have more than enough." The assistant curtsied and hurried off to bring them breakfast.

"Why do you need two packets of tea?" asked Fendton

"One for Asvik as thanks for all the tea she has been giving me, of course" replied Elentari.

Lorcan came into view with Awnrie, both beaming and carrying a bag each. "Morning all," he said, holding out a chair for Awnrie before taking the seat beside her.

"Morning. You have two bags. Does that mean you have brought me lots of clothes Lorcan? You are my favourite if you have, buying me so many presents," she said playfully

"Ha funny. You crack me up," answered Lorcan rolling his eyes at her.

"What!? Did you not get me something?" she said pouting.

"It's not for you, it's Awnrie's bag. She's coming back with us for a few dias," he said looking lovingly at Awnrie.

"Yes, I do. Awnrie, you may stay in my casa or Jasper's with him and Sarina. They are both close to Lorcan's and can choose when we arrive back. Whichever makes you more comfortable."

"Elentari! Rorien! Jasper!" an excited Rewa came running up to them, jumping up onto Rorien's lap.

"Rewa, how are you?" said Rorien

"Good. I came to say goodbye. I will miss you." She wrapped her arms around his neck, hugging him tightly.

"And to get more cake," said Jasper

"Yes," she said innocently.

With breakfast done, a basket of cakes and a quick stop for more chocolate, Elentari headed to the jeweller to purchase her necklace. As they headed into the square to say goodbye to Rewa and find Roswen when the lady from the dress shop came up to her with an older female.

"Forgive the intrusion, my mother wanted to meet you. She made your dress."

"It is fine," she said to the assistant. Turning to her mother, "Your dress is beautiful and fits me perfectly. Thank-you."

"What is your name?" asked the mother.

"Elentari, I am from Thoroneath," she answered.

"My sister lives in Thoroneath and informed me the stolen princess has returned," she said as Roswen arrived. "I made the dress with the returned princess in mind. My friend, who owns the tea shop on the docks, informed me the princess was here. You are the lost princess?"

"I am the princess who was stolen and has returned. Elentari, daughter of the King of all the lands."

"It is an honour to meet you" she curtsied, "and delighted you love my dress."

"Thank-you. I will be returning and will visit you. Hopefully, you may have a few more dresses for me."

"I will, princess. Journey safe." She curtsied and took her to leave.

"You are the princess!?" asked a shocked Roswen.

"Elentari is a princess?" said an amazed Rewa. "I am friends with the princess?" She pranced around in delight.

"Yes, I am and yes you are" she smiled at Rewa.

"Forgive me, your highness, for not knowing?" Roswen curtsied.

"Roswen, you may call me Elentari, all my friends do. There is no need for formalities unless they are called for. Please?"

"Are you sure?"

"Yes. You are my friend." She hugged Roswen and Rewa.

"When I come to visit my brother, can I stay at your casa?" asked Rewa

"Yes Rewa, you can stay at my casa." She looked at Roswen questioning.

"I told her last night," said Roswen quietly, her eyes on the ground in front of her. "I thought she should know."

"Thank-you," said Rorien to Roswen. He grabbed Rewa and swung her up into the air before hugging her. "You can stay with both of us when you visit, little sister."

They said their goodbyes and headed off with Lorcan and Awnrie in front, Rorien beside her and Jasper with Fendton behind. Lorcan was beyond excited to have Awnrie travel back with them, all jittery and anxious and wanting to move quickly to get home.

"Lorcan, will you slow down. We are spending the night at the clearing and we will be home on the morrow," said Elentari

He groaned, slumping his shoulders forward and shuffling his feet.

"If I said you two could go ahead and be home tonight would that keep you happy? And stop you from agitating me?"

"Yes."

"Then go but Awnrie stays at Sarina's tonight." He kissed her cheek, grasping Awnrie's hand and headed off at speed, their feet hardly touching the ground.

"He is going to cause you grief for a while you do know that don't you?" said Jasper

"If he is going to act like Rorien did when we first meet, then yes I know," she sighed "Lucky I have three extra guards to watch out for me."

As they neared the clearing, they could hear laughter. Elentari hoped Peana would be there and hoped her kindness was the start of mending the hatred between the two beings. A war so many years ago seemed senseless to be still tearing them apart. This area was a part of her lands and she would protect all who dwelled in her lands, wanting rifts between kinds to be mended and Peana was the beginning of a friendship between them all.

The clearing was alive with little fauns playing, their laughter filling the air and could be heard throughout the bush. It was such a wonderful sight to see them enjoying themselves running and jumping, playing King of the castle and chasing each other. Older fans were sitting around listening to one play the flute, a light, mellow wafting rich sound so clear and graceful penetrating the heart with such a brilliant poetic shrill.

"Elentari, your back" squealed Peana as she came crashing through the clearing. "I told every faun about you. They wouldn't believe me," she said eyes downcast.

"Mmm they are missing out," smiled Elentari hugging Peana "It is good to see you Peana. Have you been staying out of the water?"

"Yes," she said, moving her foot in the dirt. The music had stopped playing and all eyes were on them, searching them as the little fauns came over to them being inquisitive and nosey.

"Hello, little ones. It is lovely to see you all playing and having fun." They said their hellos and headed off chasing each other again their inquisitive minds satisfied with who they were. Elentari turned to the older faun's. "I am Elentari and these are my friends Rorien, Jasper and Fendton." The fauns said nothing, cautiously watching them. This was not going to be an easy task and she wasn't expecting it to be. "You play beautifully. Your music is wonderful. Will you keep playing, please? It was such a wonderful sound for the ears." The faun shrugged and started playing again.

"Elentari, you are back," said Rhen coming from the bush with a cup of tea in her hands. "Come have a seat and tell me how you have been. Where is Lorcan?"

"Thank-you, Lorcan found his link, Awnrie and they have headed back to Thoroneath," she said as she sat down.

"Oh, he is going to miss out. We have music and stories around the fire tonight. Will you stay?" Rhen gestured to the faun playing music and to the fire.

"Thank-you we will. I shall enjoy a bit of fun and learning your ways. We do have some food with us to share too if you need it." Elentari opened the basket.

"Please tell me you have those delicious cakes," Rhen asked with the palm of her hands together against her chest.

"No, I haven't any more of those cakes. They are the best, aren't they? These are from a shop in Rhunduin." Elentari removed a plate of cakes from the basket and placed it between them.

"Elentari, your name is unusual. I know of only one child who had that name." Rhen's eyes narrowed and her head turned slightly sideways as she studied her.

"I know of no one who shares my name. Whom is it you knew?" Elentari stared across the clearing, avoiding all eyes.

"The King of all the lands had a daughter but she was lost, stolen and never found," she was still studying Elentari, trying to search for answers.

"Yes, the King had a daughter who was stolen and taken to another land. That was 20 anoks ago. It was her link who recently found her and brought her back." Elentari's face showed no indication of her thoughts.

"We heard whispers of her return. Is it true? She has returned?" Rhen relaxed.

"Yes, it is true. The King's daughter returned." Still, Elentari's face was void of emotion.

"And you are her?"

"Yes," she said, not moving.

"It is said you yield the power of all four elements?" Rhen lent forward towards Elentari.

"Yes"

"Why did you not dry Peana with your power?" asked Rhen as she straightened herself.

"If I dried her quickly the rift between our kinds would not begin mending," said Elentari as she turned to face Rhen. "The warmth around the fire was my doing and kept it warm all night for you."

Rhen was quiet as she sipped her tea lost in thought. Elentari kept quiet watching the children playing, waiting patiently.

"Why do you want to mend the rift?" she asked, as she turned to her.

"I am the future Queen of all the lands, I will protect all who dwell in my lands," she said as she turned to Rhen. "I am not here to rule, I am here to protect. That is how I wish to sit on the throne, the Queen who protects. How can I protect them all if they will not trust me?" Her head tilted sideways.

"It would be hard." Rhen went back to her thoughts and Elentari sat waiting. "You have shown kindness and did protect Peana until we arrived. You have shown you can be trusted. You have my trust," she said nodding.

"Thank-you." Elentari bowed her head to Rhen.

"Mending the rift with Hoofington will be much harder." She let out a deep breath.

"Hoofington?"

"Yes, Hoofington" boomed a voice from the bush, startling Elentari. From the edge appeared a minotaur, half man half bull. "Who are you to invite yourself into our clearing?" he demanded stopping in front of Elentari. His massive human-looking body stood 9 feet tall making her feel very small. His large bulls head had horns almost a meter long and his fur the brown colour of an oak tree blending him into the bushland.

"My name is Elentari. I came to check on Peana. She fell in the creek the other dia and I kept her warm and dry until her parents found her." He was huge and quite frightening. She was very unsure she should continue and wanted to run and run fast.

"I invited her Hoofington," said Rhen cowering in fear.

"Silence." He glared at Rhen and she hunched over more.

'You know how I said I need you to protect me and always will, well now is one of those times' Elentari said along with the link

'I can see you have gotten into trouble. I am here.' He replied feeling her fear on the link and attempted to keep his fear from her.

"You are not welcome. Leave." He stood bending down over her to try and intimidate her. It was working but she would not give in…she hoped.

"May I stay awhile to hear the music? The faun plays such beautiful music. I have not heard such an amazing sound. It must be wonderful to be able to listen to such beautiful music when you like?" she stood her ground. '*You had better have my back. He is huge!*'

'*You are doing great. Stand your ground. I am here as are Jasper and Fendton. You have this*' Rorien replied

"I said LEAVE," he said, taking a step closer.

Elentari could feel his hot breath in her face and she moved to step around him and be closer to the fauns. All eyes were watching them. The children had stopped still and were watching from where they stood. It seemed the only one breathing was the flute player and his eyes were darting between the two of them.

"I am staying a while to listen and then I shall take my leave." She sat closer to the fauns, almost amongst them. "Please keep playing. Rhen come sit with me." She turned to Rhen patting a spot beside her hoping he wouldn't hurt her if a faun sat with her and she was near them.

'*I am doing this for the right reasons, aren't I? I am not being stubborn, am I?*' she asked Rorien on the link.

'*You are being stubborn but you are doing this for the right reasons. Hang in there. I am here, we are here.*'

Rhen looked at Elentari and to Hoofington before gingerly moving towards Elentari hunched over and frightened. She slowly took a seat beside her watching Hoofington and glancing to Elentari. As she sat Duggit came over and sat on the other side of Elentari. The fauns began to shift uncomfortably, afraid of what was to come and the children began to play quietly keeping their eyes on them.

"You are NOT WELCOME!" he boomed. Leaping in front of her his hand raised to strike her.

Rhen stood quickly yelling "She is the lost princess! Don't hurt her!" The whole area stopped still, all eyes on them. "Yes, she is the princess.

If you hit her you WILL start a war. Don't hurt her. Please don't hurt her. She is my friend." Rhen turned to Elentari "You are my friend."

"You are not the princess, the future Queen of all the lands is gone." He stood up with his hands at his side.

"I am her. My link found me in another world and brought me home." She straightened up.

"I don't believe you. You LIE." His nostrils flared and his eyes filled with rage, his face inches from hers and she could feel the anger in his breath as it hit her face hard and fast.

"Whether I am lying or not, would you risk all these beings' lives to hurt me?" Her hand waved across the area signally to all. "I have not been cruel or unkind to any being here. I helped Peana when she was wet and cold and wanted to make sure she and her family were ok." Her hand stopped at Peana.

'Make sure you stop me before I go too far.'

'I will. I would like to see my next birthday. Not fussed about you, just me,' he ribbed her on their link, *'You are doing great.'*

"They are fine. They have me to protect them." He stood tall staring her down. The children kept playing quietly, slowly running and chasing each other, keeping their eyes focused on Hoofington.

"They are lucky to have such a strong male to watch over them. How is it you came to watch over them?" Elentari's demeanour changed. She was soft and quizzical. *I hope this works*, she thought. *'When is your birthday? That hasn't been something we have discussed'*

"Why should I explain myself to you?" he straightened, still not backing down.

"You do not need to. As I have not lived in this world for 20 anoks, I do not know the history and am most interested to know how my friends have been so lucky to have a strong male to protect them. From what Duggit has informed me, they would be most thankful for some being to help them." Eyes were focused on Hoofington.

'Another 3 mesik till it is my birthday. The 24th of the 8th month.' Rorien said.

"Of course, they are grateful." He sneered. "They were left without anyone to help them. Gornack and Leelan were of no help and hurt them. They would have continued to hurt them if I hadn't been here." His eyes were focused on her.

"You saved them? How?" The fauns began to go back to their activities as the tension was gone and nothing was going to happen, ignoring the two of them. Her guards were still focused and ready and had not moved, staying ready to strike if needed.

"Of course, I saved them. Why wouldn't I? They are happy, kind beings who deserve to be treated right. That irresponsible Gornack wanted more slaves. He had come back to entrap more fauns for his dirty work. I took him down and freed those he had shackled."

"That was the bravest and kind of you. Were all fauns enslaved freed?"

"Yes. We stormed his casa, freed all who were chained in dungeons and took down his casa." He relaxed.

"When you say 'we' is that yourself and the fauns?"

"It was myself and my friends and faun's who wanted to help with every being choosing to fight, none were forced." He sat down opposite her.

"How many of your kind are there?"

"There are many. We live on this side of the mountains with the fauns."

"Do you have a partner, a mate, a link? I am not sure of what you would call her," she asked her forehead creased.

"Yes, I have a mate."

"I shall very much like to meet her," she smiled.

"Hoofington, please invite the minotaur's to join us for festivities tonight. It will be the most wonderful thing to have all here." Pleaded Rhen.

"As you wish. It would be nice to relax a bit. I notice your guard has not relaxed yet," he said pointing his horns towards them."

"Is that better, Hoofington?" Elentari released their oaths and the guard relaxed. "Please may I introduce to you the princess' guard

Jasper, Fendton and Rorien who is also my link. Not yet complete." She pointed to them.

"So, you are definitely the missing princess, future Queen of all the lands?"

"Yes, I am."

"I shall return," said Hoofington leaving and the fauns began to relax and enjoy themselves. Music, singing and dancing were going strong when Hoofington returned later with the other Minotaur's and more fauns causing the clearing and bush around to be overflowing with beings enjoying the music and merriment.

It had been a great night. The faun's and minotaur's began to open up and let them in, chatting with them and getting to know them. They all danced and sang, listened to the music and stories, they ate and drank. The fauns showed them their dance moves and taught them some songs and the adults joined in a few games of chase with the little ones. All through the night, Elentari kept the clearing warm, her contribution to her new friends.

As the night grew late and the little fauns had long ago fallen asleep, Rorien and Elentari finally found a spot away from any being to rest. Jasper and Fendton were still hard at it with other male fauns, minotaur's and a few females. Mostly the females had slipped away throughout the night to find a place to sleep and to tend to their children. Rorien held Elentari and she snuggled into him feeling safe and protected. He watched her, running his fingers through her hair, rubbing her with his air and stoking their link lovingly. "You are beautiful," he murmured, kissing her head.

"Mmm. I like this." She turned her face, looking into his eyes. He moved his lips to hers kissing her deeply. She broke away. "We have company. Either we stop or move further into the bush away from every being."

"We will stop." He kissed her and closed his eyes breathing in her scent. Gone were the perfumes and smells she used in her world and all that was left was her real scent. She smelt of lotus flowers amongst the moss growing beside a waterfall. He loved that smell.

CHAPTER 17

They left early before sunrise, heading for home, the four of them enjoying the crisp morning, listening to the bush beginning to awaken. Each of them, quiet and lost in their thoughts.

"Am I always going to have to save you like that?" asked Jasper, turning to her.

"Oh, you saved me, did you?" she said with a half-smile.

"Yes. Without me, you would have been his breakfast." He grinned, turning and walking backwards to watch her.

"Is that right? You tamed the beast and protected me. Ok. You may let Sarina know that and that is all. I shall inform all others of what truly happened, shall I?" She looked at him with one eyebrow raised, relaxing she said, "No. Hopefully, you won't have to save me like that again. He was massive and really scary. My heart was pounding so fast."

"I agree with Jasper. Don't ever put yourself in that situation again," said Rorien pulling her into him. "I could feel her and she was petrified, the link trembling."

"She wasn't the only one," said Jasper as he turned back walking in front of them.

"What I am hearing is that you lot will protect me if the big scary mean side is smaller than you?" her bottom lip protruding out and eyes sad as she pushed Rorien off her.

"Yes. That would be a good start," said Fendton from behind her.

Elentari laughed, turning to glance at him. "If you keep me informed of any other big, mean beings and where to avoid, we may not have to have another saving." Her hand found Rorien's and held it.

"There are giants in the south," said Fendton

"We shall avoid the south for now," she replied. "What confuses me is he said he was there to save the fauns from Gornack. That would make him thousands of years old. How long does a minotaur live for?"

"I don't know, ask him next time you see him. At least one question will have an answer." Grinned Jasper.

"Or the Scholars may have an answer," she said.

They continued home taking their time enjoying the dia and spotted the fields in the distance as all were beginning to stop work for a lunch break.

"Do you two want to head home without us?"

"Yes. I would like to see Sarina well before supper," said Jasper.

"Then off you go. Supper at my casa." Fendton and Jasper said their goodbyes and headed off. Partway down the mountain, they found a spot which overlooked the fields and to Thoroneath and the mountain range beyond stopping to enjoy the view, gazing at the beauty which lay before them when Rorien took Elentari's hand in his hands.

"Elentari, I know our worlds are different and you are used to your world. I am not sure how to ask you properly in your world. Here we just ask." He bent down on one knee removing a box from his pocket. "Let's set a date to complete our link," he said, opening the box. Inside lay a ring to match her new necklace.

"YES! YES! Yes, let us set a date." She yelled, her face was full of joy and her grin wide as she grabbed him and kissed him. In this world, they didn't propose, as such, they agreed on a date to complete the link and did it. He had remembered in her world the male proposed and gave a ring to confirm. She took the box from his hand, admiring the ring. "Ooo, it is beautiful and perfect." He took the ring out and she held out her hand for him. He placed it on her finger and it fitted perfectly.

"Do you like it?"

"I love it, it is perfect and you remembered how males propose in my world." She wrapped her arms around him and kissed him. He responded, wrapping his arms around her kissing her deeply.

"Which dia do we choose to complete our link?' he asked

"I don't know. In my world, you can be engaged for anoks. I'm not liking that idea. It is bad enough it has been near two mesik. How long does it take to organise?"

"We can do it on the morrow, as long as the King and Masters are free. We need them to perform the ceremony. As you are the princess, I am guessing we will have to invite specifics," he said kissing her.

"How about we choose the 1st which is in eight dias, a vika. Hopefully, that will be enough time for those who are to attend can. The first of the mesik will be like a new beginning. Beginning of a new mesik, beginning of our lives together, our first dia with our link completed." She kissed him

"The first dia, I like that. Plus, the moon is new, new dia, new moon, new lives together. Let's keep going and inform the King?" He kissed her.

"Who do we tell first? After Papa of course." She asked as she transported them to the other side of the field and the outskirts of Thoroneath.

"All our friends will be at supper, let's announce it then."

"Ok. Papa will be in the royal hall." Elentari kept raising her hand to admire her ring, her engagement ring, her completing the link ring as they made their way to the hall.

"Will you always be admiring your ring?"

"Maybe." She smiled as they entered the hall to find the King busy with the Scholars. They paused partway waiting for the King to finish, he acknowledged their arrival and, finishing up, he summoned them forward.

"Hello Papa, we have returned. May we speak with you more privately?" asked Elentari

"Yes." The King rose and they entered the private rooms. "What is it, daughter?"

"Papa, if I was to complete my link how long would I have to wait? Are there specific dignitaries you are required to invite?"

"Well the kings in our other lands must attend and the King in the south takes about four dias to get here. Invites will take time. I would say you would need to allow two vikas. Why do you ask Elentari?"

"Rorien and I have decided to complete our link. He proposed as we do in my world and gave me this completing ring." She held out her hand to show her ring. "We were hoping to complete the link on the 1st."

"You are in luck as this mesik is the januel kings meet. This meeting all the kings are bringing their families with them to meet you. You will be able to have your dia as the meeting is on the 39th and 40th."

"Oh, perfect." Elentari hugged her father. "Our linking vows will be the 1st," she paused as her face went from happy to hesitant, "Papa, am I going to have to attend the meeting?" She looked concerned. Meeting all the other four kings of their lands and their families was not something on Elentari's agenda. She planned to visit each land over the next four anoks and meet them one at a time.

"Yes. You and the future kings will be attending this meeting. The rest of the families will enjoy themselves exploring our cuedel. I shall organise the invitations."

"Ok. Papa, I have something to explain to you which happened on the trip. Please can you listen till I am finished."

"Yes, explain daughter."

Elentari explained how she met the fauns and her scary encounter with Hoofington and the minotaur's. How she made friends and began to mend the rift. The idea of what she wanted their lands to be and how she would sit on the throne. The King sat still and expressionless listening to her story. When she finished, he turned to Rorien.

"You allowed her to do this?"

"My King, I had no control over her actions. She asked me to make sure she would not go too far. By that stage, she was already far. At all times we were on full guard."

"She has made friends and has begun mending the rift?" he asked, his eyebrows raised.

"Yes. She was amazing and will make an amazing Queen in the very, very, very far future," he said as his hand moved as if to point into the future.

"Mmm. I cannot talk you out of doing something like this again, can I?" the King directed his question to Elentari.

"No Papa. If a situation is going to present itself for me to mend our lands, I will take it."

"Lucky you have your FOUR guards. You are going to need them."

"I also yield the eight powers. I think I will be ok."

"Seven powers, not eight." Corrected the King.

"It is eight Papa. I can shift and have found my animal guide. It is a dragon." The King looked surprised.

"Yes, my King she holds all powers," said Rorien

"Once you have taken the linking vows and your mesmoon is done, you will train with the shift master."

"Ok, Papa. Is there anything else? May we go?"

"There is nothing else. I shall see you for supper and we can discuss your linking dia further."

"Bye Papa," Elentari said as she kissed the King.

"Let's go find the others. See how Awnrie is enjoying her time here." Rorien said holding his arm out for her.

"Yes, let's," she said, taking his arm.

They were gathered at her casa discussing their trip to Rhunduin and meeting Rorien's sister and Hoofington waiting for Lorcan and Awnrie to arrive. As they entered, Elentari whispered in Fendton's ear, "Fendton, things have changed even more." Fendton looked at her quizzical. She nodded towards Rorien.

"Since we are all here, I would like to let you all know Elentari and I are completing our link on the 1st," said Rorien.

"Oh my gosh! Finally!" Sarina raced to Elentari grabbing her in a big hug.

"Yes, finally. Will you help me organise everything? I have no idea what to expect here. I know how we marry in my world but here, I have no idea what a linking dia involves."

"Yes. I would love too."

"Let's start after breakfast."

"This means you are not leaving?" asked Fendton excitedly.

"Yes, Fendton. I have no plans to leave and I never did. I found out how to get back so I could visit my parents. But not knowing if it is possible or what would happen or if I could visit more than once, I haven't."

"I am glad." He hugged her "Congratulations." He kissed her cheek

"Do you want to visit your parents Elentari?" asked the King.

"I did, Papa. With everything that was happening and with Rorien so distant, I wanted something familiar and advice. I would love it if they could attend our linking dia. I understand it is not possible and have accepted it. This is my life now and I do like it but I do miss them."

"Mmm. Shall we eat and I can take my leave afterwards?"

"Papa, we should invite your guard to eat with us. It seems mean to leave him out there. After all, this is a personal time with friends and he is your eldest friend."

"Good idea. Trad, come in." The King's guard entered and bowed. "Leave your duties at the door and join us as friends."

"Thanks, Adtarian. I would be delighted to sup with you all," said Trad.

"Lorcan, can you grab two more chairs from your casa please?" asked Elentari.

"I'll help," said Trad.

"Papa, I am thinking, after our linking dia we should open up the parestala for festivities each night and invite eight families from each area to sup with us. In my world, it was an honour to meet the Queen, to eat with her would have been amazing."

"Why do you wish to do that?"

"Few reasons. One - this dining area is becoming too small. Two - we can all sup together including the Masters, Scholars and generals. Three - every being would love to be invited to sup with you and the princess. It would make them feel special."

"Mmm. You raise good points. I shall think about it."

"If it is not the royal parestala, maybe a smaller one and we can call it the Princess parestala?"

"My answer will come after your linking." Adtarian and Trad took their leave after supper. "Rorien, please see me in the morning in the royal hall. I have royal duties for you to perform," said the King as he left.

"What is that about?" asked Fendton as he moved to the lounge.

"I have no idea," Rorien shrugged, "The answer will reveal itself when needed." He smirked at Elentari.

"You lot are becoming annoying. Picking on me and using my words in jest. Yes, the answer will be revealed when needed."

The night continued with them getting to know Awnrie and chatting about the fauns. On the morrow, Sarina hadn't even stepped in the door before Elentari was questioning her

"What happens? I know nothing of these traditions and ceremonies" panic in her voice.

"Settle down. We will go through step by step and work it out. We will have it organised before lunch. Now let's eat." Sarina laughed.

"Ok. But I am afraid we won't have enough time."

"You will have plenty of time Elentari," said Jasper "Calm down. It's refreshing to see you out of your depth. I could get used to this."

"No, you won't. This is the first and last time I will be out of my depth and without answers. Don't want to see you gloating again. Now you males head off and leave us, females, alone. Which one of you wants to spend the dia doing female things?"

"Fendton," they all said, pointing at him as they raced out the door.

"Guess you are my guard for the dia Fendton. So have a seat and help out." Fendton groaned slumping into a chair. "Shall we start?"

"No." grumbled Fendton.

"Sarina, can you run me down on a typical dia?"

"Ok, you both walk the length of the parestala together through all the guests to meet your Masters and King. The Master performs the ceremony with the King overseeing and giving you your linking rings. Once the vows are taken you walk back through the parestala to the room where you complete the link...alone." She nudged Elentari grinning. "The good bit. Once you two are done, linking is complete, the celebrations begin. That is about it."

"What happens during the ceremony?"

"There are four stages, lighting the candle, binding of the hands, drinking cups and pouring sand, last is the linking rings and celebrations follow when you return."

"Mmm. Is there anyone else other than Rorien and the Masters?"

"No. Just you two and the Masters. Why?"

"In my world, we have bridesmaids, groomsmen, pageboys and flower boys. There are MC's and ushers."

"Oh. No extras, it is just you and your Masters."

"Well as I am different, I am having a bridesmaid and flower girl. What do you wear?"

"Robes in the colour of your yielding power."

"I am not wearing eight robes. Generally, on earth, brides wear a white dress or a dress in a shade of white. Maybe we should see the seamstress and see if she has an idea on a dress to suit me and fit in with tradition here. I guess Rorien can wear what he likes as long as I agree." She smiled.

"Why not have him wear a robe to match you?" said Awnrie.

"Good idea. The seamstress could do something which will keep his colour distinct. Yellow is not quite the colour I would like at my wedding...linking dia. This could work." She clapped her hands in delight.

"What is a bridesmaid?" asked Sarina.

"A bridesmaid is the bride's, me, best friend who is there for her helping her get through the dia and making sure everything runs smoothly. I would love it if you would be my bridesmaid, my linking maid."

"Not sure what to do, but love the idea."

"What are groomsmen?" asked Fendton.

"Sarina, you are already doing what a linking maid does, help me to organise this dia. Fendton, a groomsman, is Rorien's male to help him."

"Will he have one?"

"No idea. Doubt it."

"Shall we find the seamstress and get your dress?" asked Sarina.

"Yes. Plus, one for you and Rewa. Awnrie, do you have something to wear?"

"Not here."

"Then we shall find you one todia as well. Plus, we need shoes and jewellery. Shopping dia. Yay!" She said as they left the casa.

The rest of the morning was spent organising and adjusting their linking dia to suit both worlds and all those wanting to attend. It seemed every being in the cuedel wanted to see her and Rorien complete their link and help to organise the parestala. Between them all, they came up with an idea to allow all to view a part of their day. She spoke to all the Masters who came up with an idea to include them all. The seamstress was excited to design her dress and something to match for Rorien as well as one for Rewa and Sarina. Shoes and accessories were found and Asvik agreed to design a cake. Everything was ready and it was just after lunch. She was amazed at how quickly everything came together.

CHAPTER 18

"Good morning my King," said Elentari entering the royal hall.

"Good morning Princess. Please take your seat, our guests will be arriving shortly," the King said, indicating to her chair. "Each King and his family will greet us before being assigned to rooms. Who will be your guard todia? I see all of them are with you."

"Yes, my King. All will be on duty todia. I have five sets of eyes as I do not want to miss anything, no matter how small," she said, taking her seat. "They will be scrutinising the families and relaying any information they notice for me while I get to know the kings and princes and who they are."

"Very well Princess. Is everything organised for the 1st?"

"Yes, Papa. Rewa and her parents will be here on the morrow and everything else is set. All Masters are honoured to be a part of our linking dia and have designed a specific agenda for them all. It is very exciting what they have planned. Are you ready Papa?" she asked, placing a hand on his.

"No. My daughter is too young to be completing her link. I have only known her for three mesik." He smiled. A family entered the royal hall and the King introduced her to King Malik and Prince Baldric of Ennoril, the King in the east and the rest of his family. King Malik was in his early 600's and had been on the throne for 300 anoks. Prince Baldric was a similar age to her father. He and her father took their linking dias in the same anok and grew up together as Princes before Adtarian became King 200 anoks ago. Their friendship was still strong. She liked Baldric, he was kind and gentle. His son, Lannis was courteous and thoughtful, very cheerful and amusing and aged 73. She was going to like spending time with him.

King Heinrich and Prince Leopold of Norlona, the northlands, arrived next with their large family. The King was in his final anoks and the prince had been taking on more duties in readiness for taking the throne. Prince was in his 700's and his son Theonry was in his 500's. He was taking on royal duties as the next Prince and would be attending the januel. Theonry's son, Jahan, was more her age but would not be attending the januel.

King Reagan and Prince Sven of Wamrion, the west lands, arrived after lunch by themselves. King Reagan was of similar age as her father. Reagan, Baldric and Adtarian all grew up together creating havoc throughout the lands, spending many anoks exploring all the lands together by themselves and with their linked. Reagan became King at age 393, almost 100 years after Adtarian. Sven had a gentle sympathetic nature and his jubilant jest made her laugh. He was 47 and another prince she would enjoy being Queen with.

Last to arrive was King Rian of Seatheas and the twin princes, Prince Cormac and Prince Emmett and Cormac's link. King Rian's linked was no longer with them. Prince Cormac was very arrogant and believed he was better than every being and made sure to put those around him down. Elentari had touched their black hearts and searched both their minds. Both spent more time warming other beds than their own. His link spent all her time attempting to get into other males' beds and had been checking out her guard from the moment she walked in. Elentari did not like Cormac or his link and he certainly was not a good fit for a King, too harsh and uncaring. His brother Emmett was much nicer. Emmett had a kindness about him and took interest in the King and her. His heart was light and she preferred him to be King and began to plan a way to enable him to sit on the throne. The twin princes were 68.

Dinner was in the great hall with all the King's, their families, guards and assistants. Each King, queen and prince had a guard and an assistant. There were more assistants than kings and princes. Not that she could talk with her four guards and her new assistants Sarina and Awnrie, while she was here.

Each of her guards made sure to meet with two princes to get to know them and relay any information to her. Sarina and Awnrie were assigned to meet the princes linked. Having her guard spread out meant she would get to know them all without having to spend too much time with them. Elentari spent her time getting to know Sven, Lannis and Emmett. She did like them and enjoyed their company. They would make great kings and would work well with her except Emmett was not to take the throne, Cormac was next in line. She had to make sure Cormac did not sit on the throne. His idea of being King was that you rule and rule harshly with every being there to entertain him, be at his call and not speak. Emmett was charitable and kind-hearted, always looking for the good in everything. His upbeat personality brought happiness to those he spoke to. He was much better suited to be King and she had to find a way to ensure he did.

The Januel Kings meet was long and boring. It felt weird to be the only female in the room with five kings and seven princes. It seemed kings only had males as children. The kings were boring her with all their boasting and gloating and she spent more time talking to Rorien on their link to keep herself awake. If it wasn't for Rorien keeping her calm, she may well have put a few on their backsides with one of her powers. Gloating was not how she believed a King should be. Sven, Lannis and Emmett were the only princes who were humble, not trying to outdo each other and showing a caring side to those who lived in the lands.

"I am so glad this is only once an anok. I would hate to have to deal with them all more than once an anok," said Elentari as she and Rorien sat together on the couch alone in her casa for once.

"You spent most of the dia talking to me. I got nothing done," said Rorien

"You had nothing to do other than be my guard."

"I wasn't your guard for the whole dia."

"No, you weren't. Couldn't put any of you through a whole dia of boredom like I had to endure. Those pompous, self-opinionated presumptuous kings and princes are what nightmares are made of."

"Sven, Lannis, Emmett, Baldric and Reagan are not bad."

"No. Baldric and Reagan most likely won't be kings when I take the throne. They are the same age as Papa. Cormac is going to be my biggest issue. I do hope we can find a way to make Emmett King instead."

"Yeah. Emmett will be a much better King. When will Rewa arrive on the morrow?" he asked, changing the subject.

"Around lunchtime, they should be here. I have duties in the morning and a boring lunch with the kings and families before the rest of the dia is mine to enjoy. Papa has you doing some royal duty in the morning hasn't he?"

"Yeah. I won't be able to communicate with you for about an hori. It is so intense and lucky the morrow is the last of them."

"For both of us. What are we going to do for our mesmoon? Other than the obvious, are we going to go anywhere?"

"I don't think we will have any time. The obvious is going to take up most of it," he said kissing her. Their passion soared and he pulled away from her. "I had better leave."

"I will be glad when we are linked. This is torture." She sat back with her arms crossed, frown on her face. "Make my blood race and leave me hanging like this. Torture!"

"Not the only one this is torture for." He looked at her lovingly. "Two dias and no more of this torture. A different torture will take its place." He grinned

"Get out, you pain!" she threw a pillow at him. He laughed and headed to the door.

'*Love you*' he said on their link as he left.

'*and I you*' She answered '*until the morrow*'

By lunch, Elentari was ready to scream. "How can they be even more arrogant? I am over this belittling just because I am a female. Things are going to change dramatically in the future. Right now, I am being the perfect princess, quiet and not speaking. Let them think they can walk all over me. They are yet to meet me and they will be sorry they did," she said to Lorcan as she stormed out from lunch.

"It wasn't that bad," answered Lorcan.

Elentari stopped dead, "were you not listening to them!?" her voice raised and hand-stretched towards the royal lunch room. "There was too much male ego in there. All trying to outdo each other and that was just from six of them. Thank goodness the other five are sensible."

"See there was a positive to the dia."

"You are beginning to annoy me too right now. Don't give me this garbage. Just agree with me and say 'yes they are horrible'," she said with her hands on her hips.

"Yes, they are horrible. Is that better?" he said rolling his eyes.

"Yes and no. Next time don't roll the eyes." She grinned, grabbing his arm and walking back to her casa. "How is Awnrie going? I feel like I've been neglecting the females the past few dias. It has been so full up with royal business and having to be such a perfect little princess, I haven't had time to see them."

"She is good. Loving being here and fitting in fantastic." He sighed

"Does that mean…?"

"Maybe. It has been playing on my mind. We shall see." They entered her casa to find Sarina, Jasper, Fendton and Awnrie waiting for them.

"Mmm, I think I may have to rethink this open-door policy after the morrow."

"What? Don't you like us greeting you when you come home?" grinned Jasper.

"It is so good to see you all. I am over being on show and having to put up with male egos. The first of you males who shows any maleness is out the door. Understand!?" she shook her fists at them.

"Yes. I'm not interested in seeing you angry," said Jasper. "Plus, I saw how they treated you and my fuse is at its end. I was ready to take them down."

"You are sweet. Thank-you. At least one of my guards understood how horrible they were," she said directly to Lorcan.

"Yeah, yeah, they are horrible," he answered as they both burst out laughing.

"Rorien not back from completing whatever royal duty he had?"

"No. Haven't seen him yet. He's not contactable on the link?" answered Jasper

"No. He has blocked it while he is doing whatever. Apparently, I am a distraction," she rolled her eyes. As much as the males tried, they could not hold back the laughter. "Thanks, you lot. I am beginning to wonder if you were a wise choice."

"We are. Your life would be boring without us," said Fendton, hugging her as there was a knock at the door. Elentari opened the door to find Rewa, Roswen and Havid standing there.

"Elentari, we found you." Screamed Rewa jumping up to hug her.

"Rewa, Roswen, Havid please come in. It is so good to see you. Was the trip good?" Elentari carried Rewa inside.

"It was long but easy. Glad to be here," said Roswen.

"Where's Rorien?" asked Rewa.

"He has duty for the King to do. He will be here soon."

She settled them into Rorien's place and Rewa tried on her flower girl dress, excitement filling her as she danced around feeling like a princess. Elentari showed them part of the Cuedel as she checked on all the arrangements for the morrow. The parestala was beautiful and everything was in order. The females had done a marvellous job with flowers suspended above cascading down creating a beautiful overhead scene. When the wind gently blew, the flowers swayed creating a calming, soft flowing environment, the colours complementing each of the stages of the vows. Somehow, they managed to line the path they were to walk along with moss. Leaves covered the rest of the parestala hiding the bare ground. Table clothes matched the flower colours, coloured candles were ready to be lit, origami coloured ribbons lined the tables, glasses etched with their names sat in place and taking centre place on each table were bottles filled with coloured sand art depicting parts of their lives and journey together. The whole parestala came together to create an enchanting area to captivate their linking. She was overwhelmed with how wonderful the females were and how mesmerising it made her feel.

They were sitting in her lounge discussing the link dias agenda when she felt Rorien tug their link.

'*I am at home. Hurry up. Rewa is here*' she said.

'*Be there soon. Just finishing up. I missed you todia.*' He replied back

'*I missed you too. It was aggravating sitting with the pompous kings and arrogant princes, not having you to talk to.*' She replied as the door opened and Rorien entered with her father and behind him came her parents.

CHAPTER 19

"I have a job for you to do as a linking gift to Elentari from me. I need you to work with the Master to find her parents and bring them here to see you two take your vows. As you are the only one who has met them, they will trust you. Are you willing?"

"Yes, my King. That will be an amazing gift for her. I will find the Master and get to work." Rorien bowed and went off in search of the Master finding him in the ancient library pouring over books along with many other Masters and apprentices. He looked up as Rorien approached.

"What is it I can help you with this time?" asked the air Master concerned as Rorien slumped into the chair pretending to be perplexed.

"The King wishes to gift Elentari with her parents at our linking dia. I need to head back to her world, find them and bring them here for a time," said Rorien as he scanned the open books on the table.

"The King mentioned you would be seeing me. The dia you set your date, the earth Master had found information on returning and informed the King. You may return to her world as many times as you wish and she can visit her world any time for a maximum of seven dias each time. At least this time I have answers and you are not troubled." The Master said as Rorien grinned

"How are we going to find her parents? I have no link to them," he asked, a little worried.

"The codes you found which pulled you, the eight final codes, we will use them first and see where they take you. We will allow half a hori for each to give you time to know where you are and if you are close. On the return door will be written a code in the ancient text. Take it down each time. I will need this to create the doorway for them to enter our world, hopefully to this point."

"I have the map of her world you wanted in my casa. Will that help us?"

"Yes. We can work out where each code leads you on her map, we may be able to create a code to bring us directly to her parents. Go retrieve the map, any codes you have and any information which may help. Meet me here in an hori."

Rorien took his leave and headed to his old casa. The code and map of her world he had left there thinking he would not need them again. He stood outside his old casa looking at the bare façade. It was basic compared to where he lived now. Elentari had the stonemasons create beautiful artwork on each of their facades and gardeners planted plants to blend in with the stonework. She had designed and worked with the masons and gardeners to create a scene where the five facades blended together when viewed from afar. The scene centred around her dragons and each of their animal guides was represented as well as every power and each façade could be viewed by itself to tell a story. The masons and gardeners had designed a spectacular scene. Standing here looking at his old place, he was glad to have her in his life creating beauty, warmth and love.

He entered and went to the bedroom removing the bottom drawer to reveal a hidden compartment. He grabbed the code, the copy of the old map and her world map. In the drawer was the notebook he used when he was finding her. He had jotted down his frustrations, questions, achievements and answers he came across. He opened it to read a few lines, memories came flooding back of long stressful nights, of wanting to give up and of the excitement of finding her world. She loved her mark in the library and this will make a good gift for her, giving her insight into his journey. He bundled it with the other parchments and replaced the drawer. He stopped as he went to close the door and scanned the room. He had no desire to return and felt no sorrow in leaving. It was bare and unappreciated. He didn't know how he lived in such an unloved place. He closed the door and smiled. The door on his old life has reached an end and a new beginning with the most amazing, wonderful, loving female is about to begin.

"Master, here is her code, copy of her old map and her new map." He placed them on the empty table beside them. He had changed into the clothes he brought from her world.

"You traced the map? Great idea. Good thinking to change."

"As it could not be removed from the library, I wanted her map and hence traced it to keep."

"With everything you have gone through in the mesik since she arrived, you still have it. You are a complicated male Rorien," said the Master shaking his head.

"Your life would be boring if I wasn't." Grinned Rorien

"Let's start. These are the other seven codes. These are the last two which gave you trouble in finding her. We will start with these. Quickly find where you are when you arrive. Take a quill and parchment to scribe the returning door code, remember to scribe the symbols EXACTLY as they appear. You will have half an hori before the doorway appears." The Master handed Rorien the potion, he drank it and spoke the ancient text.

The doorway appeared and he stepped through into her world. He had entered her world between two tall buildings and walked out from between them into a clear grass area. Quickly scanning the area, he saw similar style buildings varying from single story to five-story buildings moving about quickly he attempted to work out exactly where he was. They had not come here and nothing was familiar. All the people were of young age carrying books, backpacks and sat facing the same way in each room. He guessed they were students and this was her uni and continued searching for something to confirm it. A road blocked his path and he followed it, leading him to the main road when he noticed a sign on the building just as the doorway appeared. Grabbing the quill, he jotted down the door code and stepped back into his world.

"This code is where she attends uni, I think. The doorway appeared before I could read the sign properly. This is what was written on the door," said Rorien as he handed the Master the parchment. "Her uni is here." He pointed to a spot on the map, "and her casa is here." He moved his finger on the map.

"Good. This will give us a start. Here is the next code and potion."

He took it, drank and spoke.

Stepping through the door he was in a narrow alley behind shops walking down the alley he approached a street and scanned both directions finding nothing but shops on both sides. Deciding to turn left, he hurried along the street, scanning the shops hoping to find something familiar. Reaching the corner, he scanned the streets, more shops lined both ways. Nothing was familiar. He turned left and continued his search, stopping as he passed a shop front. There was something about the shop front which caught his eye, it was filled with buses, planes, maps, animals, suitcases and bags. The sign above said 'travel agent'. This was her job. *Brilliant,* he thought. He quickly rushed back to the alley, taking the quill and parchment ready to scribe as the doorway returned.

"This is the code for her work which is here."

"Ok. Here is the next code and potion. Are you ready to return or do you need a break?"

"I'm right to continue," he said as he took the cup.

He stepped through and was standing outside homes. He began running scanning, looking for anything familiar. There were no shops or tall buildings, just homes along every street. He stopped at the corner and surveyed further trying to find something familiar, anything which would give him an idea of where he was. Noticing the mountains, he knew he was not near her parents, the casas in their area were on flat ground, and he guessed he must be near Donna. Elentari had said to him that Donna lived on the other side of the mountain and this must be where Donna's casa was. He grabbed the quill and found a secluded spot to wait for the doorway.

"This is Donna's, her best friend's place. It is here, in this area. Next code." Rorien was eager to keep moving. Only four more to go. He grabbed the bottom code as the Master looked quizzically at him. "It seems every time I am searching for something it is always the last." He smiled. The Master shook his head and waved him off.

Rorien stepped into a shopping centre. It was a large centre he had not been in before and searched for the exit to take him to the street. Finding the escalators, he hurried down to the ground floor and out into the street. All around him were many tall buildings and shops. *This must be her main cuedel, the one we went through to her parents, not helpful and too far away. Only three more to go. I shall find them soon,* he thought. He headed up the street, finding a secluded spot to wait for the doorway.

"This is her main shopping district here in this area. Her parents are over here." He pointed to where he needed to be. "All the codes are keeping me close to her casa and not close enough for me to get to her parents. Her casa to her parents takes about 10 horis to run and that's if I remember how to get there."

"Hopefully one of these will bring you closer."

This time Rorien was on a mountain. Nothing around him was familiar, it was cold and far away from anything. In the distance, he could see small villades and more natural land. This area was not anywhere they went or of an area, she spoke of and he was nowhere near either her cuedel or her parents. He was confused and eager to get back as this code was useless to him. He paced waiting for the doorway to return, the half an hori seeming to take ages.

"No idea about this area. It is in the mountains somewhere. The mountains are all around here. It could be anywhere."

"We will leave this door code aside. It may be useful later. Second last code."

He stepped out onto the mountain again, his hope waned until he heard a waterfall nearby. He raced towards the sound and intercepted a path beside the river, racing down the path, he hoped this was where Elentari was found. It was not long before he came to the spot where Francis and Beth found Elentari and his excitement soared. *Excellent. If the last door is unsuccessful, I can get to them from here,* he thought, *it will take time but at least it is closer than from her place.*

"This is where she was found. I can get to her parents from here but it will take a couple of horis. If this code is no good, we will have to use this one. How is the code going to bring them here?" he asked.

"Slowly. Each of the doors has matching words and I have been able to create part of the code. It may take a few horis to get the code right. We will have it by 40th and they will be here for your linking dia. Now get a move on and check the last code."

Rorien scanned the area, it was familiar. He began to race in the direction of her parent's place or he hoped it was the direction to them. He took a few wrong turns but finally found their casa and raced to the door, continually banging loudly until her mother answered it.

"Rorien?"

"Hi, not much time. I will be back to explain but we are getting linked and want you to attend. I am working with the Master to enable you to come back..." he trailed off as the door arrived. Grabbing the quill, he quickly wrote the code. "I will be back in an hour" and he stepped through the doorway.

"This is near her parents. Make it so I have an hori. I need to return to finish explaining. I had no time as I was disorientated trying to find their casa."

The Master made adjustments to the code. "Here. This will give you an hori."

"Excellent. I will see you after lunch."

Once stepping through, he raced directly to her parent's place and calmly knocked on the door.

"Rorien, come in," said her mother, "and explain. We want to see Elentari and you two marry." She led him into the kitchen. "I will make us some lunch. How long do you have?"

"About half an hour. We marry in seven days and the Master is working on a code to bring you to our lands for a week. You can attend our linking, our marriage and spend some time with us before you return. The King has requested you attend."

"Oh, an invite from the King? How unusual? Does he know Elentari's family?" said Beth turning around to face Rorien.

"He is her father."

"What!? Our daughter is the King's daughter? A princess?" blurted out her father.

"It is a long story which she can explain when you visit if you decide to visit?"

"Yes, we want to see you marry our daughter and see where she lives. What do we need to do?" asked Beth as she returned to fixing lunch.

"I will return in six days with everything you need to reach our world. Make sure you have a bag and that is all," he said sitting down at the table.

"What about Donna? I know she would love to be there and Elentari would be thrilled if she could." Her mother moved to the wall and marked the date on the calendar. "We will be ready. Is there something we can give her for her wedding? Something you need?"

"Having you will be enough and Donna if we can. We have plenty and do not go without, she is the princess, remember."

They continued to chat while eating while waiting for the doorway to return, and Rorien filling them in on what happened since they left them.

"See you in six days." He grinned waving goodbye as he stepped through to his world.

"Master, they are eager and will be ready. Are we able to have three to visit?"

"Yes. Why?" the Master asked, looking up from studying the codes.

"Her best friend Donna. Her parents want Donna to attend. Her and Elentari grew up together and have travelled together. I know she would love her here," he said as he sat down.

"It shall be done. Three to arrive." The Master returned to the codes.

"How is the code coming?" asked Rorien as he scanned each of the parchments.

"Nearly there. I shall have it ready and the potion for them on the morrow."

"Excellent. I will return to get them on the morning of the 40th. Until then." Rorien bowed and took his leave.

He was eager for the next few dias to finish and for the 40th to arrive. He had almost let it slip that her parents were coming during the janual. The excitement he felt waking up on the morning of the 40th was hard to contain, especially around Elentari. Keeping such a big surprise from her agony but thrilling, knowing how ecstatic she would be. He met the Master in the ancient library.

"Morning Master. This is an exciting dia, bringing Elentari's parents to visit. She is going to flip out when she sees them, I can't wait," he said, his face beaming.

"This is the code they will need to speak to enter our world. All three will need to drink the potion, only one needs to speak to open the door. I have produced a map for them in case they do not enter the ancient library. Have them to ask the very first being they see to be taken directly to me, here. Make sure they open their portal well before your doorway is due to appear. I am unsure if there will be complications if they are opened close together. Good luck with sending them here." The Master handed Rorien a bag containing bottles of potion, the code and a map. Rorien drank his potion and stepped through the door.

"Rorien, it is good to see you. These past days have been long waiting for you. It will be wonderful to see my daughter again, is she good?" asked Beth as she opened the door for Rorien, leading him into the kitchen.

"Yes, she is. This morning she is busy with royal duties and has a few preparations to check after lunch. We will find her mid-after high sun and she has no idea you are coming. Your visit is the King's gift to her."

"How exciting. Do we follow you through your door?"

"No. You will have a different door. This is the code to speak to open your door. I will follow later. We are not completely sure where you will enter, use this map and ask the first being you see to take you to the air Master in the ancient library. Here." He pointed to a spot on the map as he glanced at the unknown female across the table and guessed she was Donna.

"Air Master in the ancient library" repeated her mother. "Have you met Donna?"

"No. Hi Donna," he said glancing at her.

"Hi." she answered.

"Yes, air Master in the ancient library. Can you read the code?" he asked looking at Beth.

"Yes," she answered.

"Are you ready?" they all nodded excitedly. "Ok. Drink all of this and Beth, speak the code." They drank and Beth recited the code for the door to appear. "Remember air Master ancient library, now go." They each picked up their bag and stepped through the portal and into a room.

"Beth? Francis? Are you Elentari's parents?" They turned to the voice.

"Yes," They both answered, staring at an old man dressed in yellow robes. "Are you the air Master?" asked Beth.

"Yes. You have entered where we hoped you would. That is a relief. This is the ancient library. Welcome to you all. Come we are meeting the King in his private casa." He led them out. "He will meet us there when he and Elentari are finished with royal duty. It is an honour to meet the guardians of the princess. You have raised a wonderful female." He continued to praise Elentari and the wonderful things she had accomplished since she had arrived, explaining the area around them and pointing out things for them.

They entered a home and the air Master settled them in the kitchen to eat, making sure they were comfortable, as they waited for the King and Rorien. The Master continued with his general chat, giving them a rundown on what was to happen while they were here, about the cuedel and how Elentari was settling in as Rorien entered with the King.

"Rorien, you made it back." Beth grabbed him hugging him.

"Yes, Beth, I came as quick as I could. Hope it's not too daunting for you and the Master has looked after you."

"It has been a bit daunting. The Master fed us and has relayed much information," said Francis.

"Beth, Francis please may I introduce you to the King. My King, these are Elentari's Earth parents Francis and Beth."

"I am most pleased to meet you, Francis and Beth. You have raised a wonderful daughter. She speaks highly of you both," said the King

"Hello, your majesty," said Beth curtsying.

"Hello," said Francis, bowing, unsure and looking uncomfortable.

"My King, this is Donna, Elentari's best friend, the one she is constantly talking about and grew up with."

"Hello, Donna. You have had an interesting life together" said the King turning towards her.

"Hello King. Yes, we've had manu adventures together," replied Donna curtsying.

"Come let's get you settled at Sarina and Jasper's place before we surprise Elentari," said Rorien as he grabbed Beth's case and headed for the door. "They live beside her and will take care of you while we are occupied. The King will be with you on the morrow as well as Sarina and Jasper. We will see you the following day. Donna, you will stay in Lorcan's casa with Awnrie, his link. He is staying at Fendton's." Rorien showed them to their rooms and tugged the link. "She is waiting for us. Are you ready to surprise her?"

They both nodded. Beth's eyes were filled with tears. Rorien took her hand and led them to Elentari's door.

"Mum, Dad, how...what...your...Rorien...Papa?" she was flabbergasted. How can her parents be here?

"Keep surprising her like this Rorien. I do love her when she is lost for words." Laughed Jasper

"Elentari, you wanted your parents to come for you linking dia. I have fulfilled your wish," said Papa.

She raced to them grabbing them tight, her eyes filled with tears. Her mother was sobbing quietly as her dad held her tightly.

"Papa, thank-you, thank-you, thank-you. You spoil me," she said moving to him to give him a hug. "Thank-you Rorien for finding them and bringing them here," she said before hugging her parents again.

"Anything to keep you happy. It was the King's idea, all his doing. All I did was step through the doorway."

"Mum, Dad, have you got outfits for the morrow? I hope they are not just something you dug out of the wardrobe," she asked stepping back holding her mother's hands.

"Well, we did buy new clothes for your wedding."

"Mmm, let's get you something else. Dad, you will need something to match the wedding party. After all, you will be walking with me. Mum, I know what style you tend to like and you will need something better too. Before we go let me introduce you to all. These are my guards Jasper, Fendton and Lorcan. Rorien is also one of my guards. Sarina and Awnrie are my friends. This is Rewa, Rorien's sister and her guardians Havid and Roswen."

Pleasantries were exchanged between them all. Questions asked and answered.

"Dear, we have a gift for you," said her mum.

"Having you here is enough of a gift. You did not need to get me anything." Rorien moved from the door as Donna entered.

"Donza!" screamed Elentari

"Anza!" screamed Donna

Both girls erupted screaming, racing towards each other, talking rapidly over the top of each other, questioning, answering, explaining, hands flailing about, hugging and touching each other, not breathing, holding two different conversations at once. The group stared wide-eyed at the scene before them.

"They can do this for hours," said Beth unfazed at what was happening. "It is nothing unusual for them when they have been apart to speak this way. We gave up years ago trying to understand them," she said, shaking her head. "It is like they are having two different conversations at once. Most unusual."

"Will they stop soon?" asked the King his eyes wide at the scene before him.

"If we leave them alone, they may still be like this in the morning. We have had to intervene every time. Once Donna's parents picked her up and carried her to the car and the girls were still going."

"Oh," said the King with concern.

"GIRLS!" shouted Francis forcefully. Her dad was inspecting the stonemasons' work on her walls. The two girls shut up, stood straight side by side facing her dad. "That is better. Annie, you are now Elentari, the princess of all the lands, now behave as such," he said, his eyes not moving from the stonework.

"Yes Dad," said Elentari.

"Donna, you are the best friend of the princess, practically her twin. Behave as such." His eyes were still scanning the stonework taking it all in.

"Yes Dad," said Donna.

Both girls bursting out laughing and hugging again. "Thank-you Papa and Rorien for my gift. Thank-you Mum and Dad for my gift. This is most awesome." She kissed them all. "And you lot, close your mouths. Donna, meet Sarina. She is my linking maid, I don't have a bridesmaid, you're not interested, are you?"

"Hell Yeah! I am so being your bridesmaid!" screamed Donna jumping up and fist-pumping the air.

"Excellent. You can assist Sarina on the morrow as my bridesmaid. We better head off and meet the seamstress and get you all fitted up. Papa, are you coming?"

"No, I shall take my leave and meet you later for supper." He kissed her and left.

"We shall meet in the parestala nearby, the princess parestala." She smiled

"The princess parestala? We have not discussed this as yet. I will organise food to be brought to the PARESTALA and meet you there. Enjoy seeing our cuedel Francis and Beth, I shall meet with you later," he said as he waved goodbye.

They headed off to find the seamstress and to check on the preparations for the morrow, making sure everything was in order and running through what was to happen, informing her parents and Donna their rolls. The King had organised supper in the princess parestala and they settled every being into their room before retiring. The morrow was going to be a big dia.

CHAPTER 20

Linking dia morning arrived and her casa was buzzing. The seamstress arrived with her parent's and Donna's outfits and maids arrived with breakfast. Elentari had the males move tables and chairs outside amongst the casas for all to eat breakfast together and out of her crowded casa. Excitement filled the air as every being spent the morning getting ready and her mother taking many photos. The Masters arrived a little after breakfast.

"Are you ready Princess?" asked the fire Master. "It is nearing 2 hori after sunrise."

"I believe so Masters. Rorien and I are. Not fussed on the rest" she said grinning holding Rorien's arm and hand.

"Exceptional. Shall we begin?"

"Yes, Masters. Please head to your required area and we shall meet you there." The Masters bowed to the princess and King and headed off.

"Ok. Is every being ready?" asked Rorien.

"All those not part of the linking party, it is time to head off and find your seat," said Elentari. "Sarina please take Rewa and Donna. Mum and Dad, you will be following with the King. He will show you where you all are sitting. Rorien and I will be behind you all. I know you have been snapping away all morning, Mum have you got your camera?"

"Yes dear, I have it," said Beth holding up the camera.

"Then it is time for us to go so we can complete our linking," she said as Rorien held out his arm for her.

"Your dress looks amazing and my outfit is perfect. You have chosen well," said Rorien as they walked to the east parestala, the first part of their walk-about linking ceremony. This was the way for every being to view their linking, a walk-about ceremony where a part was performed in each of the four main parestalas.

"I know. The seamstress did a marvellous job. I had nothing to do with design," she said '*You look fantastic*' she said along the link and with that comment they spent the rest of the ceremony on their link pointing out things to each other and discussing their amazing dia.

Her marbled coloured dress had a cowl neckline with a plunging back and every power colour was represented. It was loosely fitted with an A-line skirt flowing to her ankles, from her shoulders hung a long scarf gathered at the shoulders, falling down her back to the ground where it dragged along the ground creating a train. In her hair, she wore a halo of flowers. Rorien's traditional styled robe matched hers, every power colour marbled together with sleeves of yellow representing his power.

Sarina, Donna and Rewa had matching dresses with a sweetheart neckline and A-line skirt in the same material as Elentari but with lighter colours. They carried baskets filled with petals to spread across the path in each parestala. The seamstress had a dress for her mother which matched the bridesmaid's dress style in a blue colour with intricate needlework around the neckline and on the bodice. Her dad wore his dark blue suit with a cummerbund and tie to match her dress.

The East parestala was adorned in yellow and white to represent air and sight powers and was full to overflowing, it was as if every being from the Eastside was here. Not a spare seat was to be found with many standing to fill the voids. All wore either white or yellow to match the décor and the power represented. The flowers, ribbons, candles and clothes were all yellow and white. At the end of the path stood the Master of air and Master of sight.

'*It seems every being dressed to match the décor*' she said to Rorien.

'*No. Every being here is either an air or sight yielder*' he replied.

'*That would explain how they all have robes to match.*'

Sarina, Donna and Rewa walked the moss path throwing yellow and white petals in the air before taking their seats at the front beside Jasper. The King and her parents followed and took their seats. Rorien and

Elentari stood waiting for the Master of air to nod before they began their journey to complete their link. Music began, 'The Feather' song gently played through the parestala.

'Oh my, Donna is awesome to remember this is the song I wanted for my wedding. She is the best.'

"Welcome all. Todia we witness these two complete their link and begin a life together. Their lives till now have been very different, living in separate worlds. Their journey to this point has not been an easy one. Todia they will leave their separate lives and become one," said the air Master. He opened the book in his hands and read from the ancient text.

hul sini sua yao pamwens
om bli kuw
pamwens moja inte vides
masha pende xan nie

Closing the book, he looked at Rorien and Elentari.

"I connect," they spoke. Elentari felt her link vibrate, a soft humming feel. It continued, not ceasing. Rorien felt the same. Their link was humming.

Three candles sat on the table in front of the Masters. The Master of sight stepped forward and handed the yellow candle to Rorien and the white candle to Elentari. The candle of blended white and yellow sat in the centre of the table. Stamped into the candle were their names. The Master lit their candles.

"The two separate candles represent the separate lives, families and worlds of Rorien and Elentari. As they light the centre candle, they are joining their lives together as one, one life, one family and one world," said the Master as they lit the middle candle together. "The candles they hold are extinguished representing their single lives are no longer." They extinguished each other's candle. "This one light cannot be divided and neither will their lives be divided." The Master held up the candle, handing it to Rorien and Elentari.

The parestala broke out in cheers and applause as they together held the lit candle high in the air and kissed. More cheers and applause broke out. Rorien and Elentari turned to the centre, smiling to all, yielding airpower to air kiss all those within the parestala as they began the walk to the south parestala, holding their combined candle in their hands. Behind them followed the Masters, her parents and their friends, chatting together as they all walked.

Sarina had removed the white and yellow layer of petals from the baskets to reveal the next layer of blue and orange petals and guided Rewa forward along the moss path with Donna following throwing blue and orange petals. The King and her parents followed behind them. The Master of water nodded to Rorien and Elentari to begin their walk to the next step in completing their link. Again, the parestala was overflowing with beings wearing blue and orange to match.

The Master of water and Master of healing was standing behind a table with the Master of air and sight joining them. They placed their candle on the table.

"Finding your link is usually an easy task. For these two it has been a long and hard journey, a journey which spanned two worlds and nine anoks. Todia they link their spirit, coming together as one," said the Master of water. He opened the book in his hands and read from the ancient text.

roha ges rito samman
flod vloi pamo pamo
koppel bunna geb
geur kamo som

"I bond," they answered. Rorien felt a chain linking the two of them, humming between them. He looked at Elentari knowing she too felt the chain.

On the table were two bands, one with blue ribbon wrapped around it and one with orange ribbon and a chain joining them, leftover ribbon dangled from the bands. The Master of healing stepped forward and clutching the bands he said: "These bands represent the lives of these two, two joined together by links forming a chain." He placed the orange band over Rorien's clasped hands. Elentari linked her arm through his and the Master placed the blue band over her hands. "Their arms represent links in a chain, linked and bound together they have become one." He wrapped the orange ribbon around Elentari's wrist and the blue ribbon around Rorien's and raised their hands high for all to see their connection and devotion to each other.

As the parestala erupted in cheers and applause as Rorien kissed her. Elentari glanced at Jasper and together they yielded water power creating many water bubbles to float over the heads of every being. All eyes turned skyward to watch the water bubbles dance above, Jasper nodded and the balls exploded into snowflakes falling gently to the ground. Rorien picked up their candle and guided Elentari to the west parestala, walking awkwardly bound together.

The west parestala was overflowing with beings wearing red and purple. The Master of fire and Master of shift was standing waiting for them as the four Masters joined them. On the table were two jugs and a cup in the centre. There was nothing special about the jugs, however, the silver cup was stunning etched with the marks of each power, the oval face protruded from the cup with their names and date in purple surrounded by a band of red flowers.

"We are born, our life and blood our own. Todia we witness the combining of these two as one. The blood and bodies combining to be one," said the Master of fire opening the ancient textbook and reading.

binasie kws bili
sanue cora kamo dumo
rando diras ene vermung
unihul ses ligga moji

"I combine." It felt like there was fluid in the link, flowing along the chain and moving between them.

The Master of shift handed them each a jug filled with wine. "The jugs represent their lives and blood, separate and single. Pouring their blood into the cup blending the wine into one, blending their blood as one and their bodies as one." Rorien and Elentari poured the wine together into the cup to fill it. "The empty jugs symbolising their single bodies no longer and drinking of the wine symbolises the sharing of experiences together, both bitter and sweet as one." Rorien took the cup and held it for Elentari to sip from and she held it for him to sip.

Cheers and applause rang out through the parestala as Elentari placed the cup on the table and kissed Rorien. She glanced at the King and Lorcan and together the three yielded fire flames to dance across every being's head before shooting high and exploding into fireworks.

Rorien held the cup and Elentari held the candle as they headed to the north parestala, still bound together. It was already awkward walking with their arms bound and holding an item each became even harder. Lucky this was the final part of the ceremony before they headed off alone to complete the link. Along the way they found Asvik waiting for them with a table of food and tea.

"Thank-you Asvik. This is most welcoming," said Elentari putting the candle down and taking a cup of tea as Rorien put the linking cup down and took some food, both finding it difficult to eat or drink bound together and burst out laughing.

"Here, let me undo one so you can eat," said Donna undoing Elentari's band.

"Sarina asked me to set this up for you. She thought you may need something before continuing. I agreed, it has been a long morning and is yet to finish. You look beautiful," said Asvik

"Thank you, both of you." Every being enjoyed the little break and a quick bite of food and tea before continuing for the final part.

The North parestala was beyond full and spilling out onto the paths with beings in green and black with all the kings and their families dressed in their traditional power colour robes. For the final part of the ceremony, all eight masters stood waiting for them.

'I am glad this is the final ceremony and I get you to myself' said Rorien on the link.

'I agree. This linking ceremony is too long and tiring. I hope I have enough energy after this' she teased giving him a little push with her elbow.

'You better' he smiled.

They placed the candle and cup on the table beside three glass containers, the largest container empty and the smaller ones filled with sand, one with green coloured sand and the other black sand. The Master of earth stepped forward.

"The final step to completing the link is the combining of the physical. Two mesiks ago, we did not believe we would be here, thankfully Rorien came to his senses and we can witness their final commitment to each other." He read the ancient text and stepped back.

fisist solwim tussnie dae
kwim pantos
tando kom ja
parnie te tengwi

"I commit." The chain became solid linking them strongly together. He could feel her heartbeat in his link and she could feel his. They were one, committed, combined, connected, coupled.

"The ground is our foundation. The sand represents the ground and the strong foundation on which Rorien and Elentari's new life will begin. As the sand combines together, coming together not to be separated again, as one." Rorien and Elentari poured the sand into the empty container filling it using all the sand.

The Master placed the lid on the container sealing the sand inside, using the melted wax from the yellow and white candle to seal the lid shut. The King stepped up and Rorien and Elentari turned to face him. He removed the bindings and handed them to the Master who arranged the table from left to right, the lit yellow and white candle, blue and orange bands, red and purple cup and the green and black sand jar.

"Your left arms please."

Rorien moved behind Elentari, taking her left hand in his and presented their arms to the King. His right arm wrapped around her waist pulling her into him. He never wanted to let her go. She leant back resting against him feeling his warm and strong body and her head slightly turned into him to rest on his chest.

"These bands are to show all you have completed your linking, that you are connected and committed to each other." The King placed a silver band around Elentari's wrist and a matching band on Rorien's. "The bands have been specially made to represent you both. Set around the band are eight gems representing the Princess and her abilities. Etched into the band are symbols of air to represent Rorien's ability, the air symbols surrounding the gems and flowing through them, the combining of the two of them." The King yielded his firepower to seal shut the band and cover the opening.

"May I present to you, Princess Elentari," the King said as he placed her crown on her head, "and her linked Prince Rorien." He placed a crown on Rorien's head and held their wrists up as the parestala exploded in whistles and accolades. Rorien dipped Elentari and kissed her passionately. Her arms wrapped around him, holding him close and enjoying their first kiss as his linked. Straightening up, Elentari nodded to Fendton.

Using his earth power, he lifted the stone they were on and floated it to the completing casa, placing it on the doorstep. Rorien placed his hand on the doorknob and grinned at Elentari. She nodded and they changed to hawks, soaring above the parestala before flying off.

They landed not far from the cuedel as planned for she was not comfortable with Rorien taking her in his bed with every being outside knowing what they were doing. They decided to complete their linking away from every being, somewhere private and away for any being hearing them. During the vika, Rorien had found them a secluded spot and set it up for them in readiness. Only they knew of this change in agenda.

Now, here they stood facing each other to finish the last step in their ceremony. She raised her hands to her shoulders and slowly pulled her straps off down her arms, letting her dress fall to the ground and exposing her naked body. Rorien quickly removed his robe, hungrily taking her in not taking his eyes off her body. He closed the gap between them and kissed her. She opened her mouth to him inviting him to take her. His arm moved around her waist pulling her close to him. Her arms wrapped around his neck, fingers running through his hair pulling him to her. He picked her up and gently laid her on the blankets laying partially on her and beside her.

His mouth moved to her neck, kissing and sucking it as she moved her head to expose her neck to him, inviting him in. His hand moved to her breast to caress it.

"This is much easy to get at" he grinned at her

"I wasn't interested in wasting time having you work out how to get it off," she said, grabbing his head and pulling him in to kiss him. His tongue flicked against hers as his hands explored her body, caressing and rubbing her.

"Take me please" she begged. He moved between her legs, positioning himself ready to take her, rubbing against her. She moaned and he took her.

Together they moved, pleasuring each other. He was bringing her to the edge of no return when she felt the earth move beneath her, moving in unison with her. She had lost all control, lost in how great he felt and how he excited her beyond what she knew. Her legs were wrapped around him as he brought them to climax and she bit his neck as he bit hers, both speaking the ancient text into their mark as their bodies shuttered and spasmed.

The earth beneath her vibrated from her rippling out from them. Fire and water twirled together rippling away and air blasted from them. She had lost control of all her element powers as they exploded from her across the land with them as the epicentre.

He rolled off her and onto his back and she turned on her side placing her arm over his chest and her head on his shoulder with a leg over his. They lay there enjoying the peace, gently caressing each other, enjoying the moment.

"Is that going to happen every time?" he asked, tilting his head to look at her. She glanced up at him.

"I don't know," she said as she moved to straddle him. "Shall we find out?" She guided him into her, moving to pleasure him and bringing them both to the brink of no return.

"Nope. Just that one time. It must have been all the built-up tension you gave me," she said as she lay beside him.

"And you gave me. The strength it took me not to finish what started was amazing. The tension you caused me…" they burst out laughing.

"We should get back. We have four parestalas to visit and far too many to speak too," she said, not moving.

"Yes. Or we could stay a bit longer, enjoy just us." He began kissing her shoulder continuing to her neck, moving his hands down her body.

"Maybe we can wait," she said as she opened herself for him.

This time as they finished, she stood up and clothed herself. "We do have to go back, quicker we are back, quicker we get through everything and the quicker we get back to OUR casa."

He jumped up and dressed quickly. "You're right. The quicker we get back to our casa, the quicker I get to finish this," he said as he kissed her neck.

She looked at him, taking him in, all the answers she needed standing in front of her.

He thought he was complete when she said she was coming home with him. That was nothing compared to the feeling he had now. Feeling her on his link made him know he was complete, settled and calm. He was hers and she was his, forever combined, entwined together always.

ABOUT THE AUTHOR

Whilst some may say Dee Verhagen's major accomplishment would be raising her children, others might say it is her National Service Medal. Dee would probably argue that publishing her first novel, A Distant Land Beyond, is fairly awesome considering she just passed Year 12 English!

Originally from rural NSW, and spending the bulk of her life in Victoria, the now Tasmanian mother of two has drawn on her world travels and love of sci-fi novels and movies to complete this intriguing tale.

The sequel book is already in the making, with a third being mapped out.

www.ingramcontent.com/pod-product-compliance
Lightning Source LLC
Chambersburg PA
CBHW072354030726
47505CB00014B/1811